BLOOD IS BLACK

BY

SCOTT PRATT

© 2023 Phoenix Flying LLC

All rights reserved. No part of this book may be reproduced or transmitted in any form or by any means, electronic or mechanical, including photocopying, recording, or by any information storage and retrieval system, without permission in writing from the copyright owner.

This is a work of fiction. Names, characters, places and incidents either are the product of the author's imagination or are used fictitiously, and any resemblance to any actual persons, living or dead, events, or locales is entirely coincidental.

ACKNOWLEDGEMENTS

Thank you to Dan Pratt and Travis Johns for helping me bring this manuscript to completion after Dad's death. It was a long, difficult road.

To Mom and Dad – Save me a seat by the lake and have a Bud Light waiting on me if it isn't too much trouble. In a bottle. I'll find you when the time is right.
I loved you both before I was born and I'll love you both after I'm long gone.
—Dylan Pratt

This book, along with every book I've written and every book I'll write, is dedicated to my darling Kristy, to her unconquerable spirit, and to her inspirational courage. I loved her before I was born and I'll love her after I'm long gone.
—Scott Pratt

"To the victor belongs the spoils."
—New York Senator William L. Marcy, referring to the election of Tennessee's Andrew Jackson in the presidential election of 1828.

PROLOGUE

My name is Presley Myers.

I'm in bed, a twelve-year-old girl with twelve-year-old girl problems. I've just gotten my period, which frightens me a bit and makes me confused, embarrassed, and irritable. Anyway, it's close to 1:00 a.m., and I've been in bed since ten thirty. It's a Wednesday, and I have to go to school in the morning. I've barely closed my eyes, and I can still hear my younger brother, Aaron, breathing heavily across the hall. He's afraid of the dark, so he sleeps with a night light and his bedroom door open, but once he falls asleep, there is no waking him. I can hear a breeze blowing outside. A tree branch scratches the house as it moves back and forth in the wind. I get up to go to the bathroom and see my mother turn out the light in my parents' room. I walk over to the top of the steps and look down. A dim light slips out from beneath the door of my father's study. His name is William Myers, but everyone calls him Bill. He's a lawyer who practices criminal defense and often works late. I rub my eyes, finally feeling sleepy, and go back to bed.

A little after two in the morning, I hear footsteps on the wooden deck outside the front door. My heart rate accelerates when the hinges on the front door creak. The footsteps are now in the foyer at the bottom of the stairs, moving in the direction of my dad's study. My gut tightens as I roll out of bed and creep toward the landing.

I hear muffled voices—my father's voice and the voice of another man—as I creep silently down the stairs. It's a short conversation. And then the gun blast. One shot. It reverberates through the house like a cannon. I freeze. Then a tall man wearing a long black overcoat and a black ski mask walks out of daddy's office. The sight of him petrifies me. He squares his shoulders to me once he realizes I'm there, and I can see the outline of a pistol hanging loosely from his right hand. I know for sure he is going to shoot me. I lower my eyes and wait for it. But there is no loud bang. No pain. Only footsteps as he approaches and pats my head. It feels gentle, pure, and honest. Like he cares. It confuses me, so I look up. The two holes in the man's mask focus my attention on his eyes, and that's when I see it. One eye, bright blue. The other, dark brown. It's just a glimpse, because almost as soon as our eyes meet, the man walks quickly out of our house. Taking my life as I know it with him.

It doesn't take long after the shot for the house to explode with movement. My mother hurries down the stairs and asks if I'm okay. I can't form an answer, but the nod of my head reassures her enough that she continues into the study.

That's when I hear her scream. It raises goosebumps on my skin and hairs on my neck. And, like the gunshot, there is only one.

Then the quiet.

That's when I put one foot in front of the other until I'm standing in the doorway of the study. I stare at my mother, who is staring at my father. He's sitting in his cracked-leather desk chair, leaning forward with his arms hanging at his side, face down on his mahogany desk. Blood is beginning to form a pool around his head. I am shocked at how dark the color is. Blood is bright red on television and in the movies. But in real life, blood isn't red at all. In real life, blood is black.

"Is Daddy okay?"

No answer.

Then I hear my brother's sleepy voice calling out annoyed from his room at the top of the stairs: "It's the middle of the night, what the heck's going on down there?!"

I step past my catatonic mother and pick up the receiver of my father's phone, just now being swarmed by the creeping pool of black blood. I call for help but help never comes. Only people to clean up the mess.

I'm alive and my father is dead and there's nothing I can do about it. There is nothing I can do.

PART I
TWENTY YEARS LATER

CHAPTER ONE

The Williamson County Courthouse is on Fourth Street in the middle of the quaint downtown area of Franklin, Tennessee. It was built in the 1850s in the antebellum Greek Revival style and has been through several renovations. The courthouse site is rich in cruel history, having been used for public hangings and beatings. Mostly of untried criminals. If my father had been alive back then, I believe he would've fought for the accused. He would've stood up for the meek, the poor, the innocent, and yes, even the guilty.

As a child, I would often hear him talking on the phone in his study, telling a client or reporter that he believed everyone, yes, everyone, deserved the best representation available to them. That was my father. Whether someone had millions of dollars or was flat broke, if my father believed he could help, that's what he did. For his entire legal career. Right up until he was shot in the head.

Having just turned 32, I'd already made a name for myself as a criminal-defense lawyer in and around Nashville. Not on the level of my father, but I was working on it. A person might think the child of a murdered criminal-defense lawyer would go into law enforcement, or prosecution, or some other field altogether, but my father was a criminal-defense attorney, and I knew early on I would be one, too. He was dead, after all, and there was his legacy to uphold. A legacy I was obsessed with preserving, and, hopefully, building upon. He could no longer defend the oppressed, but I could. He could no longer win hard-fought judgements for the wrongly accused or reduce exorbitant sentences for the guilty. But I could. And I did. I also kept my maiden name—Myers—for my law practice. Doing so ensured his name would stay alive in the profession he loved. My husband, Mack, wasn't happy about it, but he knew my father would've been proud.

The clock on the wall above Judge Lester Givens's bench read 9:45 a.m. when he called my aggravated assault case. Givens was the youngest judge I knew. His father was a Criminal Court judge and his grandfather had been a chancellor. He was a prosecutor's judge who loved to send people to jail, no matter how minor the offense. The overcrowding in the Franklin County Jail be damned. He had sandy-blonde hair, cobalt-blue eyes, and had it not been for a nose the size of a ski slope, he would have been handsome. It was hard to get past that honker, though.

My client's name was Willie Higgins. Willie had done a ten-year stretch for aggravated assault in the Morgan County Penitentiary and had only been out of prison for five days when he was arrested for slicing up a redneck named Donnie Blue. It took more than two hundred stitches to sew Donnie back up after Willie got through with him that day two months earlier. I was appointed to represent him because he had no money and no job. Naturally, I was excited for the challenge.

Willie Higgins, who I'd come to like very much during my visits with him at the Williamson County Detention Center, had taken an interest in knife fighting as a boy growing up in rural Williamson County. His grandfather, who had served in a commando unit in World War II, taught Willie everything he knew. He'd apparently learned his lessons well, because the ten years Willie spent in prison came about after he got into an altercation in a bar in Lebanon, a suburb of Nashville best known for being the corporate headquarters of Cracker Barrel, during which he'd used a small pocketknife like a surgeon uses a scalpel. He'd claimed the fight was over his victim welching on a pool bet, and that his opponent tried to hit him with the cue after he tried to collect. Others backed up his account. They even said Willie's opponent outweighed him by at least sixty pounds and had started the fight. Still, after seeing photos of the scars from the wounds Willie inflicted on the "victim," a jury convicted him.

Willie was thin as a rail, about five feet ten, had dark hair and eyes, deep acne scars, and yellow teeth. He'd always been pleasant around me, but there was a dangerous aura about him that matched the "Don't Tread on Me" rattlesnake tattoo on his right forearm.

The assistant district attorney, a brash, impetuous young man named Carl Jones who strutted like a peacock and dressed like one, too, called Donnie Blue as his first and only witness. After speaking with my client several times and having my investigator make some inquiries, I'd attempted to talk to Mr. Jones about the case in the hope that he'd be reasonable, but he wouldn't listen to anything I said. He simply waved me off when I went to his office and gave me the lame old, "See you in court, counselor." I just shrugged my shoulders and left.

His mistake.

I'd subpoenaed Donnie Blue's former live-in girlfriend, a real prize named Wanda Blaylock, and planned to call her as a witness. It was an unusual move in a preliminary hearing. Preliminary hearings in General Sessions Court are held so the judge can make a determination as to whether there is probable cause that a crime was committed and that the defendant was the person who committed said crime. If, after hearing the witnesses, the judge finds there was probable cause and that a crime was committed, he then binds the case to a grand jury, and they vote whether or not to indict the defendant and send the case to Criminal Court. They do so nearly 100 percent of the time because they operate in closed sessions and only hear from the investigating officer and prosecutor. Defense attorneys are not allowed in the grand-jury room. Unfortunately for criminal defendants, the old saying that a prosecutor can indict a ham sandwich is true. But I wasn't planning to let things get that far with Willie.

Before I could call Wanda, however, Carl Jones took his turn with Donnie Blue. Donnie sat down in the witness chair and took the oath that he'd tell the truth, the whole truth, and nothing but the truth. Almost immediately after that, he began to lie.

"Mr. Blue," Carl Jones said, "do you recognize the defendant, Willie Higgins?"

Blue was in his late thirties and pudgy, his thinning sandy-blond hair made darker by the hairspray he used to hold his comb-over in place. He had the jowls of a bulldog and a double chin. He was wearing a black sweater and blue slacks.

"I do," Blue said. He pointed at Willie Higgins. "He's sitting right there next to that red-headed lady."

"Let the record show the victim pointed out the defendant and his lawyer, Mrs. Presley Myers," Jones said. He turned back to Blue. "Tell the court how you know the defendant."

"He sliced me up like a Christmas turkey two months ago."

"Did you know Mr. Blue prior to the incident during which he cut you?"

"No, sir. Never laid eyes on him before that day."

"And this incident occurred on January third of this year here in Williamson County, correct?"

"Correct."

"Please describe for the court what happened that day," Jones said.

"Well sir, I was just driving along Southall Road on a Saturday afternoon, minding my own business after doing some work on my car at a friend's house, when I run upon this joker. He was driving about fifteen miles an hour or so. The road's pretty narrow, and it's curvy, and I didn't want to pass him, so I honked my horn at him to try to get him to speed up. Next thing I know he's got his arm hanging out the window, givin' me the finger. I honked at him again, and he slowed down to about five miles an hour. Then he just plumb stopped his vehicle right there in the middle of the road. Like I said, it's a narrow stretch right there. It also drops off on both sides, so I couldn't get around him."

Carl Jones nodded, urging his star witness to keep going.

"So, I sat there a second, and I seen him get out of his car and start back to mine. I locked the door, and he started cussing me up one side and down the other through the window. He was yelling like a crazy man, saying all kinds of terrible stuff. Called me everything but a good Christian man, which is exactly what I am. I rolled the window down a little and told him to stop acting a fool and let me pass, but he called me a gutless coward and started kicking the side of my car. I reckon I should've stayed put, but I just couldn't let the man call me a gutless coward and do nothin'. If I would've backed up or just stayed in the car, seemed to me I would have pretty much proved his point, so I opened up the damn—sorry, dang—door and got out. Next thing I knew, I saw a flash, and he was movin' like a whirlwind. I felt burnin' on my arms and then my chest and stomach, and then I saw the blood and I knew I's being cut. I couldn't do nothin' to stop him, neither. I mean, that boy was fast. I tried to hit him a couple times, but it was like trying to catch a cracked-out cat. So, I jumped back in my car and locked the door, then I put it in reverse and started backing up as fast as I could. When I come to a driveway, I turned around and headed straight for the hospital in Franklin. I didn't have no cell phone—I'd accidentally dropped it in the toilet the night before—so I couldn't call 9-1-1. I didn't have no other option but to start a-prayin', so that's what I done. I just kept prayin' to God and whoever else'd listen to not let me bleed to death."

"How did you identify Mr. Higgins as your attacker?" Jones asked.

"When the police came to the hospital, I told them he was in an old silver Dodge Dart. I had a pen in the console of my car, and I wrote his tag number down on the palm of my hand as soon as I saw him stop his car in the middle of the road and get out. Glad I did, too. Turned out the car was registered to his momma, and he didn't have no driver's license, but when the police went and talked to him, he admitted to cuttin' me."

"How severe were your injuries, Mr. Blue?"

He stood up and pulled his sweater off to reveal a white tank-top underneath, then lifted the undershirt and turned in a circle. There were ugly pink scars on his arms, chest, stomach, and back. "Two hundred and thirty-four stitches severe," he said.

"Thank you, Mr. Blue," Jones said. "Please put your shirt back on and answer the defense counsel's questions."

I stood. "Mr. Blue, do you have a girlfriend named Wanda Blaylock?"

Blue stiffened. "No," he said.

"Do you understand the meaning of perjury, Mr. Blue? It means lying under oath in court, and it's a felony."

"I ain't lyin' or perjury-ing."

"Good, then I'll ask you one more time. Do you have a girlfriend named Wanda Blaylock?"

"No."

"Let me rephrase. At the time of this incident, did you have a girlfriend named Wanda Blaylock?"

"Don't see how that's any of your concern."

"Will the court please instruct the witness to answer my question?"

"Answer the question," Judge Givens said.

"I kicked her out months ago."

"But at the time of this incident she was living with you, wasn't she?"

"I object to this," Carl Jones said. "Mrs. Myers is badgering the witness, and I fail to see the relevance as to whether this woman may or may not have been living with the victim at the time of the incident."

"She witnessed the incident, Your Honor," I said. "And if she tells the truth, Mr. Blue here is going to be facing arrest for perjury. That is if Mr. Jones cares anything about the integrity of the legal system."

"I resent that," Jones said.

"Enough," Judge Givens said. He turned to Donnie Blue. "Answer the question and do so truthfully."

"She was my girlfriend, but I kicked her out," he said. "I don't recall if it was the day I was cut, or a few days before, or after, or what."

"I have a couple of photos I'd like to show you," I said. "May I approach the witness?"

"Go ahead," the judge said.

"Is this the Dodge Dart you spoke of earlier?"

"Appears to be."

"Was all that damage to the rear of the vehicle there before you encountered my client, or did you run into his car?"

"Must have been there before, 'cause I didn't run into his car."

"What about the back windshield? Do you deny smashing it with a claw hammer?"

"Claw… I didn't do no such thing."

"And this second photograph," I said, "the Plymouth Barracuda, whose car is that?"

"It looks like mine."

"There's quite a bit of damage to the front. How did that happen?"

"I let my little brother drive it, and he got drunk and ran off the road through a fence."

"So, your sworn testimony is that your car *wasn't* damaged because you rammed it into the back of the car my client was driving?"

Donnie nodded, weakly.

"See those two places near your right headlight? Does that look like silver paint to you?"

"Those are just scratches from the fence. I done told you I didn't run into nobody's car."

"I don't have any more questions for this witness, Your Honor, but I've subpoenaed Wanda Blaylock and would like to call her now, if Mr. Jones is finished."

The judge looked at Jones, who rose to his feet. "May I ask the relevance of the witness's testimony?" he said.

"I just told you," I answered. "She was there. She was an eyewitness."

"Call her," the judge said.

CHAPTER TWO

The bailiff went out into the hallway, and a couple seconds later, in walked Wanda Blaylock. She was in her midthirties, a touch overweight, with bleached-blonde hair, brown eyes, and breasts that stretched her black Lynyrd Skynyrd T-shirt to the limit. Her court attire was completed by tight blue jeans, cowboy boots, and a face covered in an inch of makeup. Her lips were smothered in candy-apple-red lipstick. I'd spoken to her about the penalties for perjury when my husband, Mack, showed up with her at the courthouse that morning. I sometimes used him and his status as the Williamson County Sheriff to bring in witnesses I didn't trust to show up on their own.

"State your name, please," I said after she took the oath.

"Wanda Jean Blaylock."

"Miss Blaylock, I've spoken to you about perjury and the importance of telling the truth in court, is that correct?"

She nodded, her eyes looking down.

"You have to say yes," I said. "This is being recorded."

"Yes, you talked to me about perjury and that I need to tell the truth."

"Back in January, did you witness a fight between your then boyfriend, Donnie Blue, and my client, Willie Higgins?"

"Yes," she said quietly.

"Where were you when you witnessed the fight?"

"I was in the car."

"Whose car were you in?"

"I believe it belonged to Willie's momma."

"Was it a silver Dodge Dart?"

"Yes."

"Would you tell the court how you happened to be in the car with my client?"

"Well, I was at home at about eleven o'clock that morning—it was a Saturday—when one of my girlfriends pulled into the driveway. She came to the front door and asked if Donnie was home, and I told her he wasn't. As usual, he'd stayed out all night drinking with some of his buddies, and I figured he was either sleeping it off or had already started cracking 'em open for round two. That's what he always does, so I figured that's what he was doing. So, when she asked me if I wanted to come and party with her and a couple of her friends, I told her yes. I mean, why not? Like I say, Donnie did it all the time. Why couldn't I have a little fun? She told me one of the friends she was with had just gotten out of prison and might be a little on the randy side, if you know what I mean. Shoot, Donnie didn't ever want to have sex. I didn't even think he could, if I'm being truthful about it. I don't mean to be talkin' bad about nobody, but a woman can only take being ignored that way for so long. Anywho, I grabbed my purse and headed out the door. When I got to Linda's car—Linda Goodin is my friend that came that day—she told me to get in the back seat. There was a man in the front named Benny Emmert that I'd known for quite a while. He and Linda partied together some, so that was nothing new. I didn't know who the man sittin' in the back was, though. I guess he turned out to be your client, Willie Higgins."

"Had you ever met Mr. Higgins before?"

"No."

"What did you guys do?" I said.

"We drove to the convenience store about a mile down the road from where me and Donnie lived and bought a case of beer and some cigarettes, and then we went to Linda's trailer, which was about six or seven miles away. We started drinking and talking and listening to music, and we were just having a good time. Nothing crazy, just a fun time, you know? After a couple of hours, Linda and Benny disappeared into a bedroom in the back, but before she went back there, she told me there was another bedroom and that me and Willie could use it if we wanted to."

"Did you?"

She blushed. "Like I said, Donnie ain't never been much in that department. So, yeah. We did. We were in there for quite a while. She was right about Willie being randy, too. I guess being cooped up in a little ol' cell for ten years will do that to a man."

"What happened next?"

"We came out after a couple of hours, but I wasn't really ready to go home, so Benny and Linda took Willie and me over to his momma's, where he was staying. He asked me if I wanted to ride around for a while and drink some more, and I said that sounded like fun. So that's what we done. Later on, we stopped by that same convenience store because Willie was taking me home, and I needed more cigarettes. As I was walking back out to the car, I looked up and saw Donnie pulling into the parking lot. I just about fainted. I got in the car real quick hoping Donnie hadn't seen me and told Willie we better get out of there because my boyfriend had just showed up. So, Willie got us out of there in a hurry. I thought we were in the clear, but all of a sudden, this car rammed into the back of us. I turned and looked and sure enough, it was Donnie in his old Plymouth. Willie asked me what I wanted him to do, and I told him to try to get away, so he hit the gas, but that little Dart didn't have nothing for the Barracuda. Donnie rammed us again, and almost pushed us off the road. Finally, I told Willie to pull off into the parking lot of this abandoned sawmill off Southall Road, and I'd try to talk some sense into Donnie. Willie pulled over and parked, and next thing I knew Donnie smashed the back windshield out of Willie's momma's car with a claw hammer. Willie jumped out of the car, and so did I. He was trying to tell Donnie we didn't do nothing and that he didn't know I had a boyfriend, but Donnie went at him and tried to hit him with that hammer. I saw Willie's hand go into his pocket, and then I saw a knife, and then it was like a magic show. I've never seen anything like it. He was like a Tasmanian devil with that thing, and in no time at all, he had Donnie bleedin' like a stuck hog."

"Miss Blaylock, I'm not asking you what was in Mr. Blue's mind, but from where you were standing, did it appear Mr. Blue was trying to hurt my client?"

"Hurt him? He tried to take his head off with that hammer."

"What happened next?"

"I guess Donnie realized he was hurt pretty bad, because he all of a sudden jumped in his car and tore out of there."

"And what did you do?"

"I had Willie drive me to my sister's."

"Why didn't you call the police?"

"I was scared, and I was embarrassed, just like I am now. I didn't want to get involved with no police."

"Thank you, Miss Blaylock. Please answer Mr. Jones's questions."

"Mr. Jones doesn't have any questions." The voice came from the bench. Judge Givens looked livid.

"Your Honor," Jones said, holding his hands out as if to say, *What the hell are you doing?*

"There isn't any point," the judge said. "I find Miss Blaylock to be a credible witness and the victim to be untruthful. You can still indict Mr. Higgins if you want, but this is a clear case of self-defense, and if you indict Mr. Higgins, you'll be wasting the taxpayer's money and your boss will get a call from me. I'll also file a complaint against you with the Board of Professional Responsibility. I also expect to see an indictment against Mr. Blue for perjury. There isn't a jury in the world that would convict Mr. Higgins on this testimony. The court finds there is no probable cause that aggravated assault was committed. This was mutual combat and self-defense. The case is dismissed. Mr. Higgins, you're free to go."

Winning felt good. With each victory, the Myers legacy and reputation grew.

After the court had cleared, I finished packing my briefcase and passed my opposing counsel, Carl Jones, on his way back in to retrieve a brief he'd left on the prosecution table.

"Congratulations," he said, as we passed each other.

"I tried to warn you," I said. "I gave you an out."

"I guess you're right," he said. "I'm just a house dog, and I should've known better than to tangle with a wolf."

"Okay," I said, not knowing if the odd comment was meant to be a compliment or an insult.

"Really," he continued, as he picked up the file, "I lost to a much savvier, much meaner breed." He paused as he passed me, then whispered low. "You might win more fights, Presley. But guess who's gonna have a longer, happier life?"

CHAPTER THREE

The comment ate at me the entire ride home. What did Carl Jones know about me? Besides that, I had made a habit of kicking his ass in the courtroom. And what did he know about a happy life, or what makes one, or who has one? I was happy. I was doing what I loved to do, and I was married to a handsome, strong, smart man who loved me unconditionally. Mack had, eventually, supported me keeping my maiden name for my career in law. He had been there for me when my brother, Aaron, fell hard into drugs and alcohol. He even went so far as to vouch for him in court to help me convince a judge that probation, not prison time, would be punishment enough for my troubled sibling. And I'm sure what was most difficult for him was being right by my side at the doctor's office when she read the results from my fertility test. It was me, not Mack, who was the problem. I was the reason we were childless. He comforted me, told me it didn't matter, and said he loved me no matter what.

When the doctor told me I was barren, I expected a rush of despair, anger, and frustration. Instead, what I felt was relief. It was all I could do to suppress a smile of joy. I had never wanted kids. At least, not after my father was murdered. I was a child before the killing, but as soon as the man pulled the trigger, patted my head, and walked out of our house, a veil had been lifted. And once it was pulled away, I no longer saw through a child's eyes. I saw the world as it was: a chaotic, cruel place where no one was safe. Not even at home, working late in a study.

So, for the past twenty years I put my head down, finished first in my class at Vanderbilt Law, started a terrifically successful firm, and carried my father's torch, feeding the flame with every courtroom victory. Screw Carl Jones. Let him live his lazy, hound-dog life.

I liked being the wolf.

CHAPTER FOUR

The man's name was George Willis. He'd traveled almost three hundred miles from Elizabethton, Tennessee, to my law office in Franklin to meet with me. I'd spoken to him on the phone two days earlier and tried to discourage him from doing what he wanted to do, but he was insistent. I finally relented and agreed to meet. It was Thursday, August 15, at 11:00 a.m. when he showed up. I'll never forget that date because that's when my life changed forever.

"It's nice to make your acquaintance, Mrs. Myers," he said, as he sat in the overstuffed chair in front of my desk.

My office was a small two-bedroom house that Mack and I bought cheaply and renovated. It was bright, clean, and homey by design. I wanted my clients, many of whom were facing long prison sentences, and sometimes even the death penalty, to feel at ease when they met me. So, I hung pleasing photographs of the Smoky Mountains, the Ryman Auditorium, and other local landmarks on the walls in place of family photos or diplomas. That was the only thing I did differently than my father as far as my law practice was concerned. Daddy had every inch of his office wall covered with pictures of me, my brother, Aaron, and our mother, Delilah Jean. When I asked him as a child why he put up so many photos of us, he simply replied that we made him happy. His whole life was on display, and somehow, after seeing him shot to death in his study, I connected the two. Did the killer visit my father's law office and see the family photos on the wall? The picture of us on our front step, with the house number on the door? Is that how he knew where to come and kill my hero? I didn't know and wouldn't know until I figured out who murdered him. Which was, along with becoming the best defense lawyer in the state, what I'd vowed to do with my life. Those two things would make my father the proudest, so those were the two things that occupied most of my time. Often to the detriment of my health and my marriage.

Regardless, the familiar generic photos put the clients at ease and provided me with some level of privacy. I wouldn't even display a picture of our dog, Abby.

"How was your trip?" I said to Mr. Willis.

"The drive from Knoxville to Nashville is the longest stretch of road on the planet," he said. "It just seems like you're never going to get from one place to the other."

It was rural and mountainous, the interstate was full of trucks, and there were often wrecks, especially when the weather was bad.

"Well, it looks like you made it in one piece."

He was a short, pale man who looked to be in his midfifties. His light-brown hair was thinning and beginning to gray. He had dark circles under his eyes and appeared to be exhausted.

"I have to tell you, Mr. Willis, I've given a lot of thought to what we talked about. I also took a close look at your son's case. I think you're wasting your time. I don't want to make you angry, but do you have a clear grasp of what he did?"

He nodded and offered a weak smile. "You're not making me angry. I know exactly what Junior did. He shot his ex-wife and her boyfriend sixteen times. Reloaded a two-shot Derringer seven times to do it."

"He broke into her house at four in the morning," I said, reading the brief I had prepared before his arrival. "He was arrested, then tried before a jury a year later and convicted of two counts of second-degree murder. His conviction was upheld by the Tennessee Court of Criminal Appeals, and the Tennessee Supreme Court refused to review the case. His sentence is 20 to 40 years, Mr. Willis. He's served what? Four? How do I possibly go about justifying executive clemency for him?"

"We have a new governor," Willis said. "I think he'll look favorably on the matter."

"Why is that?"

Willis cleared his throat. "Because we're old friends. We were roommates at college, and I'm his patronage chief in Northeast Tennessee—or political adviser if you want to be by-the-book-correct about it. He also knows and loves Junior."

The new governor, Lonnie Black, had been in office for thirteen months. I'd read quite a bit about him prior to the election. He'd come up poor in McNairy County and worked his way through Middle Tennessee State where he majored in business. After graduation, he went back to McNairy County and started a string of very successful used-car lots that made him very rich. He used all that money to run for state representative in his home district and won easily, served two years, then ran for the United States House of Representatives. He thumped a long-time incumbent Democrat in the primary, ran unopposed in the general election, and served three terms in Congress before announcing he was going to run for governor.

He rolled into the Tennessee governor's mansion riding a wave of unprecedented popularity, promising—as they all did—to look out for the working men and women of the state. And, of course, to take care of the elderly and the children. To me, though, he was disingenuous. He reeked of sleaze and corruption. But the fact remained he'd never been charged with doing anything illegal. Still, something about him made me uneasy. As did Mr. Willis's connection to him.

"Plus," Mr. Willis continued, "Lonnie's a Democrat and Northeast Tennessee is Republican through and through. I got him thousands of votes. Turned the election for him. He owes me."

"He won by a landslide," I said. "He didn't need much help."

"I got him a lot of votes," Willis repeated. "He'll want to show his appreciation."

So, there it was. A patronage connection. Classic cronyism. I knew it. Still, I didn't think the governor would go so far as to release a convicted double murderer just because he and the murderer's father were former roommates.

"What do you do for a living, Mr. Willis, if you don't mind me asking?"

"I own an aluminum extrusion plant. It isn't glamorous, but it's profitable."

"So, you're wealthy."

"I'm very wealthy. I'm about to become even more so after I sell my plant."

"Good for you. I suppose you also made financial contributions to the governor's campaign."

"I did."

"All of them legal, I hope."

"Of course. I donated through Political Action Committees."

"What did your son do for a living? Did he work for you?"

He nodded his head and looked down. I could tell it was a sore subject.

"Junior worked for me, yes, but he was having a hard time when this happened. He was trying to find his way, trying to recover from his divorce. I think he'd started using drugs, and I know for certain he was drinking too much. I tried everything I could to help him. I don't know what went wrong. He just seemed depressed all the time."

What I was hearing was a daddy enabler speech. George Willis's son was a ne'er-do-well, enabled by his father's money and willingness to make excuses for him. Now he'd committed double murder, and his father was still trying to make sure he wasn't held accountable.

"The children were in the house when he killed their mother," I said, pushing my own memory of a similar situation out of my mind.

"That's right, and as far as I'm concerned, it's more evidence of how far gone he was. He didn't even run after he shot them. Just went into the kids' room, laid down in bed with them, and waited for the police."

"He was also highly intoxicated," I said. "What I read said he was passed out drunk when the police arrived. Voluntary intoxication isn't a defense for murder."

"But temporary insanity is. And he was temporarily insane. Junior isn't violent."

"Says here you had a psychiatrist testify at trial. The jury obviously didn't buy it."

"The shrink they used was ugly and inarticulate. I asked the lawyer why he hired him, and he said he was an old friend. I still think the jury would have felt differently if Junior had testified."

"Why didn't he?"

"His lawyer wouldn't let him. He said it was always a bad idea for a defendant to testify in his own defense."

"I would have disagreed," I said. "I think every jury wants to hear a defendant testify." There was one caveat I didn't mention, however. If the client was guilty and I knew it, or if I thought the client would be chewed up and spit out on cross-examination, then I advised them to exercise their right to remain silent.

"The lawyer thought Junior was stupid and wouldn't be able to stand up to the prosecutor's cross," Willis said. "I'll admit that Junior isn't brilliant, but he isn't stupid, either. I should have never hired that lawyer. Charged me a hundred thousand dollars and didn't do squat."

"Why did you hire him?"

He dropped his chin and shook his head again.

"He's my nephew. My wife's brother's son. He'd been practicing law up in Elizabethton for ten years, but he was in way over his head on Junior's case."

"What about me?" I said. "Of all the lawyers in Nashville, why did you choose me?"

"You're young, Mrs. Carter," he said, before stopping. "Um, should I call you Carter or Myers?"

"Carter is fine," I said.

"Well, Mrs. Carter, you have an excellent reputation. I know you graduated magna cum laude from Vanderbilt, and that you were the editor of the law review. I've been told you're honest, aggressive, and effective. Everybody I talked to spoke very highly of you. And speaking of Myers and Carter, I'm hoping your apple didn't fall too far from your father's tree."

It didn't happen that often anymore, hardly ever, but some clients did know of my father and mentioned him to me. It always made me proud to talk about him.

"He was something special, but I do my best."

"Well, I'm hoping you'll do your best for my son, Mrs. Carter," he said, as he laid a thick manila envelope in front of me. "How much would you charge me to file the petition?"

"What's this?" I said, hoping it wasn't full of cash that he expected me to deliver to some sleazy character in a trench coat. I wasn't going to be a part of bribing anyone.

"There are a hundred letters in that envelope from people in the community who know Junior," he said. "They're letters asking for executive clemency. They're from all sorts of people. Church folks, business owners, a couple of lower court judges, even the Carter County Sheriff…" His throat caught, and he sucked back his emotion. His son had killed his wife while his children slept in the next room. His son was a bad man. But Mr. Willis loved him. Always would. To him, that bad man was his child. His child who just needed a second chance. A third. A fourth…

I took a deep breath and let it out slowly. I felt sorry for the man sitting in front of me, but executive clemency for a convict who had committed premeditated double murder? I didn't think it was possible. At the same time, I thought of my father's words. The words I had heard him say to hundreds of clients as a young girl spying on his meetings: "Every man, woman, and child in this country deserves a proper defense if they find themselves charged with a crime."

"Two thousand dollars," I said. "And I'll tell you again that I don't think we have a snowball's chance in hell of getting your son out of prison. But, if by some miracle the board wants to hold a full-blown hearing, and I have to call in witnesses, it'll be double that. At least."

He stood up, pulled his wallet out of his back pocket, and started counting out hundred-dollar bills. He set the stack of money on top of the envelope and reached out his hand.

"Thank you, Mrs. Carter," he said. "I appreciate you not gouging me on the fee."

I stood and shook his hand, but something didn't feel right.

CHAPTER FIVE

The bar was called Nappy's, a honky-tonk in the truest sense of the expression. It sat off a two-lane state highway on the outskirts of Goodlettsville, a small town twenty miles north of Nashville. The outside of the building was concrete block and painted pale blue. A purple neon sign was perched on the flat roof above the door. Neither of the *p*'s worked, so when the sign was lit at night it read, "Na y's."

There was a narrow walkway between the barstools and the six booths. The interior block walls were also painted pale blue. On the opposite side of the bar was a pool room with only one table and a pinball machine that paid out if you knew the owner, Eli "Nappy" Sparks. James "Whitey" Cornett sat inside the booth in the furthest corner. Cornett was a lifelong criminal in his mid-forties, just shy of six feet tall, thick and muscular.

He spent much of his free time under a bench press and ate anabolic steroids like jellybeans. Cornett's blond hair fell below his shoulders, and his face was sharp and well defined, but full of pockmarks from old acne scars. His eyes were the color of the cinderblock wall, and he liked to brag to anyone who would listen that women of a certain age always told him the blue color reminded them of the old movie star, Paul Newman.

In the booth across from Cornett sat Junior Willis's father, George. Like George Willis, Cornett had been a patronage chief for the Governor and organized a strong voter turnout. Also like Willis, Cornett had donated thousands of dollars to the Black campaign and political action committees. As a thank you, Governor Black had appointed Whitey Cornett as the new state Transportation Commissioner.

When Cornett raised his long-neck Blue Ribbon bottle, George Willis noticed that every finger on his hand boasted a large gold ring, encrusted with various diamond designs. All, that is, except his left thumb.

"How's it gonna work, Whitey?" Willis said as John Prine's "Crazy as a Loon" played in the background.

"You hire the lawyer yet?" Cornett said.

Willis lifted his club soda and took a long drink. "I did. She'll file the petition on Monday."

"It'll happen in a roundabout way," Cornett said. "A lot of asses have to be covered. They have to make it look legit."

"But it'll happen? You're sure of it?"

"Did you bring what they asked for?"

"Thirty thousand cash," Willis said.

"Then it'll happen."

"I would have paid twice as much," Willis said. "It would have been worth it just knowing Junior is out of that dungeon he's been in for the past four years."

"Do you realize the kind of hell that's going to get raised when ol' Junior walks out of jail?"

"I've done a lot for the Governor," Willis said.

"I know you have. Otherwise, he wouldn't do this. He believes in taking care of his friends."

"For a price."

"C'mon, George. You know ain't nothing free in this world."

"So, I should stay in town?"

"If you want to be there when Junior gets out."

"I do."

"Then stick around."

"You'll call me when it's done?"

"No," Cornett said. "I'm not sure who'll notify you, but the less communication between you and me, the better."

Both men swigged their drinks, then swigged again.

"Just remember, George, that the most important thing is silence. This conversation never took place. You never paid a dime to nobody."

"Won't anyone hear a peep out of me," Willis said.

"What about the lawyer?"

"She won't be a problem."

"She better not be," Cornett said, before draining his beer bottle. "Or else she'll end up like her daddy."

CHAPTER SIX

As it turned out, I was right about them denying Junior's clemency and not calling a hearing. But I was wrong about that being the end of it.

Late Wednesday afternoon, I received a call from the governor's general counsel. His name was Reginald Gray. He had a high-pitched voice that was grating and Southern. "I wanted to be the first to congratulate you," he said.

"Congratulate me on what?"

"The governor is commuting Junior Willis's sentence to time served. He'll be released first thing tomorrow morning."

I damn near fell out of my chair. "You're kidding."

"I'm as serious as I can be."

"The Parole Board agreed to this?"

"No."

"I don't understand," I said.

"They called the governor after your petition came in and expressed concern, before recommending Junior remain incarcerated."

"So why is the Governor letting him out?" I said. "It was such a serious crime—"

"It's completely legal," he said, cutting me off. "It's within the Governor's power under the Tennessee Constitution. Governor Black has been told by the Supreme Court and plenty of members of the legislature that our prisons are overcrowded, so he's just… alleviating that particular problem."

"But isn't that—"

"I'm sorry," he said, interrupting me again. "I have a lot on my plate today, so I have to go. I just wanted to call and be the first to congratulate you. You, in turn, can be the first to call Mr. Willis and share the good news."

With that, he hung up. I immediately dialed the number George Willis left with me after our meeting.

"Are you sitting down?" I said to him, after he answered my call.

"As a matter of fact, I am. On a barstool in the Gulch."

"So, you're still in Nashville?"

"I went to see Junior over the weekend," he said. "Decided to stay in case something good happened. Has it?"

"The Governor commuted your son's sentence," I said. "He'll be released in the morning."

"What good news," he said, surprisingly calm. "Thank you for your help, Mrs. Carter. I'd expect a few calls if I were you."

"Why would anyone call me?"

"You filed the petition that got him released," he said. "The press is going to want to know how it happened, and my guess is they'll start with you. I suggest you stick with 'no comment.'"

That uneasy feeling that started with our final handshake was back with a vengeance. My heart was beating faster than normal, and my vision was beginning to tunnel. I couldn't help but feel like I'd been used, and that made me angry.

"Did you pay anyone besides me to get your son out of prison, Mr. Willis?"

"Of course not," he said, "but I don't think that's a question you want to ask again. Ever."

"What's that supposed to mean? Is that a threat?"

"Not if you're a good little gal and keep your mouth shut, it's not," Willis said. "Thank you again for what you did. Good night."

Click.

Good little gal? That son of a bitch had some nerve threatening me. I hung up the phone and stared off into space for a few minutes before buzzing my secretary-slash-paralegal, a forty-year-old black woman named Cheri McKinney.

"Everything okay?" she said.

"No. I'm leaving for the day."

"Where are you going?"

"Home," I said. "And don't call. I'll be drunk."

CHAPTER SEVEN

It was the beginning of the end of summer, and for the first time in months, there was a slight chill in the air. I was sitting on the back deck in a Vanderbilt sweatshirt and was halfway through a bottle of wine, when I heard my husband's S.U.V. pull into the driveway.

It was 6:00 p.m., and he usually didn't get home from work until, at the earliest, eight. During our first few years of marriage, we made it a point to eat dinner at home together at least four nights a week, but since then, the pressure and long hours of both our jobs had led to less and less of those sit-down dinners with long conversation, and more and more to microwave meals in front of the television. I missed those earlier days. Cooking together, laughing, planning our future. Things were simpler then. Less pressure. More fun. Sure, there were problems. Some of those problems still persisted.

Namely, kids.

After we found out that I couldn't have them, he suggested we adopt. It was a logical solution, and one we could easily afford, but I bucked. I used our jobs as an excuse. He was a sheriff, and I was a lawyer. I didn't see where a child would fit. But, of course, that wasn't it. Despite my best efforts to find my father's killer, he was still out there. Free as the wind. Maybe he would come back for me one day. Maybe he would come for my family. There was no way I was going to bring a child into the world to go through that. To see what I saw. To feel what I felt. To always be looking over their shoulder and wondering if today is the day the killer comes back. Mack and I had a safe, stable, happy life. Aside from the occasional nightmare. There was no reason to complicate things with kids.

Besides children, we would talk politics, philosophy, and music. Even poetry. Mack loved poetry, especially Robert Frost. It was unusual. I'd dated my share of guys before him, even had a few serious boyfriends, and out of every one of them, exactly zero liked poetry. That was part of the reason I fell in love. Mack was unexpected. Even after being together for years, he still had the ability to surprise me. To take a side on an issue that I didn't expect. To play a song I never would've imagined him liking. It was nice. He was an original. An anomaly. I hated lying to him.

We met at a wedding five years ago. I had recently graduated law school and wasn't looking for romance at the time, let alone a husband, but there was something that drew me to him. Something besides his butt, which was magnificent. We were introduced by a mutual friend, and before long, we were dating. We talked a lot. Well, I talked a lot. But as time went by, he began to open up. He had earned a football scholarship to Vanderbilt as a tight end, but he told me that after the World Trade Center towers fell in 2001, he started doing research on how to become a Navy SEAL. Then, at the end of his freshman year, he quit the football team and dropped out of school. His father went ballistic, and they nearly came to blows. He screamed that Mack was ruining his life. That he would regret the decision forever. That if his mother were alive to see what was happening, she would be terribly disappointed. And, finally, as the last straw, he told his son that if he went through with his decision, he would never speak to Mack again. He'd held true to his word. At least so far. They hadn't spoken in ten years.

The road to the SEALs is among the most difficult, unforgiving ones on the planet, so, of course, that's the road Mack chose. He received his Special Warfare (SEAL) pin and spent the next five years being deployed on missions all over the world. His military career ended in a fiery helicopter crash in the mountains of Afghanistan. A Taliban rocket took down the chopper carrying Mack, six other SEALs, and the crew. Only three of them survived. Mack was burned severely from the knees down. Three of his vertebrae, his pelvis, and both of his femurs were fractured. Even with the injuries, he managed to drag one of his buddies out of the helicopter before it exploded. He was awarded the Navy Cross for heroism, then spent a year in rehab hospitals in Germany and the United States before being discharged.

After a few months of dating, he told me he wondered why he was spared and the others killed. I admitted to having the same feeling about my father. We decided to see a therapist, and sure enough, we were both diagnosed with Post Traumatic Stress Disorder and survivor's remorse. Strangely, we decided to tie the knot a few months later after the two of us woke up screaming, each from our own nightmare. Funny how shared dreams of death convinced us to officially start a new life together.

Even after Mack's injuries, he worked so hard to recover that he still moved like a cat. I'd never met anyone who was more self-disciplined. I worked out with him and prided myself on keeping up. I was a cross-country runner in high school and college and could still run a marathon if I trained for a couple of months. I could do push-ups, pull-ups, and sit-ups. I just couldn't do as many as Mack. He even taught me several different styles of self-defense used by the SEALs. After one particularly hard session, he called me a green-eyed, red-headed, five-foot, seven-inch, 130 pound badass. Maybe on a lifeless punching bag, I thought, but I had serious doubts whether I could throw those same punches into flesh and bone.

Mack had gotten himself elected sheriff of Williamson County the year he returned home from the Navy. He'd already served a six-year first term and was in the fourth year of his second after running unopposed. He was wearing his uniform when he stepped out on the porch with a beer in his hand.

"Cheri ratted you out," he said, as he sat beside me.

"Needed to think."

"Think or drink?" he said, looking at the nearly empty wine bottle on the table. "What happened?"

I took a long sip of the wine and told him about my encounter with George Willis.

"That's the petition for clemency you worked on this weekend?" he said. "The one you said didn't have a chance?"

"I was wrong. I got a call from Black's lawyer today. The honorable Governor is commuting this double murderer's sentence to time served, which is only four years, and he's being released tomorrow. I called his father to tell him, but I swear he already knew. I asked him if he'd paid anybody besides me to get his son out, and he told me I shouldn't ask that question again. Ever."

I saw Mack's eyes narrow. "He threatened you?"

"Well, not directly," I said. "I took it as a veiled threat, though, to keep my nose out of the governor's business."

"Black's dangerous, Presley," he said. "Dirty and dangerous."

"I know he's a blowhard and a cheat, but dangerous? How do you know? Do you have proof?"

"Not yet. But the rumor is the governor has ties to the Dixie Mafia."

"The Dixie Mafia?" I said, chuckling. "Is that even a real thing? I thought they were just a myth."

"They're no myth," Mack said. "They've actually grown over the past decade, and now one of their lead guys is the governor's Commissioner of Transportation. Which means he'll control the road-building racket, the airports, the river, and the railroads. His name is James Cornett, but everybody calls him Whitey because he's blonde and pale."

"Original."

"Maybe not original, but they're growing. Up until now, they've been known primarily for trafficking drugs and guns. They also own strip clubs all over the Southeast and are getting into bid rigging and influence peddling on a huge scale. It doesn't hurt either now that they have a very good friend in the most powerful position in the Tennessee state government."

"Are you telling me that the people of Tennessee elected a gang member as governor?"

"He's not exactly a member," Mack said. "It's not a tight organization like that. They're more like a bunch of good ol' boys who take advantage of opportunities when they run across them and operate together when it's beneficial. That's why they've been so hard to pin down."

"Somebody oughta change that," I said, finishing my third glass of red.

"What happened to you today is probably just the beginning. Every appointment he's made and will make will be corrupt. I wouldn't be surprised if people start disappearing. Hell, some may even end up murdered. Especially people they suspect might be working with law enforcement."

"Damn, Mack, why haven't you told me about all this before?"

"I didn't think you'd ever be involved."

"Thanks. Now I really feel like a sucker."

"Come on, now. You had no way of knowing Black would grant that petition."

"So, what do I do now?"

"You're going to leave it to law-enforcement folks that know how to deal with them. He'll make a mistake, and they'll nail him."

"Maybe he already has," I said, feeling drunk. "Maybe he shouldn't have messed with Presley Carter."

"Don't you mean Myers?" he said.

I punched his arm. "I'm serious, Mack."

"That's just the booze talking."

"It might be, but if they come back and want me to file another petition because I'm so squeaky clean, I'm going to figure out a way to get in."

"Get in? What do you mean, 'get in'?"

"I'll figure out a way to get close to him."

"And then what?" Mack said. "You plan to get him in the sack and record the pillow talk?"

"Funny."

"Not really."

"*We'll* figure out a way to get close," I said. "We'll bring in whoever we have to, and then we'll sting his ass."

"Why do you keep saying *we*?" he said. "Have you forgotten you're a defense lawyer?"

"Willis told me to be a good little girl," I said. "A good little gal, actually."

"Damn. Lucky for him it was over the phone. But you gotta let it go. You don't want to start anything with these people. Believe me."

"I didn't start it. They came to me and got me involved. They suckered me, and you know what? I don't like being suckered."

"So, you're going to take the governor of Tennessee down, single-handed?"

"Maybe not single-handed," I said. "But if I get half a chance, you're damn right I'll take his ass down. And this 'good little gal's' gonna enjoy doing it."

CHAPTER EIGHT

The next morning, a reporter from the Nashville *Tennessean* called me at 9:15. I was in the office nursing a hangover and going over some materials that pertained to a murder trial that was scheduled in a month. The reporter's name was Marie Robinson. She covered state government for the paper—specifically the executive branch, which was now led by Governor Lonnie Black—and had been doing so for twenty years.

I took the call, and after introducing herself, she asked about the petition. Her voice was deep and her tone aggressive.

"What about it?" I said.

"Who hired you to file it?"

"His father. And just so you know, I was as surprised as everyone else when I heard it went through."

"So you didn't have any idea the fix was in?"

"I don't know what you're talking about. I'm not a fixer. I didn't do anything wrong. I simply filed a petition after being hired to do so by a client."

"Were you paid?"

"Of course, I was paid. I don't work for free."

"Do you mind if I ask how much?"

"Very little. I thought the petition would be rejected out of hand by the Parole Board, and it was. That didn't seem to matter to Governor Black."

"Do you know how it worked?" she said.

"All I know is that I filed it on Monday and forgot about it. Then I got a call from the governor's general counsel yesterday afternoon informing me that he was commuting Junior Willis's sentence to time served."

"And you were surprised?"

"Surprised? I was shocked. But the state constitution is very clear that the governor has the power to grant executive clemency if he sees fit."

"How do you feel about being a part of allowing a double murderer to go free?"

"That's an unfair question," I said. "It implies I knew executive clemency would be granted. Lawyers file these petitions on behalf of incarcerated clients all the time. I don't know the percentages as to how many are granted, but I suspect it's very few."

"Then why did you file it?"

My blood pressure shot through the roof in half a second, and it was all I could do to keep my cool. "Because I was hired to do so."

"Why did his father hire *you*?"

"I asked him the same thing. He said I have a good reputation."

"Actually, I've heard the same thing," she said. "Good stock. So, I was surprised to hear you were a part of this."

"I was simply doing my job, Ms. Robinson, I had no part in anything other than that."

"Would you like to talk about it on the record?"

I paused, thinking. Did I really want to get into this? Did I want to take on what was undoubtedly a corrupt, and perhaps dangerous, governor and his administration? I'd spewed my drunken bravado to Mack, but did I have the courage? Did I have the stomach for it? I knew it would get nasty, and that I could be risking my reputation, my legal career, or even my life. Finally, I made my decision.

"No comment," I said, then hung up the phone.

I needed some advice.

CHAPTER NINE

Ruthie Mae Potter was an icon among criminal-defense lawyers in Nashville. She'd been practicing for more than thirty years and was the first female practitioner who concentrated solely on criminal defense. I remembered hearing my dad speak of her often when I was a child. He had a tremendous amount of respect for her, and so did I.

Ruthie Mae was the kind of person you couldn't help liking. I loved her not only for her brilliant mind and quick wit, but for her quirky personality and the way she dressed. More importantly though, I loved her for her deep sense of commitment to her chosen field. She viewed criminal defense as helping people who were in dire need. If she took your case, you could rest assured you had an aggressive and highly capable advocate. But most of all, I loved her because she took me in when I was a rookie and showed me the ropes. One of the most important things untaught in law school is how to actually practice law. Ruthie Mae taught me how and sent some work my way. I could call or visit her anytime, day or night, and she was more than willing to help.

I called her office and told her secretary, a tall, young blonde named Brittany, that I needed to see her as soon as possible. She was an extremely busy woman, but when Brittany came back on the line, she told me if I'd drive up from Franklin immediately, she'd give me as much time as she could.

When I walked into her office on Second Avenue in Nashville, just a couple blocks from the Adolpho A. Birch Building, which housed Nashville's Criminal Courts, she was sitting behind her massive quartz desk, on the telephone, spreading syrupy sweet Southern charm all over the ear of a Nashville prosecutor. She motioned for me to sit down, and I happily watched her work her magic.

She was wearing a black-and-white striped blouse, but I couldn't see her skirt under the massive desk. She was in her midfifties but looked ten years younger, with silver hair and dark blue eyes. Her skin was smooth, her body toned. A gold cigarette pack sat on her desk, which I knew contained Virginia Slims. She smoked them using a polished mahogany holder that was about six inches long. Smokers usually looked older than nonsmokers. Not Ruthie Mae.

Her beauty and success were awe-inspiring, and as a young woman, made me assume she was married to a beautiful, successful man and had a beautiful, successful family with beautiful, successful children. When I mentioned that to her, she laughed the fantasy away. "You can have a whole helluva lot, my dear," she told me. "But, as much as it pains me to regurgitate a cliche, you in fact cannot have it all." I shrugged it off as cynicism then but find it harder to argue now.

A couple minutes later, she hung up.

"Those young ones are putty in my hands, sweetie," she said in a perfect low-country drawl. She'd been born and raised in Charleston, South Carolina, and had wound up in Nashville after accepting a full academic scholarship to Vanderbilt. Then, like me, graduated at the head of her class at its law school. "I just got him to dismiss a second-degree murder."

"You got a Class A felony kicked?" I said, dumbfounded.

"Sure did."

"I hope you charged your client a ton of money."

"It's an appointed case. The police didn't know my client had a nanny camera in the house that showed her drunken husband trying to stab her with a butcher knife before she put a bullet in him. Didn't believe her when she told them, and she had the good sense to keep her mouth shut about the camera until she got a lawyer. I probably won't even file the paperwork to get paid. It isn't worth the trouble. Anywho, what brings you up here in such a rush, dear? You look distraught."

"I'm thinking of accusing the Governor of being corrupt," I said.

"That's like saying a skunk stinks. It's not an accusation. It's true."

"I don't have any proof of it, really, but I just got off the phone with a reporter from the *Tennessean,* asking me about—"

"The petition you filed for executive clemency?"

"How do you know about that?"

"Lawyers are worse than a sewing circle, Presley. Congratulations on getting your man out, by the way."

"He bought his way out."

"Seems pretty obvious to anyone with half a brain," she said. "It's not like you to stir the pot, though. It must've really gotten under your skin."

"If I talk to a reporter, could they get me for libel?"

"I don't think so," she said. "If someone asks you for your opinion, I don't see how anyone can sue you for giving it to them. As long as you're careful about how you word things."

"What about lawsuits?" I asked.

"Black's a public figure, so I'm not worried about him suing you," she said. "But he isn't going to be pleased, either. If you do speak up, you're going to have a bunch of powerful enemies when the paper comes out."

I had spent my entire life up to this point avoiding making powerful enemies. Staying out of trouble. Doing what was right. What was expected. What my father would do. If Governor Black had the power and connections to get a multiple murderer out of prison without blinking an eye, what could he do to a nosy lawyer accusing him of being a criminal? I was scared, but I was angry, too.

"They used me, Ruthie," I said. "They used me to help them get away with it. And I don't like being used."

She reached for her gold cigarette case and took out a Virginia Slim. She put it in the cigarette holder and lit it with a gold Zippo. The tip of the cigarette was a good eight inches from her lips when she took the first puff.

"You don't mind, do you, sweetie?"

"Your lungs," I said.

She blew a smoke ring, then exhaled the rest through both nostrils, like a dragon. "So, what do you want to do about it?"

"I want to take Black down," I said. "I just don't know how."

She grinned and took another drag. "You'll have to have the Feds' help to do it," she said. "You can't go to the Tennessee Bureau of Investigation because the governor appoints the director. You can't go to the Highway Patrol for the same reason. And you can't go to the Nashville Police or the Davidson County Sheriff's Department because they just wouldn't have the juice to get anything done. Not to mention the conflicts along the way, including your husband. Your only choice is the FBI. Even then, I think you'll run into some problems."

"What kind of problems?"

"Going up against a governor is political," she said. "The FBI likes to think they're not political, but they are. We have a Democrat in the White House right now. The green light for an investigation into a sitting governor would have to come from Washington, and I don't know whether they'd be too serious about trying to take down a member of the same party. After all, the man in the White House has the power to fire the director of the FBI. I could be wrong, though, Presley. This governor is special. He doesn't seem to think any laws apply to him. He wants to get all he can get while the gettin's good. So maybe he's brash enough to become an embarrassment. Politicians hate to be embarrassed. Maybe they'll go after him."

"But not because I ask them to."

Ruthie Mae shook her head and twisted her cigarette holder.

"You're one of my favorite people, and you've become a damned fine lawyer. But you don't have the juice to take on Black by yourself. What you need to decide is whether or not you want to fire the first shot in what will probably become a very political, very dangerous war."

I thought it over for a few seconds. "What would you do?" I asked.

She thought about it, then pulled the cigarette out of the holder and smashed it in her crystal ashtray. "I'd aim for his balls."

CHAPTER TEN

After I left Ruthie Mae's office, my mind was racing and my stomach was growling, so I ate lunch at Barney's Country Kitchen on Eighth Avenue South. The food is served cafeteria style, and like others of its kind in Nashville, is called a "meat and three." Which is pretty much what it sounds like: one meat and a choice of three vegetables. It's some of the best food I've ever put in my mouth. My father first brought me here as a young girl, and I've been coming back ever since. The owner, Ardean Barney, a slight, quiet woman in her seventies, has been running the place as long as I can remember. She loved my father, especially after he got her husband, Lou Jack Barney, out of trouble when he was booked on multiple federal charges for moonshining and tax evasion. After that, she always greeted us with a smile and a hug every time we walked through the door. Even better, she always gave me a free slice of peach cobbler with homemade vanilla ice cream. Still does. The line at lunch usually goes out the door, and when you get to the end of the tray line and pay for your food, the place is so packed you wind up sitting at one of the long communal tables with strangers. I've overheard some of the happiest, saddest, and strangest conversations of my life eating at Barney's. But usually, you've made a friend by the time you've stuffed dessert down your throat.

In fact, I met my secretary, Cheri, at Barney's years ago. She was a server who always had a sunny disposition and a kind word. Plus, she worked as hard as anyone I'd ever seen. So, when my business picked up and I needed a secretary, I asked her if she'd be interested. Miss Ardean didn't like that I was stealing one of her best workers and withheld my free dessert for a few days afterward. She eventually came around and gave Cheri her blessing. We've been together for four years now.

I got back to Franklin around one, and Cheri informed me I had a visitor waiting in my office. He didn't have an appointment, and when I heard his name, I had mixed feelings about seeing him. He introduced himself as Special Agent Lawrence Beard of the FBI and asked if he could speak to me about Junior Willis. I'm sure my mouth fell open given the conversation I'd just had with Ruthie Mae, but I tried to maintain some semblance of composure.

Agent Beard, at first glance, was pure Fed. He had short brown hair parted perfectly on the side, the ill-fitting navy-blue suit, the ugly tie, and the air of superiority, despite the smell of dried sweat hovering around his neck and shoulders. He sat down across from me and got right to the point.

"We've opened an investigation into the governor's commutation of Junior Willis. Am I correct in assuming his father hired you?"

I had repeated this information multiple times to multiple people already, and I didn't want to say it again. I knew I didn't have a choice, though, and it put me in an aggressive mood.

"Am I a suspect or a target in your investigation?"

"I'm not sure yet," he said. "The answers to the questions I ask you will have a lot to do with how we proceed."

"Fire away," I said.

"Who hired you to file the petition?"

"Junior's father, George."

"How much did he pay you?"

"Two thousand cash."

"What did you do with the money?"

"I deposited it in my trust account, just like I'm required to do. I'm above board, Agent Beard. I do things the right way."

"Would you be willing to provide me with a copy of the deposit?"

"Maybe, if you're nice." That comment burrowed straight under his thin skin. I quite enjoyed it.

"Were you given any other money to deliver to anyone?"

"No."

"How can I know that for sure?"

"Because I'm not a liar."

"How did you learn that your petition had been granted and the governor had commuted the sentence to time served?"

"I received a telephone call from Governor Black's general counsel. A man named Reginald Gray."

"What did he say?"

"He congratulated me."

"That's it?"

"Yes. It was a short conversation."

"What did you do then?"

"I called Mr. Willis and told him what the governor had done."

"Did he sound surprised?"

"I think he knew what was going to happen before I did."

"Why would you say that?"

"Because he wasn't surprised."

"How do you know he wasn't surprised?"

His tone was beginning to annoy me. He was a stuffy jerk. "I'm pretty good at reading people, Agent Beard. The man was having a drink at a bar. He knew the petition was going to be granted. He was hanging around Nashville waiting to hear when, not if, he could go get his son out of jail."

"Were *you* surprised?"

"Completely. If I ever used the word *flabbergasted*, which I don't, that's how I would describe my feeling."

"What else did Mr. Willis say?"

"He was my client, so I can't get into specifics. I will say this, though. I may have made an inquiry as to whether he'd paid someone besides me to get the petition granted."

"And his response?"

"Hypothetically, he may have told me it was dangerous to make such inquiries."

"So, he threatened you?"

"In a roundabout way."

"But you have no proof that he paid anyone, how much he paid, or who he paid."

"I don't, but I'm not the FBI agent, am I? I have to tell you, though, I don't think it would be all that hard to figure it out. It had to be someone who could make it happen, and that's a short list of people. He either paid the governor's general counsel or one of his general counsel's assistants because they prepare all the paperwork."

"Or the Pardon board."

"They denied the clemency," I said. "Why would he pay them?"

Beard furrowed his brow. "Do you think you'll be getting more requests to file petitions?"

"I think when word spreads, others will come."

"And what do you plan to do?"

"Politely refuse," I answered. "I'm not going to be a part of any of the governor's corrupt schemes."

"Schemes? Do you have specific knowledge of others?"

"No, I don't, but I've been told this governor has a history of corruption, is connected to the Dixie Mafia, and that you people haven't been able to pin anything on him. Is that true? And if it is, is it going to change now?"

The crow's feet at the edges of his eyes tightened, as did his jaw. "I think that's all I need from you at this time. If you hear from any of Black's people, or receive any other petition requests, I'd appreciate it if you'd give me a call."

"And why, in God's name, would I put my career, hell, my life on the line for a sleazy politician and a sweaty fed?" The overreaction spewed out of me like a geyser. His attitude had caused some of my simmering anger to boil over.

"How would alerting me risk your career or your life?"

"It wouldn't," I said quickly, collecting myself. "I'm afraid I'm putting the cart before the horse on where that phone call could lead. I'll give you a ring if anything comes up."

He stood. "They say your father was the kind of person who'd take a stand for what's right," he said, before nodding to the nameplate on my desk. "Since you use his name for work, I guess I was hoping you were that kind of person, too. Should the need arise, and you call me, of course."

My mind was racing with razor-sharp comments. I wanted to hurt this smug man. I wanted to cut him down to size for even mentioning my father. But, if I was honest, I had to admit I'd asked myself the same question. If it came down to it, would I stand up and fight for what was right? I still wasn't entirely sure. After a few more seconds of awkward silence, he turned to leave.

"Who knows," he said. "Maybe courage skips a generation."

With that, he walked out and closed the door behind him.

I sat in silence, stunned. Agent Beard had unknowingly provided the push I needed to send me over the edge. I didn't need to sit around waiting for the phone to ring with another request for a clemency petition. I didn't need Beard or the FBI, either.

I made my decision. Marie Robinson, the famed political reporter from the *Tennessean*, answered my call after the first ring. I was ready for battle, and I wanted to fire the first shot.

CHAPTER ELEVEN

The following morning the story Marie Robinson wrote was on the front page of the *Tennessean*, above the fold. The headline read: "Attorney Accuses Governor of Corruption in Release of Murderer." There was a photo of me that one of the paper's photographers had taken outside a Nashville courthouse a year or so earlier after I successfully defended a vehicular-homicide case that involved the daughter of a famous country-music singer.

Mack and I sat in silence in front of cold eggs and toast with the paper laid out between us. He had been furious that I hadn't called him before making the decision to talk to the press. He had seen whistleblowers hurt, even killed, and felt betrayed that he was left out of such an important decision. I agreed and apologized, but there was no going back now.

"Be careful today," he said, before grabbing an apple and kissing my forehead. "Call me if there's any sign of trouble." With that, he left for work.

I stayed at the breakfast table reading and re-reading the article. The governor's press mouthpiece denied any wrongdoing and said my comments were "spurious and irresponsible." George Willis, Sr. refused comment, as did the FBI, which made me like Agent Beard even less than I already did. Upon his release, Ms. Robinson reported toward the end of the article, George Willis, Jr., headed straight for the Nashville airport and boarded a plane for Los Angeles.

It sounded familiar. Junior had done what my brother, Aaron, had done two years ago. They had left for very different reasons, of course, but it was true, both men had boarded a plane from Tennessee to Los Angeles, a city that was about as far away from home as either of them could get and still be in the country. Reading the news brought on melancholy thoughts.

I hadn't spoken to Aaron in over a year, but I thought about him every day. I had sent him a hundred dollars every week the first few months he was in Los Angeles. After two of my envelopes were returned with an official yellow sticker from the Postal Service slapped across the front claiming no such occupant resided at the address, I stopped. We spoke less and less, until eventually he drifted away completely. I occasionally tried to reach him, but his phone number had been cut off for months.

As I finished reading the story for the last time, I looked up to see my mother walking through the door. Her name was Delilah Jean Myers, and she was fifty-eight years old. She lived just up the road from us on a fair amount of land she purchased after my father's life-insurance policy paid her $750,000. At first, the insurance company suspected she had a hand in his murder. Eventually, after a year of investigations, delays, and threats of lawsuits, they paid her the money.

She didn't put away a penny of it for Aaron or me, but she did deed us each an acre. Aaron sold his the second he was legally able to, then blew through the money buying drugs, alcohol, and a tricked-out F-150 he promptly totaled after smashing it into a hundred-year-old pine tree. After Mack and I were married, we built our house on my acre.

She also ended up with our family home since my father had willed it to her. She sold the house once Aaron and I had graduated from high school, then took that money and built a small house on the land she'd already bought about three miles away. She told me at the time she couldn't continue living in the house where her husband had been killed now that her kids were of age, but she still felt as though the area was a part of her. She didn't want to leave.

My mother was an attractive woman—I'd always thought so, at least—but she was, to be polite, a bit on the eccentric side. And more often than not, her demeanor was cold. Her hair was strawberry blonde, now heavily streaked with gray, and her eyes were large and turquoise and always seemed to be looking off into the distance. She had a prim nose and high cheekbones, and she had turned herself from a stout meat eater into a lean vegetarian.

She was also obsessed with Elvis Presley. She owned more than a hundred of his albums and singles, all of which she kept in pristine condition. She had backups she played every day on a stereo Mack and I bought her when the old one she'd had for nearly three decades finally died. She had photos, prints, and paintings of

Elvis, his parents, his wife, Priscilla, and his daughter, Lisa Marie, in every room of her house. She'd been to Graceland at least a dozen times. Against my father's wishes, she'd named me Presley and my brother Aaron, which was Elvis's middle name.

She walked in the kitchen, took off her coat, and made herself a cup of tea. "I read about you in the paper," she said. "You're a celebrity."

"Like Elvis," I said.

"You can't sing, and I've never seen you shake your hips the way he did."

"When did you start reading the paper?" I said. "I thought you hated news."

"I decided to give it a try a couple of months ago. Thought I needed to be better informed about the goings-on around here. But to be honest, I was planning to cancel my subscription. It's all so depressing."

She was wearing a yellow-and-green floral-print dress, the kind of clothing she favored. Unlike my father, she was a hippie. My mother was also an excellent artist and photographer. She painted landscapes in oil and watercolor, she did charcoal and pencil drawings, and she stalked birds and photographed them everywhere she went. She had developed both skills through the years and now made a decent living selling her art and photographs at local shows and on the internet.

"I wish you hadn't seen the article," I said.

"Well, I did, and I have to ask you a question. What made you decide to take on the most powerful man in the state?"

"Somebody has to."

"Do you want to wind up like your father?"

"I have no intention of letting anyone kill me."

"I don't know that you'd have much of a choice if they decide you've stepped over some imaginary line or are bringing a bunch of pressure down on them from the police."

"Mother, please. Just stick to your work, and I'll stick to mine."

"I don't want to see anything happen to you. Is that so hard to understand?"

"Daddy would be proud."

"He probably would be, but that's enough reason to head the opposite way. He was a windmill chaser, Presley, and a frustrated one at that. You got a lot of your father in you, but I was hoping you avoided picking up that particular trait." She sipped her tea, then continued, "You and Aaron are all I have left, and he's in California, which means he might as well be on the moon. I don't want to lose you, too."

"You're not going to lose me," I said. "They'd be stupid to kill me after what was in the paper. Every law enforcement agency in the state, plus the feds, would be breathing down their necks."

"And you'd still be dead."

"Stop it, Mother." I carried my cup over to the sink, rinsed it, and put it in the dishwasher. "I have to go to work now. I'll see you later."

"I hope so," she said, dramatically.

I made the drive to my office in Franklin in about ten minutes and parked in the same spot I parked in every day. It was in a small lot across the street from my office.

When I got out of the car, I noticed a medium-height, solidly built white man wearing a black coat, white shirt, and black pants walking toward me from my left. He was moving quickly.

"Miss Myers," he said.

I knew immediately he was a stranger. I only used my maiden name for work. I turned and looked at the man. He was wearing aviator sunglasses, which struck me as strange because it was cloudy, and a blue Atlanta Braves baseball cap pulled low on his forehead.

"May I help you?"

"You certainly can," he said, then pulled back his coat to reveal the butt of a revolver in a holster on his belt. "You can keep your mouth shut about Governor Black. I'd really hate to see something bad happen to you."

I quickly reached into my purse and pulled out my phone. I intended to take a photo of him and call 9-1-1, but he jerked it out of my hand and threw it over my car. That's when instinct and Mack's training took over. I threw a jab, a cross, and an uppercut that sent the man to the asphalt, sucking air and bleeding from his nose. I was shocked. I couldn't believe I had done it. It was over before it had begun, and I stared at the man as he stood back up.

"Bitch," he grunted, then took a step toward me.

"Fire, fire, fire!" I yelled, as I took off running toward my office. I had heard on the news and from friends that yelling *fire* instead of *help* was twice as likely to get people's attention. I refused to believe the cynical thought, but no sooner did I get the words out of my mouth than a group of people started to gather. The man in the hat and sunglasses immediately ran in the opposite direction, then disappeared around the side of a building.

My heart was beating at the cadence of a fully automatic machine gun as I surveyed my surroundings. The short sprint had ended with me a yard or so from the door to my office. Sensing the danger had passed and my assailant vanished, I bent at the waist and hungrily gulped air into my lungs.

I knew it wasn't over. I had won this small battle, but the war had just begun.

CHAPTER TWELVE

I was sore and shaken by the encounter with the man in the black coat, but I wasn't terrified. It gave me a strange sense of satisfaction knowing I'd rattled the Governor's cage enough to cause him to send a goon with a gun to threaten me on the street. It gave me even more satisfaction knowing I had handled myself physically. I hadn't frozen. I had punched a grown man and knocked him to the ground. It felt good.

I needed to call Mack, and I figured I should also call Agent Beard—even though I didn't care for him personally—just to let him know what had happened. Mack would be angry and want to hunt the guy down and arrest him. Beard would want me to look at photos of people associated with Black to see if I could pick the guy out. If I did, they'd start watching him closely and try to determine exactly where he fit in the Governor's hierarchy.

All that had to be taken care of, and I would take care of it. But I had to put it behind me for now and get on with my day. I had a 9:30 a.m. meeting with a young man who had been charged with several felonies, all drug related. His name was Dustin Jackson, and he was a ruggedly handsome, twenty-three-year-old with black, bushy hair that reminded me of a horse's mane. He'd been an all-state football player in high school and had earned a scholarship to Middle Tennessee State, where he played linebacker for two years before his mother died of colon cancer. After that, he went off the rails and was finally kicked off the team for repeatedly missing meetings, practices, and failing drug tests. He dropped out of school and began selling marijuana, along with, I was certain, more serious drugs I hadn't bothered to ask him about.

Four months earlier, he'd been home alone one night when two young men and a woman broke into his rented house and attempted to rob him. One of the men shot Dustin in the right thigh. What they didn't realize was that Dustin had a gun of his own. He shot back and wounded the man who had shot him before the robbers fled. Neighbors who heard the gunshots called the police, and when they arrived, they found Dustin bleeding, plus five pounds of marijuana, eight thousand dollars in cash, and three handguns. He was charged with maintaining a dwelling where drugs were sold, possession with intent to sell, and using a firearm in the commission of a felony. He made bond (probably with drug money the police hadn't found), recovered quickly, and hired me. I was making some progress on the case with the assistant district attorney, primarily because it was the first time Dustin had been arrested.

Then he did something incredibly stupid.

Dustin and his eighteen-year-old girlfriend thought it would be a good idea to get high and visit the Nashville

City Cemetery at three o'clock in the morning. Before they went, however, they parked their car in a convenience-store parking lot where they smoked pot and drank beer. The convenience store's security video showed them pulling in at 1:57 a.m. At 2:30 a.m., Dustin went into the store to buy a pack of cigarettes. He was inside for five minutes, and the heavy-set woman behind the register smelled marijuana and alcohol. The clerk, who could be seen on the security camera peeking out the window at Dustin's vehicle several times, finally called the police, and two cruisers showed up at 2:45. Dustin and the girl were high as kites and dumfounded to be in the spotlight of Nashville's finest. He immediately fessed up to having a small amount of marijuana and gave it to the officers, which gave them grounds to arrest him and search his car. His girlfriend also had a small amount of pot, which she immediately gave over to the officers. Upon searching the vehicle, the police discovered the psychedelic drug DMT. Although it was a small amount, it was enough for the police to charge Dustin with possession with intent to distribute.

The assistant district attorney was willing to be reasonable, but Dustin had backed himself into a corner. He was looking at serious prison time. Against my advice, he'd made bond on the second drug charge and was still on the streets. I'd told him it would be best if he started building some time behind bars, since every day spent inside would count against his eventual sentence if he was convicted. Which I was certain he would be. Dustin ignored me and made the $20,000 bond on the second arrest. He'd also paid me another five thousand dollars to represent him on the DMT charge, but there really wasn't much I could do for him, other than make the best deal I could.

He showed up ten minutes late for our meeting, looking haggard.

"Long night?" I said, when he plopped down in the chair across from me. He was wearing an expensive Ralph Lauren T-shirt and a pair of $200 blue jeans full of holes.

"Having trouble sleeping," he said.

"Would you like a cup of coffee? I need you alert."

"Sure. Black."

I got up and went into the kitchenette and poured him a cup of coffee that Cheri had made earlier, walked back in, handed him the mug, and sat down behind my desk. "I have good news and bad news."

"I'll take the good first."

"The prosecutor is willing to cut you some slack."

"Cool. The bad?"

"You're going to wind up in the penitentiary."

"The penitentiary? Which one?"

"I don't know," I said. "Probably one of the mediums. My guess would be Morgan County."

"How long?"

"The D.A. has agreed to dismiss the gun charge since you shot the guy in self-defense. He wants one year on maintaining a dwelling where drugs were sold, which is the minimum. He wants the same on the five pounds of pot, also the minimum. He's willing to run those concurrently, so the effective sentence is one year."

"That's sweet as hell. I'll keep my nose clean and be out in six months."

SCOTT PRATT

"Hold your horses," I said. "On the DMT, he's willing to give you the minimum as well, but the minimum on that one is eight."

"Years? Jesus." He popped out of the chair and started to pace.

"Since you were out on bond when you caught the charge, the law requires the sentence to be consecutive."

"What the hell does that mean?"

"It means you're looking at nine years. You'll be eligible for parole in just under three. Unless you do something stupid."

He shook his horse's mane. "Damn," he said. "Three years? I can't do no three years."

"The alternative is to take everything to trial."

"Let's take it to trial then."

"We'll lose. The facts in both cases are terrible. A trained monkey could prosecute you and get a conviction. I don't have a defense to any of the charges. If you don't take the deal, you'll wind up with anywhere from sixteen to twenty years, depending on how upset the judge is after she hears the case."

He slumped back down in the chair, crossed his arms, and began muttering, "Three years, three years, three years."

"I'm sorry, Dustin. It's the best you're going to do."

"Didn't they just let a damned murderer out?" he said. "Some dude that killed two people. Didn't you have something to do with that?"

I knew my accusations were getting attention, but I was shocked this kid read the paper. "I was as surprised as anyone when he got out."

"See there, that's what I'm talkin' about. How do I get some of that love?"

"You find somebody close to the governor, then you buy your way out."

"How much would it cost me?"

"A lot, I would imagine."

"Can you hook me up with someone?"

I thought for a minute about the question. I had no intention of hooking him up with someone corrupt, but I thought about Agent Beard and the power of the FBI. It was daunting, and a little scary, but I was in now. There was no turning back.

"You'd have to enter a guilty plea and go to prison," I said. "But I might be able to help you get out. Do you have someone you trust?"

"My girlfriend. I trust her."

"Would she be willing to work with the FBI? Maybe wear a wire?"

"I don't know about all that," he said. "I don't know if I'd want her being a snitch for the feds, anyhow."

"It's either that or serve the time."

"I don't know. I guess I could talk to her."

I already knew the girl, whose name was Emma, would agree, because Dustin would talk her into it. He was a likable enough kid, but he was a drug dealer, and from the experiences I'd had with drug dealers, I knew they ultimately looked out for one person and one person only: themselves.

"Do you have money stashed?" I asked.

He nodded.

"A lot or a little?"

"I've moved a ton of product and don't spend much money, so—"

"La-la-la!" I yelled. "Too much information. Talk to Emma and get back to me."

"Would it be dangerous? For her, I mean."

"It could be. It could be dangerous for you, too, if something goes wrong and they find out what we're up to."

Dustin dropped his head and shook it from side to side. He stayed that way for a long moment before he stood and looked me in the eyes. "I'll think about it," he said.

CHAPTER THIRTEEN

I heard back from Dustin after lunch. Emma was in. She was willing to go meet with the FBI and wear a wire if necessary. As soon as I hung up, I called the Nashville FBI office and asked to speak to Agent Beard. He hadn't bothered to leave me a card when we had our little chat. I wondered as I waited whether he would pick up the phone when he heard it was me calling.

"Special Agent Beard," he said in his deep baritone.

"Guess who?" I said.

"What do you want, Mrs. Carter?"

"I want to meet again."

"Why?"

"Because I think I can help you with the case we were discussing. Do you have a private place where you meet people?"

"Do you know Percy Warner Park?"

"My husband and I run there a lot."

"You know the parking lot at the bike trail?"

"Yes."

"When is good for you?"

"I can come now," I said.

"I'll be in a blue Chevy sedan. When you get there, park next to me and come get in."

It was raining when I pulled into the secluded parking lot, which was empty with the exception of Beard's car. He had traded in his blue suit for a brown one and regarded me suspiciously when I climbed into the passenger seat.

"What do you have?" he asked me, dry as a desert.

"The governor sent a man to visit me this morning when I arrived at work," I said. "He walked up to me, showed me a gun, and told me to keep my mouth shut about Governor Black. He said he'd hate to see something bad happen to me."

"What'd he look like?"

"Hard to tell with the hat and glasses. Medium height, white, barrel-chested. Dark hair, crooked teeth."

"Did he hurt you?"

"No," I said, smiling. "But I got him pretty good."

"What do you mean?"

"Jab-cross-uppercut combo," I said, while throwing the punches in the air. "Put him on his ass, bleeding through his nose."

"You hit him?"

"Three times," I said. "Hard and fast, just like I was taught."

"Okay…" he said, wrapping his head around it. "I'll get some photos together if you'd be willing to take a look."

"Sure," I said. "But everything happened so quick, I don't know if I'll be able to pick him out. Should have a pretty good shiner on his eye, though."

"I wish you'd told me on the phone. I could have brought some photos with me."

"I want to discuss something else right now."

"Okay."

"I have a client who is looking at nine years in the state pen. He doesn't have any other choice but to plead guilty because I don't have a defense. When we were talking about it this morning, he mentioned the governor letting a murderer out of prison, then he asked me how he could get the same treatment."

"What did you tell him?"

"I told him he'd have to buy his way out."

"Now, hold on a minute, Mrs. Carter…"

"But…" I continued, "I said the only way I'd help him do it, is if he went to jail and got somebody on the outside to offer the bribe and wear a wire doing it."

"And?"

"He has an eighteen-year-old girlfriend who's willing. The problem for me is that I don't know who the governor's man is. I don't even know who his patronage chief is in Nashville. Seems to me that'd be the place to start."

"His patronage chief is a man named Biney Beals," he said. "Owns a bunch of fried fish places around town. Multi-millionaire crook. He's the governor's type of guy."

"Did you say Biney? What kind of name is Biney?"

"Old country one, I guess," Beard said. "He and Black are tight, and you're right, he'd be the man I'd start with. So, do you want me to meet with this girl?"

"I want to be there, too."

"When's your client set to go in?"

"His next court date is in two weeks."

"Let me guess," he said. "You want us to put up the money for the sting?"

"My guy has his own money. And I don't want you to bust anyone until the governor signs the paperwork either pardoning or commuting my client. I need your word."

Beard stuck his thumbnail in his mouth and chewed on it for a few seconds. I don't know why, but seeing him do that, chewing his nail like that, made me like him just a little bit better.

"I have to run it by my bosses, but I think it's something we can do," he said. "I'll get back to you."

I opened the passenger door and stepped out into the rain. "Oh, Agent Beard?" I said, leaning back in. "There's one more thing I forgot to ask you."

"What is it?" he said.

"I guess courage doesn't skip a generation after all, does it?"

Agent Beard had no answer, so I grinned from ear to ear and shut the door in his face.

CHAPTER FOURTEEN

I decided not to tell Mack about the governor's messenger until he came home that night. He'd reminded me the evening before that he had a SWAT training exercise scheduled and would be home late. He also said he'd bring sushi, so we wouldn't have to cook. After I got home, I still had an hour before he'd be back, so I went into my study and delved into something that had been a full-time obsession of mine—trying to figure out who killed my father.

The Williamson County Sheriff's Department had investigated the murder initially, but they had very little forensic evidence and only a vague description from a terrified, unreliable twelve-year-old eyewitness—me. After clearing my mother, the police were initially focused on my father's clients, especially those who had gotten out of prison around the time of the murder, but they didn't find anything that pointed to a suspect. The police pursued one dead-end after another, until finally the dead-ends disappeared. They'd never officially closed the case, but it sat there in files and boxes year after year until my own husband took over the department. It didn't matter. Mack told me he just didn't have enough guys to assign someone to work it. I was upset, and I gave him the cold shoulder for a few nights, but one day I came home from work and found piles of files and stacks of boxes, all pertaining to my father's case, waiting for me in our home office. I knew Mack had to pull major strings, and probably tell some major lies, to get those files and boxes home to me. It was a helluva gesture, and I told him I'd never forget it.

I believed the answer to who killed my father was in one of those boxes stacked floor to ceiling. Some contained two files, some as many as ten. When I had spare time, which wasn't often, I went through them, looking for something—anything—that might set me on a path toward his killer. There was one word that I searched for the most, however. I had learned it after telling the detectives about seeing the killer's one blue and one brown eye. Heterochromia, they said. That's what the condition is called. I never forgot it.

I hadn't seen it listed on any of the criminals' profiles, but I kept looking. Murder cases, rape cases, assault cases, DUI cases, drug cases, practically every crime imaginable. I'd been searching the files for years and was about halfway through the stack, but still no closer to the truth. Or to any true peace of mind.

I heard Mack and Abby come into the house a little after eight. I closed the file I was studying and walked out of the room to greet them. The dog sniffed me twice, then hurried to the living room and plopped down on her oversized bed. Mack smiled at me. His eyes still lit up every time he saw me.

"Hi, babe," I said, as I walked toward him. He set a bag of food on the kitchen table, picked me up, and kissed me as I wrapped my arms around his neck. "Good day?"

"It was fine. How about yours?"

"It was a little strange, to be honest."

He set me back on the floor.

"Something happened."

"Let's talk while we eat," I said. "Want me to get you a beer?"

"I'll take a bottle of water."

"Sure."

I went to the refrigerator, grabbed two bottles of water, and sat down across from Mack at the dining-room table. "No point in beating around the bush," I said. "But promise me you'll stay calm."

"I'm always calm," he said. It was true, too. On the exterior, Mack never appeared rattled, most likely due to his military training. But I knew what I was about to say would test that training.

"Spit it out," he said.

"A man walked up to me outside work this morning and told me to keep my mouth shut about the governor and that he'd hate to see something bad happen to me. He pulled his coat back and showed me the butt of a pistol."

"Don't suppose you have any idea who he is."

"Never saw him before, but I just assumed he's one of Governor Black's goons. He was wearing a half-assed disguise. Sunglasses and a Braves cap."

"What'd you do?"

"I pulled my phone out, but he grabbed it and threw it over my car."

"Then what happened?"

"Well…" I said, "then I kicked his ass."

"Really?"

"It was beautiful."

"What did you use?"

"My fists. Simple three-punch combo. He went down like a sack of potatoes."

"Jab-jab-cross?"

"Jab-cross-uppercut."

"Damn, Press! That's my girl."

He hugged me, then pulled back, a serious look on his face. "Are you okay? Are you hurt?"

"Hands are a little sore, but I feel like a million bucks. Just a little worried about how much I liked it."

"Did you call the police?"

"It was all over so fast, there wasn't any point."

"Him flashing that pistol is aggravated assault, Presley. It's a C felony. You should have called and at least made a report. If we can find him, you can have him arrested."

"I'm a lawyer, Mack. I know what he did was a felony. But I don't think Jake Gram would allow a prosecution to move forward."

"Why not?"

"First off, the guy who threatened me obviously works for the governor, and Attorney General Gram's a Democrat and pretty much gutless. He wouldn't cross the governor. Secondly, there weren't any witnesses. And third, he didn't take the gun out or point it at me."

"The law says if a person puts you in reasonable fear of death or—"

"I *know* the law. Please stop treating me like I'm stupid."

"Sorry," he said. "Were you scared?"

"Didn't have time to be."

Mack shook his head. "Guy threatens you with a gun and you go all fists of fury. Damn, Presley. I don't know if you're brave or nuts."

"I just did what you taught me."

"But if he'd just walked up and started shooting, I'd be planning your funeral," he said. "I'm gonna get the extra pistol out of the safe and put it in your purse."

"Mack—"

"No arguments."

"Okay," I said. "It's a dangerous world sometimes."

"Especially when you rat out the governor and whip his gangster."

"So now you're going to blame me?"

"I'm not blaming you," he said. "Not at all. I just want to find the guy. What did he look like again?"

"Like every other middle-aged white dude in Nashville. An FBI agent is going to put together some photos."

"Wait a second. You called the feds?"

"It was the agent that came to my office yesterday. I told you about him. I called him about something unrelated."

"Which was?"

"I'll tell you after."

"After what?"

"After I jump your bones."

I grabbed his hand and led him toward the bedroom.

"Don't think you're off the hook," he said. "I'm not going to forget about that."

"Enough of the serious stuff," I said. "It's been a stressful day. I need to blow off a little steam."

That night, after making love and falling asleep, I was haunted by the recurring nightmare where my father was murdered. But when I jerked awake, the paralyzing fear wasn't suffocating me like it usually did. I could breathe.

It felt good.

CHAPTER FIFTEEN

The Governor's Mansion was a three-story Georgian-style home that sat on ten perfectly manicured acres nestled in the exclusive Nashville suburb of Oak Hill. It had served as the home of Tennessee's Governor since 1949 and had been open for public tours every year since. Except this year. When Governor Black was elected, he discontinued the tours, stating that the constant stream of visitors would have an adverse effect on his ability to work for the good people of Tennessee.

On this night, however, two men strolled the outer edge of the property. One was James "Whitey" Cornett, Black's Transportation Commissioner. Besides his official title, he also organized the governor's personal security detail, and other, more clandestine jobs. Like picking up a bag of money from a released murderer's father.

The man walking next to Whitey was named Zeke Gibson. He was in a black short-sleeved polo and black jeans. Gibson's official position was Executive Director of the Tennessee Alcoholic Beverage Commission, but, like Cornett, he had other duties he performed for Lonnie Black. Like threatening loud-mouthed, nosy attorneys who don't know how to mind their own business.

"How'd it go?" Cornett said.

"I did what you told me to do. I'm sure she got the message."

"What did she do?"

"The first thing she did was pull out her phone. I guess she was gonna call the cops. But I got it away from her and slung it."

"Then?"

Gibson went quiet.

"Zeke, you got a swollen nose and a black eye. You might as well spit it out."

"She caught me by surprise," Gibson said. "Hell, I wasn't expectin' some woman to start throwing punches. Plus, she was quick as a damn cat."

"She get a good look at you?"

"I don't *think* she'd recognize me, but I can't say for sure," Gibson said. "It was broad daylight, after all."

"Did you stay on her?"

"Yes," Gibson said. He was short with Cornett. He always felt like the man talked down to him. And now it would only get worse.

"What did she do for the rest of the day?"

"She worked in the office, then later on she went out to Percy Warner and met with a guy in a blue Chevy."

"A boyfriend?" Cornett said. "That'd be good to know."

"The car had a fed tag."

"FBI?"

"I couldn't hear what was said, but it looked like it."

"Shit," Cornett said. "Who is this woman, anyway?"

"Just a lawyer on a crusade, I guess. She obviously doesn't like the governor very much."

"I want to know everything there is to know about her," Cornett said. "From her bra size to her IQ. And I want some ears in her office."

"Done."

"Tonight."

"You got it."

"We've come a long way," Cornett said. "We're in a position to make millions over the next four years. I don't want it screwed up by some righteous criminal lawyer."

"She's nothing," Gibson said. "She's a pissant."

"A pissant with a helluva right cross," Cornett joked.

"What are you tryin' to say?" Gibson said, fuming.

"I'm saying you do what I tell you to do. Lonnie's worked long and hard to get here, and he's had a lot of help along the way. It's time to reap the rewards, and if this woman wants to get in the way, we'll do whatever we have to do to take care of her. Is that clear?"

"Yes, sir," Gibson grunted.

"This conversation stays between me and you, Zeke. Lonnie has enough on his mind."

Cornett puffed his cigar, cursed under his breath, and walked back toward the mansion.

Gibson watched him until he was out of earshot, then spit on the ground in Cornett's direction. "Dickhead."

He turned and walked toward his car.

CHAPTER SIXTEEN

In three days, Agent Beard had approval from his bosses and came by my office with some photos. He placed six of them down in front of me.

"That's him," I said, pointing immediately to the man who had threatened me. "What's his name?"

"Gibson," Agent Beard said. "Zeke Gibson. He's the Executive Director of the Alcohol Commission. You sure he's the guy?"

"Positive," I said. "I didn't think I would be, but I am."

I told Agent Beard I thought we wouldn't be able to get Gibson charged with a crime, and even if we did, he wouldn't be convicted. And even if he was charged and convicted, the Governor would pardon him immediately. Beard agreed and waited at my office while I contacted Dustin Jackson and told him to bring over his girlfriend. The two of them showed up an hour later.

Emma Hodge was an innocent-looking eighteen-year-old with long, curly blonde hair and big hazel eyes. She was about my height but couldn't have weighed 90 pounds with rocks in her pockets. Her skin was pale, smooth, and unblemished, and she had an aura of sweetness about her that made me wonder what in the hell she was doing hanging around with a drug dealer. She was dressed simply in black jeans and a white blouse and sat across from me and Agent Beard with a silly looking smile.

"It's nice to meet you, Emma," I said. "This is Special Agent Beard."

I knew both Dustin and Emma would be jumpy around an FBI agent, so Beard and I agreed that I would do most of the talking.

"Dustin tells me you're willing to go see a man and offer to pay him to help Dustin get out of jail," I said. "Is that right?"

"Yes, ma'am."

"No need to make me feel old," I said. "Presley will do."

"Okey-dokey."

"Agent Beard and his fellow officers will outfit you with a tiny transmitter that will be completely undetectable, and they'll be close by recording your conversation. I hope to be there with them. If everything goes according to plan, they'll eventually use the recording to try to convict the governor, along with some other people, of various crimes. I already have the FBI's assurance that no arrests will be made until after Dustin is released."

Her eyes darted to Agent Beard, who forced a smile and nod.

"They've also assured me that if the governor is arrested, it will have no bearing on Dustin's freedom. Are you with me so far?"

She nodded her head and continued to smile.

"This could be dangerous for you, Emma," I said. "Do you understand that?"

"How could it be dangerous?"

"If the people you're going to pay somehow find out about what you're doing, if you say the wrong thing, I don't know what they might do. They might assault you. Might even try to kill you to send a message to others."

"Kill me?" she said. "Jeez."

"Nothing has been set in stone," I said. "You don't have to do this if you don't want to."

"Stop trying to talk her out of it," Dustin said.

"Sit there and keep your mouth shut," Agent Beard said. "It's our obligation to make her fully aware of the risks involved."

His outburst seemed to thicken the air in the room.

"It's okay," Emma finally said. "I promise I won't say the wrong thing. And I'm not afraid." She turned toward Agent Beard. "How is it supposed to work?"

"You'll need to set up a meeting with a man named Biney Beals," Agent Beard said.

Emma giggled at the name. I had to admit, it wasn't one you heard every day.

"Mr. Beals owns several restaurants and is close friends with the governor," Beard continued. "But first, you may have to go through an intermediary."

"A what?" she asked.

"Just someone not as close to the governor, at first, before you get to Mr. Beals," I said.

"Eventually, though," Beard said, "once you meet Beals, you'll tell him that your boyfriend has just gone into jail and that you want to get him out. He'll ask you about Dustin and his case, and you just tell him the truth. At some point, the discussion will turn to money. You'll have to ask how much it will cost to get him out. It'd be best if you could get him to talk as much as you can about how the entire process works."

"And y'all will record it all?" she asked Agent Beard.

"Yes."

"And Dustin will get out of jail?"

"That's the plan," he said.

"What then?"

"The FBI will want you to testify in court later if we end up getting indictments and making arrests."

"Who all will they arrest, again?" she said, excited and wide-eyed.

I could see the ditzy, eager girl was grating on Agent Beard. "I'd imagine several people will wind up in jail," I said. "Maybe even the governor."

Despite a nasty look from Beard, I continued. "The FBI will need you in court to authenticate the tape recording and point out the people you met," I said. "They'll want you to testify to how much money you paid, how you paid it, whom you paid, all that kind of thing. I'm sure they'll mark the money so they find at least some of it when they make arrests." I looked at her with concern. This was dangerous work. "You think you can handle all that?"

"I can definitely handle all that," she said. "No problem-o."

"Don't be too overconfident," I said. "A lot of things could go wrong."

"But you said they'll be close by, right?" She turned to Agent Beard. "The FBI people, I mean."

He nodded.

"They will, and so will I," I said. "We'll do everything in our power to make sure no harm comes to you."

She looked at Dustin, who was still fuming from Beard telling him to keep his mouth shut and winked. Then she looked back at me.

"This'll kind of be like acting," she said. "I've always wanted to try it out. It'll be fun."

"You're sure you want to do it?" I said, giving her one last out.

"Whole hog," she said. "Anything for my baby doll."

That soothed Dustin's ego.

"All right, then," I said. "Just leave your contact information with Cheri out front. Agent Beard and I will be in touch soon."

CHAPTER SEVENTEEN

The following morning, a little after 9:00 a.m., Zeke Gibson knocked on the door and walked into the Governor's bedroom in the Executive Mansion. Gibson was wearing large aviator sunglasses that hid his bruised eye. Lonnie Black was sitting at a small round table near a large window, wearing a red silk robe and eating a plate of eggs Benedict.

"We need to talk," Gibson said.

The Governor took a sip of coffee. "Mind if I keep eating?"

"Wouldn't want it to get cold," Gibson answered.

"You want an egg or anything?"

Gibson shook his head no, then said, "I think Whitey Cornett might become a problem."

"What? Why? What's going on?"

"You know that lawyer that ran her mouth to the press? He told me to pay her a visit and threaten her."

Black stopped eating and laid his fork on his plate.

"I should have asked you about it first," Gibson said, "and I'm sorry I didn't, but I talked to her on the street outside her office."

"What did you say?"

"Not much of anything. Just threatened her a little. I showed her a gun and told her it'd be best if she kept her mouth shut."

The maid walked in, and Black told her to bring Gibson a cup of coffee. "Was she scared?" Black said, after the maid walked out.

"Didn't punch like it," Gibson said, then removed the glasses, expecting the Governor to make fun of him.

Instead, Lonnie Black got serious. "That all there is to it?"

"Whitey told me to get some listening devices in her office."

"Did you?"

"Of course. I figured listening to her isn't such a bad idea. But threatening her with a gun in broad daylight? Whitey's a loose cannon, Lon. And I guess this is a little off topic, but I don't exactly love him ordering me around like I'm his houseboy, either."

The maid returned with the coffee and made a quick exit.

"I've already heard from a couple of people that he's starting some rackets on his own in the department," Black said. "I'm pretty sure he's already strong-arming contractors, too. Maybe I made a mistake bringing him in."

"So, what do we do?"

"First thing you do is tell him you work for me. Not him. If he tells you to do anything else, tell him to go to hell and that comes straight from the Governor."

"And after that?"

"Let's wait a little while and see what he does. Like I said, maybe I made a mistake. But that doesn't mean I can't rectify it."

"So, you'd just fire him?"

"I don't think I could just fire a man like Whitey," Black said. "I think it'd be smarter if you took care of it."

"I hate to say it," Gibson said, "but at this point, it'd be a pleasure."

Governor Black was silent as he broke the slimy egg yolk perched on top of his second English muffin and watched the tasty yellow liquid pool. As Black took a bite, he nodded at Zeke Gibson.

"Keep on this lawyer, and start making a plan for Whitey… in case it comes to that."

CHAPTER EIGHTEEN

Agent Beard had learned that Biney Beals's closest associate was a man named Chuck Haynes, who managed Beals's original fried fish shack. Haynes was the gatekeeper we had to get past in order to meet Biney Beals. Four days after her visit to my office, Emma Hodge was sent by Agent Beard to meet Haynes. He didn't tell me about the meeting, although I'd asked to be included.

Instead, Agent Beard called me and told me it was against bureau policy for non-FBI personnel to be included in undercover operations, and he thought it was a conflict of interest for me to represent both Dustin Jackson and Emma Hodge. I told him I wasn't representing Emma, merely advising her. He didn't budge, and there was nothing I could do. He said he'd send me a transcript of the meeting, but he wouldn't tell me the exact time or place. Apparently, Emma and Chuck were the only two people in the fish shack when she arrived. Agent Beard kept his word and sent me a transcript of their meeting. I sat down to read it as soon as it arrived.

Confidential Informant: Hi, I was wondering if Mr. Beals is in?

Haynes: Sorry, pretty girl, he ain't here today.

BLOOD IS BLACK

CI: Is there any way you could help me set up a meeting with him?

Haynes: Not sure. What would you want to talk to him about? Maybe I can handle that for you.

CI: I'd really rather not say. I don't mean to be rude, sir, but it's important that I talk to *him*. I understand he's a close friend of the governor.

Haynes: And where'd you hear a thing like that?

CI: Just a friend I know. I'd make it worth Mr. Beals's while.

Haynes: Is that right? And how would you do that?

CI: I have money. Please, I need a huge favor. I'm desperate, and I was told Mr. Beals might be able to help.

Haynes: He might. But what about me?

CI: I don't understand.

Haynes: You want me to set up a meet between you and Mr. Beals, am I right?

CI: Yes, sir.

Haynes: Chuck, baby. Just Chuck.

CI: Okay. Chuck.

Haynes: Okay, then. What's in it for me?

CI: You mean money? How much would you want?

Haynes: I don't want your money, pretty girl. I had a little something else in mind.

CI: What?

Haynes: Why don't we step into my office, and we can talk about it?

CI: I don't know if that would be such a good idea.

Haynes: Suit yourself. Have a nice day.

CI: Wait. Okay, I guess I could talk, if that's all you want.

Haynes: Just let me lock the front door so nobody don't bother us.

Every word and every sound were written on the transcript. Keys jingling, a lock turning.

Haynes: Go on back there behind the counter. Office is right there.

(The sound of a door closing and locking.)

CI: Uhhh… What did you want to talk about?

Haynes: You like snakes?

CI: What? No! I'm terrified of them.

Haynes: Well, pretty girl, I'm afraid that's a fear you're gonna have to overcome if you want to meet with Mr. Beals.

(Sound of a zipper.)

CI: What are you doing?

Haynes: I'm introducing you to my snake. If you want to meet my good friend, you're going to have to take care of it. Get on your knees.

CI: I can get you money. How much do you—

Haynes: I done told you, I don't want your money! Now either hit your knees or hit the highway.

(Silence, followed by indiscernible sounds, moaning, etc. for approximately five minutes. Sound of a zipper.)

Haynes: Wow, wow, wow… You're mighty damned good at that. I had a feeling you might be.

CI: Can I use your bathroom, please?

Haynes: Shitter's for customers only. Write your phone number on this pad right here. I'll talk to Mr. Beals and be back in touch.

(Door unlocking.)

Haynes: Have yourself a good day now, pretty girl.

(Sounds of getting into car and leaving the premises. Sounds of CI retching.)

I was so angry I was trembling when I got Agent Beard on the phone.

"You let the guy force her to have oral sex and did nothing?" I yelled. "What the hell is wrong with you?"

"First of all, I didn't *let* him do anything. Secondly, I didn't have to send you the transcript, but I'm a man of my word. She could have said no and walked out the door. I hate what he did as much as you do, but we couldn't go busting in there and ruin the whole thing before it even started. She's an adult. It was consensual."

"Bullshit it was consensual! It was coercion. You could have banged on the front door and put a stop to it. You wouldn't have had to tell him you were an FBI agent. You could have said you were looking for a freaking fish sandwich!"

"You weren't there. It happened quickly. I had to make a judgment call, and that's what I did."

"You let a pervert molest a young girl, asshole. You listened to it, and you didn't do a thing to stop it. You should be ashamed of yourself."

"You helped set this up, remember?" Beard said. "Save your judgment for somebody who cares."

CHAPTER NINETEEN

It was nearly five o'clock in the afternoon as I stood at the podium in Criminal Courtroom Five on the sixth floor of the Birch Building in Nashville, next to a nervous Dustin Jackson. I'd gone over all the terms of the plea agreement with him half a dozen times. He'd signed the forms and given up his right to appeal. He stood up straight beside me, ready to be sentenced by Judge Julia Bridgewater.

During the previous two weeks, Governor Black had given executive clemency to ten more prisoners: nine men and one woman. Four of the men had been convicted of attempted murder, four for serious drug offenses, one for armed robbery, and the woman had embezzled $50,000 from an elderly dentist. From all accounts in the news, requests for executive clemency were pouring in faster than a mudslide, and the Board of Probation and Parole was drowning in the sludge. Not surprisingly, my office phone stayed quiet. Not one request to file another petition.

Judge Bridgewater looked over the forms and began to ask Dustin questions about whether his plea was voluntary, and whether anyone had forced or coerced him into pleading guilty. Bridgewater then asked whether he was under the influence of any drugs or alcohol, and whether his attorney had been competent. Dustin said the plea was voluntary, he was sober, and that I'd done an "awesome job," which I very much appreciated.

The prosecutor read the pertinent facts of both cases, and the judge asked Dustin if he agreed to those facts. "Yes, ma'am," Dustin said.

Then the judge read her decision. "Upon your plea of guilty the court finds you guilty and sentences you to nine years of imprisonment in the Tennessee Department of Corrections as a Standard, Range One offender. You'll be eligible for parole consideration after serving 30 percent of your sentence. Bailiff, will you please take Mr. Jackson into custody?"

"I meant what I said about you doing a great job," he whispered in my ear as the bailiff approached. "I know you'll get me out."

I nodded and watched as Dustin was handcuffed and led away before I walked into the hallway. Emma Hodge was waiting. She looked different than before. Tired. Haunted. She hadn't told me what happened to her at the restaurant, and judging from Dustin's upbeat demeanor and the fact he didn't mention it, I assumed Emma hadn't told him, either.

"Have you heard from anyone?" I said to her as we walked toward the elevators.

"Yes," she said. "I got a call an hour ago. I'm supposed to meet Beals tomorrow night."

"Have you told Agent Beard?"

"I'm going to call as soon as I leave here," she said. "Have you filed the stuff?"

"There's no point in filing a petition asking for his release until you pay them."

"Are *you* going to file it?"

"No," I said. "I'll get someone else to do it after they're paid."

"Why won't you do it?"

"Because they might think something's up if I file it after what I said about them in the paper."

"What did you say?" Emma asked. "I don't read the paper."

"It doesn't matter," I said. "But don't worry, when the time comes, I'll get a lawyer to file a petition for Dustin."

With that, she started crying. It was a soft, heartbreaking sob. I wanted to tell her I knew what had happened. I wanted to tell her how sorry I was that I didn't protect her. I wanted to tell her a thousand things, but I knew I couldn't. If she wanted me to know what had happened, then she would've told me.

"Hey, hey, hey, it's okay, Emma," I said, trying my best to console the poor girl. "I promise I'll get a good lawyer to file. Don't worry, we'll get Dustin out."

CHAPTER TWENTY

I drove home and took a quick shower before I fixed an easy supper of spaghetti. Mack rolled in around eight. We ate, then watched television until we went to bed around ten. He kissed me and rubbed my cheek, then gently laid over top of me. I wanted him, but I couldn't get the disgusting transcript out of my head. When he asked what was wrong, I lied and said my stomach was upset from the red sauce. He rubbed my stomach, kissed me, and we both fell asleep. At three in the morning, my phone, which was charging on the bedside table, began to ring. I picked it up and saw that Agent Beard was calling. I answered, angry.

"It's late. What do you want?"

"Dustin Jackson was found hanging in his cell an hour ago."

"What? Oh, no…"

"It gets worse. Emma Hodge is dead, too. She was shot twice in the head in the parking lot of her apartment building."

I was too stunned to speak.

"You know what this means?" Beard said.

"Um…"

"It means that either I have a leak in my office, which is highly unlikely, or you do. You need to get it swept for bugs."

"Okay…"

"First thing."

"Yeah."

I hung up the phone, feeling a mixture of rage, sadness, and confusion. When I turned to face him, Mack had already turned on a bedside lamp.

"People don't get good news at this time of night," he said. "What happened?"

"I think I just got my client and his girlfriend killed."

"What? How?"

I felt tears form in my eyes. I rolled out of bed and put on a robe, then walked out the back door onto the deck and stood in the cool, early morning darkness.

"Tell me what's going on?" Mack said, as he walked up behind me.

"Beard said either one or both of us have been bugged. That's the only way he could've known."

"Who?"

"Black," I said. "I know it was him."

"I'll get my tech guys on it."

"It's going to be my office," I said. "I can feel it. And that makes this whole thing my fault. I should have just kept my mouth shut and gone on with my life."

"It's not too late," he said. "I hate to say it, but those two kids just gave you a way out. If you walk away now, there's no reason for them to come after you."

"Those kids trusted me, and they died. I can't live with that."

"So, what do you want to do?"

"Fight the bastards."

"And get yourself or somebody else killed?"

"Somebody has to stop them," I said. "Somebody has to do something."

"It doesn't have to be you!" He looked away, ashamed for losing his cool.

"You were right," I said. "You said people could start dying."

"And I don't want you to be one of them."

It was true. I could end up dead, too. But I had started this war, and now there were casualties. It wasn't time to run away. Now was time to charge.

"Will you help me?" I said. "Please."

Mack looked out at the dark night. Fall was fast approaching, and the weather was turning cool. The trees would soon be bright with orange, red, and yellow.

"I'll do anything for you, Presley," he said. "Anything."

CHAPTER TWENTY-ONE

My gut had been right. Mack's team found three listening devices in my office. They had been constructed by someone who knew what they were doing and were untraceable. They could hear every word, in every room. The Governor and his goons knew in advance what we were planning. The discovery made me feel violated and added another layer of guilt and fear. But I knew I couldn't wallow in self-pity. I had to find a way to fight back.

Mack showed up at my office just before lunch, and we walked to a small greasy spoon in downtown Franklin.

"I went to Nashville this morning," he said, after we were seated and ordered our food.

"Why?"

"You asked for help, I'm trying to help."

"I don't understand."

"I had an hour-long conversation with Dan Smith."

Dan Smith was the United States Attorney in Nashville. His office was responsible for representing the United States Justice Department in 42 counties in middle Tennessee. They prosecuted criminal cases, handled forfeitures, and collected debts that people owed the government. Dan had been an Assistant US Attorney, but when a new president was elected a year earlier, his boss had been fired, and he was appointed. The US Senate confirmed him two months later.

Dan and Mack had known each other for several years and had become friends. They met when Mack busted a large cocaine distribution ring in town. Dan wound up prosecuting the case, and he and Mack hit it off. We'd never actually met, but Mack spoke so highly of him I felt like he was my friend, too.

"Is that right?" I said. "How's Dan?"

"He's good."

"What did you guys talk about?"

"You, mostly."

"And why's that? Because I'm indirectly responsible for two murders?"

"Cut it out, Presley."

I took a bite of food, sulking.

"We talked about you becoming a federal prosecutor."

I dropped my fork into my mashed potatoes.

"I thought about it," he said, "and the only way you're going to get to this governor is from the other side. You can't do it as a defense lawyer, and you can't do it trying to use the District Attorney. Dan's willing to give you a job. You have a ton of trial experience, a great reputation, and he happens to have an opening. He told me he'd let you work with the FBI on the Black case, too. He's as disgusted by what's going on as you are."

I sat there listening to the words and remembered Ruthie Mae telling me the same thing about needing the

FBI. That I couldn't bring Black down alone. Still, I was having difficulty processing what Mack was saying. He was talking about a complete reversal for me career-wise.

I'd never been anything but a criminal-defense lawyer. I'd never *wanted* to be anything but a criminal-defense lawyer. It wasn't that I disliked prosecutors. They had a job to do. But becoming one? Putting people *in* jail instead of helping them stay out? I'd just never considered such a thing.

"You can close your mouth," Mack said, smiling. "I hope you're not mad. I know this would be a big change for you, but I swear, Presley, I think you'd enjoy it."

"I hate office politics," I said. "I'd be right in the middle of that kind of thing all the time."

"Just keep your head down and do your job," he said. "Think about it. You'd have the power of the federal government behind you. I know you think feds are stuck up and have superiority complexes. Hell, I agree with you. But almost all of them are smart, hardworking, and honest. You'd fit right in. With the last few of those adjectives, I mean."

"He actually said the words? He said he'd hire me and let me work the case against Black?"

"He promised me."

"When would I start?"

"As soon as you can tie up whatever loose ends you have at the office. You can start tomorrow if you want."

"I don't know what to say. I mean, thank you. I'm grateful, I really am. I'm just extremely surprised. I've never thought of myself as a prosecutor."

"You'll be great," Mack said. "If you want to take Black down, it's the place to be."

"I've got the Red Snyder trial coming up next week," I said. "Can I think about it?"

"Think all you want. You don't have to do it if it doesn't feel right. I'm not trying to force you into anything. Hell, I know better than anyone not to force you to do anything."

As I sat there, I thought about the governor letting a double murderer out of jail, and the steady flow of other hardcore criminals that were suddenly walking free with more than three quarters of their sentences still in front of them. I thought about my office being bugged and Emma and Dustin being murdered. And then an image came to mind that made my blood boil. It was of Governor Black smiling as he got the news. His rough-hewn face plastered with a big shit-eating grin. Happy as hell that Emma and Dustin were dead.

I looked across the table at my husband. "I'll do it," I said. "I'll go to work for Dan."

"Great," Mack said. "Congratulations, Press."

"There are just two things he has to agree to."

"Why am I not surprised?"

"First, he has to wait until after I finish the murder trial on Monday. I think I can win."

"I know you can."

"Second, Cheri comes with me. I'm not going to leave her without a job."

"He'd be lucky to have her," he said. "You ready for dessert?"

I shook my head from side to side. "Nah," I said. "I just had it."

CHAPTER TWENTY-TWO

The Governor's chalet was off Dowdy Ferry Road in the mountains near Gatlinburg. He'd owned it for over twenty years and mostly used it as a family vacation home. At least he used to. Now, his wife and kids were less and less interested in spending time together on top of the mountain, and more and more excited about taking first-class trips to shop in New York or relax on a sandy beach in Jamaica. The Governor missed how it used to be, playing games with his kids and dancing with his wife.

He had promised himself he'd never end up poor and scrounging like all the other families he'd grown up around, including his own. His father had never been numbers smart and ran every business he opened into the ground. His failures made him angry and bitter. They also made him poor. Which meant Lonnie was poor. Unable to face up to his limitations, Lonnie's father vilified money and constantly preached its dangers. *Money ain't everything,* his father had told him over and over, but little Lonnie realized pretty fast that was only partly true. If you lived a hand-to-mouth, second-hand-clothes type of life, then no, money wasn't everything. But if you wanted to eat steak and potatoes and wear new clothes, you damn sure needed money. Which is why Lonnie had worked so hard to acquire as much of it as possible. And why he had learned young to cut corners and bend rules to keep it coming in.

The only two people with Black today were his longtime buddies and employees, Zeke Gibson and Whitey Cornett. After realizing the FBI had come very close to infiltrating his inner circle, Governor Black had gone into full-blown paranoia mode. He decided he needed to talk privately with his two closest associates, and the isolated cabin was the perfect choice.

Black had met Cornett many years earlier during a business trip to Memphis, as a first-term congressman, when Cornett was—among other things—the owner of a strip club on the outskirts of town called The Hourglass. The men had a few things in common: they were greedy and ambitious, they had an affinity for young female flesh, and they both lacked a strong moral compass. They hit it off immediately and had stayed in touch for nearly a decade. When Black decided to run for governor, he'd turned to his old buddy for help in Memphis. Cornett's influence didn't actually swing the election in the city, but he'd worked hard and Black knew it. As a reward, he appointed his friend as the commissioner of the Department of Transportation, although Cornett knew less about road construction than Black knew about theoretical physics. But it wasn't Cornett's knowledge of the transportation department that got him the job. It was his skill as an organizer of criminal enterprises. Transportation was one of the biggest plums in the state budget at over $2 billion, and both men had discussed multiple times the myriad ways in which they could skim a few million off the top. Cornett had told Black he was implementing a fool-proof plan, but Black had yet to see any results. Meaning he hadn't seen a dime. Meaning he wasn't happy.

The men had taken elaborate measures to avoid being followed to Gatlinburg by federal agents. They communicated with throwaway cell phones, and when they drove, they doubled back often, always on the lookout for a car or person they may have seen earlier. When the three men pulled up to the chalet, which Black owned under his wife's name, they all felt certain nobody, neither the FBI nor anyone else, knew where they were.

The chalet was free-standing and private. It was a large, relatively new log cabin that hung precariously over the side of a steep mountain with spectacular views of the surrounding Great Smoky Mountains. Once the men got inside and settled, Gibson broke out the liquor. His job as the head honcho of the alcohol commission came with perks. Some legal, some not. The $3,000 bottle of scotch he was opening fell into the latter category.

"Where's yours?" Cornett said to Gibson as he watched him drop ice into two glasses. When Gibson didn't answer Cornett's question the first time, he asked it again. "You deaf?" he said. "You not drinkin'?"

"Been having stomach problems," Gibson said. "Doc told me to lay off the booze a while."

"And you're doing what he told you to do?" Cornett asked. "I ain't been to a doctor in twenty years. And if I did go, I'd do just the opposite of what he told me to do."

Governor Black watched, amused, as Gibson raised his eyebrows while Cornett opened a baggie of cocaine, dipped into the white powder with a key, put the key to his nose, then snorted.

"Really?" Gibson said. "Let's say you get shot and you have to go to a doctor. He tells you to keep the wound clean. You going to pour dirt in it every couple of hours?"

"First of all," Cornett said, as Gibson slid him a scotch on the rocks, "I can't think of anybody that would have the balls to try to shoot me. And second, even if someone did shoot me, the bullet would just bounce off. I'm indestructible."

With that, Cornett raised his shirt to reveal a washboard stomach so defined, it looked to have been manufactured in a laboratory.

"What's that supposed to prove?" Gibson said. "You've got super powers, or something?"

"Damn right," Whitey said. "Ain't that so, Lonnie? A bullet would just bounce right off."

"I'm guessing those two kids you had killed wished they'd had some superpowers," the governor said.

The room went silent.

"What kids you talking about?" Cornett finally asked.

"Why in the hell did you have to kill them, Whitey?" Black said. "What were you thinking? Look at all the heat you brought down on us."

"You're asking a lot of leading questions, Governor. You wouldn't be wearing a wire, now, would you?"

"I oughta smack you for asking me a question like that. I just want to know why you thought killing a couple of kids wouldn't be something I'd want to at least talk about before you did it."

"You didn't hear what I heard," Cornett said. "That bitch lawyer and the feds were using them to set you up. They sent the girl to Biney and were going to buy a pardon for her boyfriend. Who, surprise, surprise, was one of her clients. When the girl went to see Biney, she had to deal with Chuck. And boy did she deal with him. The feds taped the whole thing. And not for nothing. He said she worked his joint like a porn star."

Cornett laughed. Nobody else did.

"Look, Lon, I was just watching out for you, doing what I thought was best to protect you. I guarantee people will think twice in the future before they try to set you or any of the rest of us up."

"How did you even get involved?" Black said. "This was an executive clemency matter. It didn't have anything to do with transportation."

"Reggie reached out to me after the story in the paper. He was just doing what lawyers do. He was worried about you. He said he thought I'd be the best man to handle it. He obviously didn't want to get you involved, and I thought that was probably a good idea. Plausible deniability and all that. So, I had Zeke pay the lawyer a visit—which didn't turn out like I planned—and we put some listening devices in her office. Once I heard what she and her clients were working on, I thought I should do something that would send a clear message."

"I still don't get your logic," Black said. "I haven't seen it reported anywhere that those two kids were killed because they were trying to get to me. In fact, the only people that know anything about that are the people in this room. And the FBI."

Cornett shook his head.

"You're wrong, Lon. The word's out. Loud and clear. If you mess with the governor or any of his people, you wind up in a body bag." Cornett finished his drink and stood up. "I gotta take a piss. I feel like I'm on trial here."

"You're not on trial," Black said. "I just like to know what's going on, especially when something extreme is going to happen."

"Duly noted," Cornett said.

"And there's something else I need to talk to you about."

"Make it fast, or you're gonna have a puddle under the bar stool."

"Who did you use to do it?" Black asked. "You had to tell people to kill the kid at the jail. Probably had to pay them, too, right? And I doubt you shot the girl yourself. So, there are at least two loose ends running around out there who could bring us down if the feds get to them."

"I've been doing this kind of stuff a lot longer than you have," Cornett said. "And I'm talking about the hardcore stuff. The stuff you'd better not screw up. I know what I'm doing. They ain't no loose ends."

"So, there are more bodies out there that I don't know about?"

"I'm beginning to feel insulted," Cornett said. "Insulting me isn't a wise move, even if you are a hot-shot governor."

Cornett made his way to the nearest bathroom. Black looked at Gibson and nodded. Gibson came around the bar and drew a silenced semi-automatic pistol from beneath his shirt. He stepped quickly and quietly toward the half-bathroom door, which Cornett left open while he stood at the toilet. Gibson was standing directly behind him when Cornett said: "Hey! Why is there—"

Pop! Pop!

"Plastic sheets covering everything?" Gibson said, as Cornett lay at his feet. "Well, as my dear old momma used to say, 'A room covered in plastic prevents a day's worth of cleanin' up blood.'" Gibson giggled at the joke, then bent down and began to wrap the dead man in the sheet of plastic covering the floor.

The governor laid out a piece of carpet that Gibson had cut and stashed behind the bar the day before, and they both dragged Cornett on top of it.

"Roll him up?" the Governor asked.

"Yeah," Gibson said. "Let me get his watch and wallet first. If anybody finds him, they'll think it was a robbery." He took both items and stuffed them in his pants pocket, then he and Black both rolled Whitey up, taped the carpet tightly, and dragged him to the garage.

"I guess bullets penetrate his ass after all," Gibson said.

Black and Gibson stood side by side, looking at the thick duct-taped carpet on the cement floor.

"What now?" Black asked.

"Help me get him in the car, and I'll take care of the rest," Gibson said.

Black nodded, then bent down and grabbed one end of the carpet that contained his dead former friend. As the two men lifted the heavy, awkward bundle, the Governor felt lucky. His end seemed lighter than Gibson's.

He thought he must've grabbed Cornett's feet.

CHAPTER TWENTY-THREE

My last murder trial as a defense attorney lasted only three days and took place in Franklin a week after Mack told me about Dan Smith's job offer. The facts were not in dispute. My client, a 41-year-old man named David "Red" Snyder, had shot and killed another man who, up until that night, had been his best friend. The dead man was Byron Keene, also 41 years old. He and my client had grown up on the same block—directly across the street from each other—and had gone to high school together. They'd been working at the same manufacturing plant in Franklin since they graduated from high school. My client was married but had no children. The victim was divorced with two young girls.

Nine months before the trial, on a Saturday night, Red Snyder, his wife, Dee, and Byron Keene had spent three hours in a honky tonk just outside of Franklin. They arrived back at Snyder's trailer around midnight and kept drinking. At approximately 12:30 a.m., Snyder ran out of cigarettes and went out to get more. After he'd driven a couple of miles down the road, he discovered he'd forgotten his wallet and turned around to go back home. When he walked in his front door, his best friend,

Byron Keene, was having sex with his wife on the living-room floor.

Snyder was the last witness called. The state had put on all of their witnesses, including the first responders, my husband Mack—who had arrested Snyder after the grand jury indicted him and then interrogated him at the jail—and the medical examiner who had performed the autopsy. I'd called Dee Dee Snyder, who claimed she didn't remember much about the incident, but did remember Byron Keene and her husband having a loud argument after her husband returned early from his trip to the store. She also offered the tidbit that she and Keene had been having an affair for about six months prior to the shooting. I cringed when she said it, because neither she nor Red had mentioned anything about it prior to her testimony. I hated being surprised by answers during trials, especially when the witness was one I'd called. She also said her husband had threatened to kill Byron if he didn't get out of their house immediately, and that Red told Byron he'd better never come around Dee Dee again. Those answers weren't surprises.

When I called Red Snyder to the witness stand, he stood up straight and moved with purpose. He was a slight man, probably 140 pounds, with a nasally Southern twang and a thick, full head of red hair that he wore cut medium length and combed straight back. I'd helped him pick out a charcoal suit, white shirt, blue tie, and black loafers. He didn't look like a killer. He looked like an accountant. And that was the idea. His friend, Byron, weighed 250 pounds and stood six feet, three inches tall. I'd shown the jury a photo of the two men on a fishing boat during my opening statement, just so they'd get an idea of the size difference between them.

The bailiff swore Red in, and I stood at the podium. I was dressed in a navy-blue blazer and skirt that went just below my knees, a white blouse, and navy-blue shoes with two-inch heels.

"Would you state your name, please?" I said.

"David Milhouse Snyder. I go by Red 'cause of my hair."

I smiled and nodded.

"Mr. Snyder, it's been established that you and the victim were lifelong friends. Back on that terrible Saturday night nine months ago, did you set out to kill him?"

"No, of course not. We were like brothers."

"At any point while you were at the bar partying, did you think about killing him?"

"No, ma'am. Never entered my mind."

"So, you and the victim and your wife eventually left the bar, returned to your home, and continued to drink beer, is that correct?"

"Well, Dee Dee made her a Margarita, but me and Byron was drinkin' beer."

"And at some point, did you decide to leave?"

"I did. I ran out of cigarettes."

"You couldn't have borrowed them from your wife or best friend?"

"I guess I could've, except for the fact that Dee Dee smokes menthols, which I can't stand, and Byron don't smoke at all. Unless you count a puff off a marijuana cigarette every once in a blue moon."

SCOTT PRATT

"So, you left by yourself?"

"Yep. Finished my beer and headed for a convenience store that I knew was open late."

"How far from your house was the store?"

"About fifteen minutes. One way."

"Which meant you should have been gone 30 to 40 minutes, correct?"

"That's right," he said. "That's about what it usually takes."

"Objection, Your Honor, she's leading the witness," Carl Jones said. When I heard he was the competition, I licked my chops. A Labrador versus a wolf.

"I'm just setting the stage, judge," I answered.

The judge was Dean Baggett, a squat man in his late forties with a receding hair line, a flat nose, and a quick temper. He was fair, though. I'd never tried a case in front of him and walked away feeling like my client had been railroaded.

"It's close, but not over the line," Baggett said. "Overruled."

"Did you have any reservations about leaving your friend alone with your wife?" I said.

"None. Didn't have no need to."

"So, you knew nothing of the affair your wife mentioned earlier?"

"No clue."

"But Byron wound up dead?"

"He did."

"Tell the jury what happened."

"Well, I got in my truck and turned the radio on and took off down the road. A good song came on—I can't remember now which one it was—but I remember at the time it made me wanna smoke. So, I was rummaging around in the ashtray for a butt just to get a few drags on the way to the store. I finally found one that had some life left to it and reached in my pocket for my lighter. When we got home from the bar, I'd changed into sweatpants, and when I wore those sweats, I always put my wallet and lighter in the front pocket. Well, I didn't have no lighter, and I realized at the same time that I didn't have no wallet, neither. Can't buy nothing with no money, so I pulled into a driveway, pulled a uey, and headed back home."

"What happened when you arrived?"

"I parked and got out of the truck, jogged up the front porch steps, slung open the door, and there they was, buck naked, just goin' at it on the floor. Wasn't no doubt about what was happening. When they realized I'd walked in on 'em, they started scrambling around and mumbling and trying to throw their clothes back on."

"What did you do then, Mr. Snyder?"

"I didn't know what to do. I was stunned. I couldn't talk, couldn't even move for a second. Then I looked at Byron and told him to get the eff out of my house and that if I ever saw him anywhere near my wife again, I'd kill him. I reckon I shouldn't have threatened him like that, and I don't think I really meant it, but I was angry."

Red was looking back and forth between the jury and me, just like I'd told him. I had learned early on from my father that, at their core, trials aren't about truth, they're about storytelling. Red was telling a story, and he was telling it well.

"Then what happened?"

"He walked out the door, and I watched through the window while he got in his truck and left. Then I lit into Dee Dee. Just words, though. No hittin'. She was crying and saying she was drunk and she was sorry and that he'd forced her to do it, that she really didn't want to. So, I asked her if he raped her and she said, 'Sorta,' but that really didn't make a whole lot of sense to me because she appeared to be enjoying it plenty from what little I saw. Then the strangest thing happened. I saw headlights in the window and looked out and darned if Byron didn't come screeching back into the driveway. I saw him open the door, and when the cab lit up, I saw him reach back and pull his deer rifle off the rack. That's when I told Dee to hide in the closet and ran into the bedroom and grabbed my shotgun."

"Was your gun loaded?"

"An empty one ain't much good," he said. "It was loaded with shells I use for huntin' geese. They'll take down a man, too, if it comes to it."

"Had you ever fired a shotgun at a man before?"

"No, ma'am. Never aimed one at a human person."

"Tell the jury what happened next."

"Well, I turned on the light and walked out the front door onto the porch and said, 'Byron, what the hell you think you're doin'?'"

"And what did he say?"

"He didn't say nothin'. I just saw him raise the gun and heard a shot and saw a muzzle flash, but he was walking toward me and drunk, and so he missed. Barely. I felt the shockwave, though, when the bullet whizzed by my right ear."

"What did you do then?"

"I aimed my shotgun at his chest and pulled the trigger."

"So, you hit him with the first shot?"

"Yes, ma'am."

"Did he go down?"

"Yes. He staggered just a bit, but then went flat over on his back."

"What did you do next?"

"I walked down off the porch, got about five foot from him, took aim, and shot him again."

"Did you feel like you were still in danger at that point?"

"He'd just had sex with my wife, and she half accused him of raping her. Whether or not that was true, I don't know, but he'd just came back onto my property after I told him to leave and did his best to put a bullet in my head with a deer rifle. So yes, I was still feeling like I might be in danger. Plus, I didn't know if he was dead or not."

"Did you intend to kill him at that point?"

"Yes, ma'am. After he fired at me, I figured it was him or me."

"Do you regret it now, Mr. Snyder?"

He paused for a few seconds and looked at the jury.

"I regret taking a man's life," he said. "I regret taking my friend's life, that's the God's honest truth. But I don't regret the decision I made in that moment, if you can understand what I mean. I'd do it again under the same circumstances. He came onto my property and tried to kill me. If I'd gone out there and called an ambulance, and he would have healed up, who knows if he'd have come after me again. But to be honest, I wasn't thinking about all that at the time. I was just trying to survive."

"Thank you, Mr. Snyder. Please answer the prosecutor's questions now."

Carl Jones stood in his average navy-blue suit and plain navy-blue tie. I'd tried to reason with him again before trial. I'd talked to him half a dozen times about how a Williamson County jury wasn't going to convict a man defending his life and his property. Especially when that man was defending his property from another man who'd just had sex with his wife and refused to leave the property. I'd talked to Carl Jones about all that, but he laughed in my face.

He believed that once Keene had been shot the first time, the danger to Snyder had passed and the second shot was excessive and constituted second-degree murder. At least that's what he said he believed. I thought he just wanted to convict a man of murder and put a notch in his belt. Maybe he was growing tired of being a lap dog.

"You killed this man in cold blood, didn't you, Mr. Snyder?"

"Objection," I said. "Leading."

"Overruled," Judge Baggett said.

"Well, did you or did you not shoot him in cold blood?" Jones repeated.

"I don't know what that means," Red said. "In cold blood? It all seemed pretty hot-blooded to me."

"After you shot him, why didn't you call 9-1-1?"

"For one, I didn't know if he was dead. Number two, I was in the middle of a gunfight for my life. I wasn't thinking about no phone calls."

"The truth is you were so angry that he was having sex with your wife that you decided to turn vigilante, isn't that right?"

"You're forgettin' the part where he nearly blew my head off. Think he would have called 9-1-1 if he'd done that? In my opinion, he would have tried to grab my wife and run for the hills."

"Your opinion is neither wanted nor appreciated, Mr. Snyder."

"Neither is yours."

I suppressed a smile. Red was doing great.

"So, after you pumped another shotgun blast into an already defenseless man is when you finally called 9-1-1, am I correct?"

"No, sir. After I went back into the trailer to make sure that rifle round Byron shot into the house didn't kill my wife, is when I called for help."

"Are you and your wife still together, Mr. Snyder?"

"Objection," I said to the judge. "Relevance."

"Sustained."

Jones seemed to deflate a bit after that, and he wrapped up his questioning. I rested my case, the judge instructed the jury, and then they left the courtroom to deliberate. They were gone less than an hour before they came back with a not-guilty verdict. Immediately, Carl Jones stormed out of the courtroom without a word.

Red Snyder hugged my neck. His wife, with whom he was still trying to patch things up, slinked out of the courtroom and refused to speak to the press. I walked out a side door into an antcroom. Mack walked in a short time later and gave me a hug.

"Congratulations," he said. "How do you feel?"

"Like I did the right thing."

"Ready for your new chapter?"

I took a deep breath and looked around. It was probably the last time I'd set foot in the Williamson County Courthouse. I looked at Mack and nodded my head.

"Hell, yes," I said. "I'm more than ready."

PART II

CHAPTER TWENTY-FOUR

The following Monday morning, I sat down across from Dan Smith on the eighth floor of the Estes Kefauver Federal Building on Broadway in downtown Nashville. His office was impressive, with the American and Tennessee flags flanking a large oak desk. The seal of the Department of Justice was on the wall between the flags next to a large photograph of the president. The room was spacious, the chairs and other furnishings expensive. There was even a chandelier above Dan's desk. It was all quite regal.

I'd already filled out the application forms and submitted a résumé, so the paperwork was behind me. I was pretty sure, based on what Mack had told me, that my hiring was a done deal. The pay was good—a hundred grand a year starting out—and the benefits were excellent. Mack made $130,000 a year as sheriff and also had great benefits, so we were in decent shape as far as that went. Not that I was going to tell Dan this, but I would have worked the job for free. That's how much I wanted a shot at Governor Black.

Dan reminded me a lot of Mack, although he was older and about four inches taller. He was in his mid-forties, trim and muscular, with short brown hair and deep dimples in his cheeks and chin. He was a father of two kids and had been married to his wife for over twenty years. There was an easy air of confidence about him, and he immediately made me feel comfortable.

"It's a pleasure to finally meet you, Presley. Is it all right if I call you Presley?"

"Of course. What am I supposed to call you?"

"Dan is fine. Some folks around here call me Boss, some call me General, and I'm sure some of them call me names I wouldn't really appreciate hearing, but I prefer Dan."

"Okay. Dan it is."

"I read what you told Marie Robinson in the *Tennessean*," he said. "Took guts."

"Did Mack tell you my office was bugged?"

"He did. He also said you blame yourself for those kids being killed."

"I shouldn't have run my mouth to the press. It set it all in motion."

"That won't be a problem in the future," he said. "None of my assistants talk to the press. I rarely talk to them. We have a public-information officer that handles communications with the media. Anyone in this office that speaks to a reporter is subject to immediate termination. I've always found it a bit ironic, but once you become an employee of a federal law-enforcement agency, you pretty much check your First Amendment rights at the door."

"I have no desire to talk to the press. Right now, my only focus will be on bringing down Governor Black by any means available." I immediately corrected my statement. "Legal means, of course."

"Of course," Dan said. Then he smiled, leaned back, and laced his fingers behind his neck. "You know, normally you'd have to go through a grueling interview and vetting process and then you'd be assigned a mentor lawyer for at least a year, maybe two. The FBI is vetting you as we speak, but I know they aren't going to come up with anything that would cause me any concern. And with your trial experience—congratulations on the Red Snyder win, by the way—I have no problem trusting you when it comes time to go to court. How familiar are you with the RICO statute?"

"Racketeering Influenced Corrupt Organization," I said. "Passed in 1970 to help dismantle the Mafia. I know it well."

"Good. There have been questions in the past whether a sitting governor could run a criminal conspiracy from his office, but past governors from Illinois and Alabama were both convicted under RICO, so we're good to go. What about the Hobbs Act?"

"Extortion statute," I answered.

"Mack said you weren't messing around," he said, impressed. "In addition to Hobbs and RICO, it looks like we'll also be using mail fraud, wire fraud, graft, official misconduct, and bribery as we go after Black. We have a lot of law at our disposal because it appears he's breaking it right and left. All we have to do is make sure the facts fit. Any case we file against a sitting governor has to be airtight. We can't screw it up."

"So, no pressure is what you're telling me."

"Exactly. There's one problem, though, and it might be a deal breaker for you."

"Conflict of interest?"

"Exactly."

"I've thought about it," I said. "If the kids' murders or Willis's pardon is part of the indictment, I'd be conflicted out of prosecuting him. I'd be a witness."

"Both of those things will more than likely be part of our case," Dan said. "And most importantly, since we now believe the murders of your clients are part of an ongoing criminal conspiracy, we have a green light from Washington to proceed."

"Emma Hodge and Dustin Jackson are their names," I said. "Or were."

"Emma and Dustin. Of course."

"How do you see me helping?"

"We've brought in extra agents and are looking at the areas where the most money can be made through corruption," he said. "That's where we'll be focusing, and that's primarily where you'll be utilized. You'll be directly supervised by Mattie Thompson. She's been an Assistant US Attorney here in Nashville for fifteen years. I'm sure you've run across her."

"I have," I said. "Tough woman."

"Smart, too. You'll also have a couple of lawyers from the Department of Justice's Office of Public Integrity looking over your shoulder. The FBI Special Agent in Charge of the operation, which we're calling Blackout, is Lawrence Beard, whom you already know."

The name caused an automatic reaction, but I coughed and got away with it.

"He'll be coming to see you right after lunch. Mattie will swing by within the hour. Your office is at the end of the hall. We gave you a corner, so you can see the Capitol Building and dream of the day you lock up as many of them as you can."

Lock up as many as you can. I thought about that for a second. I was used to getting clients out of trouble. This was going to be so different. It might be downright strange. I wondered what my father would think. The door opened, and Mattie Thompson walked in. She was smiling.

"Stand up, please, Presley, if you still want the job," Dan said. He did the same. "Raise your right hand. Mattie is here as a witness."

Conflict or no conflict, I still wanted a shot at the governor. Dan was right, though. Even if I wasn't the tip of the spear in the courtroom, there were plenty of other ways I could help make sure Black got what he deserved.

Dan administered the oath, which consisted of me swearing that I would uphold the United States Constitution and faithfully discharge the duties of my office. When we finished, Dan and Mattie each shook my hand. I stood there for a few seconds, a bit confused. "What now?" I said.

"What now?" Dan repeated. "Now you get the hell out of my office and set up your own. Then get to work."

CHAPTER TWENTY-FIVE

Governor Black started screaming "witch hunt" as soon as he found out I'd become a federal prosecutor. He held a press conference the week after I went to work for Dan Smith and said the FBI and a newly hired federal prosecutor by the name of Presley Myers were out to get him. I had thought about using Carter as my professional name after taking the new job, but if I were to be a part of bringing the governor of Tennessee down, the Myers name and my father's legacy would become legendary.

The press conference didn't sit well with the FBI higher-ups. Dan Smith got a call later that day from Washington. The sooner an indictment could be handed down, the better.

The first thing we did was convene a special investigative grand jury, made up of twenty-three people chosen randomly from voting lists in the surrounding counties. They would hear evidence regarding Governor Black and his co-conspirators. They could subpoena witnesses and documents, and they operated in complete secrecy. The Department of Justice assigned a judge who had taken senior status (which meant she'd semiretired), named Pamela Samuels, to oversee the case. She was a 68-year-old black woman who had a long and distinguished career, both as a government prosecutor and as a district and appellate judge. From all accounts she was fair-minded, no-nonsense, and brilliant.

Once we got underway, I quickly learned that our strategy was to be the same as many Hobbs and RICO investigations: find the weakest link in the chain, make a case against them, scare the hell out of them, threaten to jail them or their family members and friends (whether we could or not, it was perfectly legal for us to lie to suspects), eventually get them working for us, and force them to lead us to a stronger link. Once we had evidence on the stronger link, we'd repeat the process until we eventually got to our target. Early on, you don't much care that the target knows you're talking to one of his underlings, especially if the underling isn't very close. You actually hope the target will be stupid enough to reach out so you can record him saying something incriminating. Black was too smart for that, and we knew it, but we wanted him to feel pressure. We hoped that as we moved up his chain, he'd become paranoid, perhaps panic, and make a mistake.

Our team set up a "war room" in a large conference room, and Mattie, Dan, and I met with the grand jury to inform them we would be issuing subpoenas for records from various state offices, and the FBI would have custody of the records. We began drafting subpoenas for documents from the Board of Parole, the governor's office at the Capitol, the governor's office at the Executive Mansion, and finally, the office of Reginald

Gray, Governor Black's general counsel. The same man who had called to let me know that Governor Black had granted my petition pardoning Junior Willis.

"I want a mass raid to gather documents," Dan Smith said. "We hit them before they know what's happening. When we're ready, we show up early and take every pertinent record we can get our hands on. We load them into boxes, put them in vans, and haul them over here."

"What about Judge Samuels?" I asked, feeling like it might be a dumb question as it left my lips.

"We'll let the judge know what's going on, but she doesn't have to sign off on the subpoenas, so we should be good to go," Dan said. "After what's happened with the pardons and commutations, if they start loading up on lawyers and try to squash the subpoenas, they'll lose. Agent Beard's guys will handle the subpoenas. Once they're drafted, we'll go over them and make sure they pass muster. Mattie, you and Presley will handle surveillance applications that will go to the judge. Once we raid them, they'll panic and start talking to each other. I want to hear every word they say."

The raid was executed the following Thursday at 9:00 a.m. sharp. Lawrence Beard and his FBI agents split into four teams and coordinated their entries into the buildings. I went with the team assigned to the governor's mansion. Governor Black didn't spend much time at the Capitol, although he maintained an office there. Instead, he chose to conduct the state's business from a spacious office in his temporary palace. To be fair, it wasn't all that unusual. Many governors preferred the

Executive Mansion to the capital. There were far fewer prying eyes, and far fewer interruptions.

My presence during the raid was somewhat unorthodox because if the Governor said something incriminating to me during the raid, I would again become a witness. But since I was probably going to be a witness anyway, it didn't matter. Besides, none of us thought Black would be stupid enough to say anything incriminating. Dan Smith agreed, and I desperately wanted to see the look on Black's face when I served him the subpoena.

After a five-minute argument at the front gate between Agent Beard and the Executive Mansion's security chief, we drove up to the beautiful home and piled out. It was a bright, chilly morning as I walked past the governor's security people—all of them former Tennessee Highway Patrol or Tennessee Bureau of Investigation agents. Passing the staring men, I had the feeling of hundreds of small darts penetrating my windbreaker. I walked into the mansion, down the hall, and into Black's luxurious office. He was sitting behind a large, decorative, solid cherry desk in a high-backed, plush, black leather chair with a large cigar clenched between his teeth. The charming-evangelical act had been tossed aside. The look on his face was one of barely controlled rage. I laid the subpoena on his desk.

"I'm Assistant United States Attorney Presley Myers," I said. "We're here to gather the documents outlined in the subpoena I just served you."

He looked down at the piece of paper, back up at me, and smirked. "I read what you said about me in the newspaper. Wasn't too nice." Then he picked up the subpoena with his left hand, wadded it up, and tossed it in a wastebasket behind his desk.

"You ever heard of Edwin Edwards?" he said. "Governor of Louisiana back in the eighties."

"No. Was he corrupt like you?"

He flashed a smug smile. "Do you know what Edwards told a reporter one time? He said, 'The only way I lose this election is if I'm caught in bed with a dead girl or a live boy.' The situation here is similar. And we both know you're not going to catch me with either."

"I'll catch you doing something, though," I said. "I promise you that. Then I'll convict you for it."

He jerked the cigar out of his mouth and leaned forward on his elbows. "You're not going to convict me of anything, sweetheart. You can't find twelve jurors in this entire state that would convict me of a damned thing, for two reasons: Number one, and most importantly, I haven't done anything wrong. And number two, the people in this state love me."

"We'll see how much they love you after we build our case, indict you, put you on trial, and send you off to a federal penitentiary," I said. "Are you going to help us locate the records we need, Governor, or would you like the agents to just ransack the place?"

"What does your husband think about you forsaking his name?" he said, with a smirk. "It must have hurt him like hell. I bet it still does."

It stung because I knew it was true. But I pushed the feeling down and focused on business. "Fine," I said. "We'll do it on our own. But I suggest you hire yourself a good criminal-defense lawyer. Unfortunately for you, the best in the state is on the other side now," I continued, smiling. "But I will give you a free piece of advice. Chances are your general counsel and most of your cabinet will wind up in prison with you, so you'd better get out there and get a good one before they're all snatched up."

He stood and pushed his fists down on the desktop, his face a muddy shade of pink. "How dare you talk to the sitting governor of the state of Tennessee like that! I'm going to have your job, lady, and then I'm going to have your ass!"

"As you know, I just got the job, so I think they'll let me keep it for a while," I said. "And if you come anywhere near my ass, you'll be picking your pearly whites up off of the floor. If you don't believe me, ask your boy, Gibson."

I turned and walked out while the agents started going through Black's drawers and files. Just before I stepped out of the office, I turned back to Black.

"Threatening me was your first big mistake," I said. "But killing those kids sealed your fate."

CHAPTER TWENTY-SIX

The raids went off without a hitch. We hauled dozens of record-filled boxes out of the four sites we hit while the government officials stood by stunned, and the media, once it got wind of what was happening, went nuts. My photo and my name were plastered on the news and the front page of the paper as the new, aggressive, and whip-smart Assistant US Attorney who was going to clean up the dirty underbelly of Tennessee politics. It felt good to be celebrated, but I was too busy to bask in it for long.

All the records we confiscated went to the war room, where the FBI agents and I began the tedious task of looking for something we could use against Black and his administration.

The raids, however, were only one prong of our attack. Surveillance was another. But, since we were dealing with corruption instead of terrorism, all the devices and equipment we hoped to use were subject to the Fourth Amendment of the US Constitution, which meant they had to be approved by a judge. Judges also had to approve warrants in terrorism cases, but the standards for approval are much lower and the secrecy is even more stringent. In our case, search warrants had to be issued for each and every device or technique, and the allegations made in the warrants had to be specific. Judge Samuels was responsible for approving the tactics, and it was the job of the FBI agents, the assistant US attorneys, and the US Attorney himself to write sworn affidavits that put forth an argument that was compelling and persuasive enough to get the judge to sign off. It was a massive undertaking, and it kept us busy for weeks.

The first round of applications we submitted to Judge Samuels were drafted largely by Mattie and me. We'd submitted them to her clerk and made an appointment five days later to give her time to go through the materials and formulate the tough questions we both knew she would ask. Her office was on the top floor of the Kefauver building, and Mattie and I walked in at 2:00 p.m. The judge was wearing a light-blue cotton blouse, black slacks, and black pumps.

She walked around her desk to shake our hands and smiled broadly revealing perfectly aligned, bright white teeth. At nearly six feet tall, she was an impressive, statuesque woman, and obviously kept herself in excellent physical condition. She had dark chocolate-brown eyes. Her black hair was neatly trimmed and streaked with gray.

"Take seats, ladies."

Mattie and I sat down across from her. Mattie was senior in the office, had far more experience as a prosecutor, and before we entered the judge's office, I readily agreed that she should do most of the talking.

"Getting the records by subpoena was a brilliant tactic," Judge Samuels said after we sat down. "You managed to circumvent the Constitution and leave me out of the process. And after reading the materials you submitted for the search warrants, I can see why you did it. Whose idea was that, if you don't mind me asking?"

"Dan's, for the most part," Mattie said.

"And he reasoned that because of the murders and the continuing executive clemencies, any attempt to quash the subpoenas by the governor or any member of his administration would be unsuccessful," she said. "Am I right?"

She addressed the question to me, and for some reason I stayed quiet and nodded.

"You're perceptive, judge," Mattie said.

"I don't mean to sound arrogant, Ms. Thompson, but a black woman doesn't get to sit on the Sixth Circuit Court of Appeals by being imperceptive."

"No, ma'am," Mattie said.

"I imagine the two of you walked in here prepared for questions, and I have to admit I was taken aback when I first began reading the warrants. This is about as invasive as it gets outside of dealing with terrorism. You'd think we were hunting the next Bin Laden."

Mattie began to speak, but the judge held up her hand.

"This isn't a run-of-the-mill graft case," Judge Samuels said. "So let me save you some time and worry. Blood has been spilled, and from what I've seen and read in both the newspapers and in your affidavits, it appears to me that the governor's office is responsible. It doesn't take a genius to infer that Mrs. Myers's clients were killed to warn off others who may attempt to cooperate with the federal government and expose what Governor Black and his people are doing. I found it particularly upsetting that listening devices were planted in your law office, Presley. I know you can't prove who placed them there, at least not yet, but we all know who *had* them placed there, don't we?"

"Yes," I said.

"I thought Dan Smith's rising star would be a little more talkative," she said to Mattie.

"She's still learning this side of the field," Mattie said. "I advised her to listen."

"Anyway," Judge Samuels said, "I want you to know that I'm going to sign all of your warrant applications. I'm going to let you go after Governor Black as though he were a domestic terrorist, which is exactly what he is. He's greedy and power hungry, and he doesn't respect the institutions or laws that are the foundation of our democracy. I know my role is supposed to be an impartial referee, but these are special circumstances, and the governor has proven that he doesn't deserve my impartiality."

She stood up behind her desk, and with us still sitting in our seats, appeared to be a superhero.

"Ladies, your warrants will be signed and ready to go tomorrow."

Mattie and I stood and shook her hand.

"Do everyone in this state and country a favor," Judge Samuels said. "Get that criminal out of office before he does any more damage."

We both thanked the intimidating woman, and then we walked out the door. We now had everything we needed to put Lonnie Black behind bars.

"You did great in there," Mattie said.

I'd said one word.

CHAPTER TWENTY-SEVEN

It was a cold, dreary day at the Governor's Mansion, and Lonnie Black was hosting a small gathering. They were assembled to discuss the recent raids on Black's offices, his lawyer's office, and the Board of Parole. Another item on the agenda was equally as important. Today, Governor Black would appoint Biney Beals as his new Transportation Commissioner, replacing James "Whitey" Cornett following his mysterious and tragic death.

A fisherman found Cornett's discolored, bloated corpse lodged underneath a low-hanging branch on the bank of a remote section of the Cumberland River. The police had come up empty. The investigating officers assumed robbery, since Cornett's wallet and watch were missing, but there were no suspects. The officers were aware of Cornett's nefarious history, and to them, it seemed that maybe his dangerous past had finally caught up with him. Regardless, it was a tragedy, and in a televised statement, Governor Black vowed to pursue the murderer or murderers until justice had been served.

Like Cornett, his successor was a lifelong criminal and close friend of Governor Black. Also like Cornett, Biney Beals had no previous experience with any kind of government position, and his entire knowledge of transportation consisted of being Lonnie Black's number-one car salesman during their early years. After Black sold his dealerships and entered politics, Beals took the people skills he'd honed on the car lot and used them to flourish in a myriad of criminal enterprises that made him a rich man. He knew he needed a legitimate business to launder all that dirty money, and that's when he got into fish. He owned and operated several legendary cash-only fried-fish shacks all over Nashville. Beals used his mother's secret recipe, and she charged him ten cents on every dollar he made. He was, therefore, not quite as heartbroken as he could've been when the eighty-nine-year-old woman succumbed to lung cancer. He was sad she was gone, of course. She was his mother, after all. But that ten-cent tax was eating into his bottom line. Especially when added to the twenty-cent tax he paid Governor Black, who had given him the fish idea in the first place.

Beals looked around at the other guests sitting in a pre-arranged circle of chairs in the Governor's library. He saw Zeke Gibson; Reginald Gray; Joseph Lettrell, who was the publisher of the *Tennessean*, the state's largest newspaper; and uncomfortably, Tulsi LaHourge, the fifty-year-old cherub-faced Chairwoman of the Board of Parole. Heady company, and Beals felt the urge to speak.

"Governor Black, I just want to first say how sorry I am for your loss, especially in such a horrific manner. And I want to reassure you that I will give one hundred percent effort to my new position and will work every day to make you glad you gave me this opportunity."

Governor Black nodded. "I appreciate that, Bine. I really do. And I have no doubt that you'll make me proud, just like you always have."

"I'll put the announcement on the front page, below the fold tomorrow," Lettrell said. Governor Black wanted the powerful publisher on hand. He wanted to prove to the man that what his newspaper had been reporting about him was untrue. He wanted to show Lettrell that he was a good guy.

"Maybe we can get a photo of you two shaking hands in the foyer before I go?" Lettrell said.

Black brightened at the idea. He loved having his picture taken. It wasn't because he was exceptionally handsome, either. In fact, at five foot ten and 165 pounds, with small acne scars and thinning brown hair, he was rather plain. All that made no difference to him. He had overcome unimaginable obstacles to become the Governor of Tennessee. He deserved to flaunt it.

Just before the election, when Black's father was asked about his son, he said, "Lonnie Black is salt of the earth. You can't truly know him unless you know where he comes from. He wasn't raised with no silver spoon, and he understands the common folk because he is common folk. He overcome all sorts of hardships as a young'un, and I ain't too proud to admit we went hungry sometimes. But that's why he's gonna make a good Governor. He'll put the people first. Always the people."

Lonnie Black won in a landslide. Two weeks later, his father died in his sleep, knowing his only son had risen above his natural station in life as a poor, rural nobody, to the highest ranked official in the state. He died happy.

The foyer photo op would have to wait, though, because Tulsi had a question. "Governor, could I ask you about some of the recent clemency cases?"

The Governor had not wanted Tulsi at the meeting, but he took the advice of Reginald Gray and invited her. Black had heard she had been asking questions regarding the recent inmate releases and had been poking her nose in places it didn't belong.

"Go right ahead."

"I don't mean any disrespect, sir, but I have to ask you about Rebecca Lynn Lowry. She murdered her parents in cold blood and would've sawed them into pieces if she hadn't been caught. How can you justify releasing her after less than four years? Against the Board's recommendation."

Governor Black didn't like Tulsi's question. He also didn't like Tulsi.

"And Junior Willis?" she continued. "He shot his ex-wife and her boyfriend to death, then went and cuddled up with his kids in the next room—"

"Tulsi, let me explain something to you, my dear," Black said, cutting her off. "Things aren't always what they seem to be. The prisons are about to burst. We can't keep stuffing human beings inside walls like cattle and expect them to have a chance at rehabilitation."

"But some of these inmates, sir, are the worst of the worst. If you're going to release people, why can't we pick some white-collar criminals? Low-level dealers. Things of that nature. Why murderers?"

"White-collar criminals, as I'm sure you know, Ms. LaHourge, are typically white- skinned criminals. If I only release those inmates, what kind of message would I be sending to the people of color in the state? 'Grow up privileged, go to better schools, be white, and when you commit crimes, Governor Black will take pity on you? Otherwise, you're up the creek?' I don't think so. If an inmate proves to me that they are sorry for their sins, truly sorry, and they've shown themselves ready to be a solid, productive member of society, then, by God, I am going to give them a second chance. Regardless of their crime, social rank, and, most importantly, their skin color."

"I'm sorry, Governor, but did you say, 'regardless of their crime'?" Tulsi asked.

"Yes, I sure did," Black said, before smiling and continuing. "Jesus don't only save the small sinners, Ms. LaHourge."

The biblical reference caught her off guard.

"No," she finally agreed. "Jesus didn't."

Later, in the white-and-black checkerboard-floored foyer, Tulsi watched the Governor and Biney Beals shake hands and smile for a photograph. She also noticed the other men looking at the Governor with admiration verging on worship, and it made her uneasy.

CHAPTER TWENTY-EIGHT

Mack and I had hardly seen each other since I started my new job. He joked that if he'd known how much time I'd be gone, he never would've butted his nose in. It was hard not seeing each other as much, and we both agreed to take a nice vacation once the case was over.

In the meantime, I lived in the war room, going through files and boxes that were seized in the raids. I'd found several pieces of evidence I thought would be helpful, but nothing strong enough for a grand jury. I needed a smoking gun. And if it was in these boxes and files, I wanted to be the one to find it. So, I spent every free moment in the war room, looking for one piece of evidence that would nail Black to the wall.

I started with the recent executive-clemency cases that had been taken from the Board of Parole. I spent entire nights rummaging through clemency files, court documents, records, and notes. I brought Dan Smith a few ideas, but he directed me to Agent Beard's office, reminding me that he was the head of "Blackout." Beard and his agents ran down my leads, but each one fizzled out.

After that, it was another few weeks of digging through files and papers, finding what I thought were other good leads, only to take them to Beard and his agents, who would report back that they were dead ends.

Finally, after another week or so, I found, to my mind, the weakest link in Black's long, corrupt chain.

"Dobb Cole," I said, as I plopped his file on Agent Beard's desk the next morning, still wearing the previous day's outfit. "Convicted of attempted murder and armed robbery. Married, father of two. Released after serving six months on a 12-year sentence."

"Okay," Beard said, with an odd tone of suspicion. "Why?"

"A few reasons," I said. "First were the constant visits from his wife. Always brought him food and photos of their small children. When she didn't visit, Dobb wrote to her. Every day. The prison had copies. They were love letters, telling her how he'd give up his arms, legs, eyes, anything to be set free and live a quiet life with the only thing that mattered to him… his family."

"So, he loves his family. What makes you think he'd talk to us?"

"It's not just the family stuff. It's the pattern to his crimes."

"What pattern would that be?" he said. "He nearly shot a man to death while robbing his store."

"Yes. But he had robbed a handful of gas stations previously and never hurt anyone. It sounds like the guy behind the counter pulled out a sawed-off, but Dobb shot first. Seems more desperate than sinister."

"I don't know…"

"He's a free man after serving six months on a twelve-year bid. I don't know about you, but if I were him, I'd do just about anything to stay that way. And guess who paid him a visit before he was released?"

Beard shrugged.

"Biney Beals," I said. "I'll go talk to him today."

"No, you won't," he said.

"What? Why?"

"Another agent already tried Mr. Cole. Spent an hour in his trailer last week."

"Why the hell didn't you say that when I first said his name then?"

"I wanted to hear your angle."

"And?"

"It didn't change my mind. Dobb Cole's not our guy."

"I disagree," I said.

"Well, you know what they say about opinions," Beard answered.

"That's it, then? You just quit on it?"

"No, we didn't just quit. We subpoenaed him to appear in front of the Grand Jury. But if he won't talk now, I can almost guarantee you he won't talk then. Oath or no oath."

"He's the one," I said. "I feel it. I can get him to talk."

"He was a good possibility, but my best agent already swung and missed," Beard said. "I don't know what else to tell you, Mrs. Carter, other than to keep looking. Have a nice day."

"But—"

Beard picked up the phone and started dialing. My signal to leave.

Dobb Cole was our man; I was sure of it. And I wasn't going back to the war room to bury my head in more files. I had done that for years looking for my father's killer, and nothing had come from it. I had another idea.

I was going to visit the convicted murderer on my own.

CHAPTER TWENTY-NINE

Mack was already asleep when I got in bed that night and was gone when I woke the next morning. As I laid there by myself, I hoped things would get back to normal soon. I thought it would. It just might take a while.

I called Cheri and told her I was feeling under the weather and wouldn't be coming into the office. Then I started getting dressed for the day. It took longer than normal since I had to search for a costume. Well, not a costume, but for anything to make me look the part I was about to play. Sequins would work, I thought, as I pulled out an extra-short skirt and a low-cut, sequin-stitched tank top Mom had made me during one of her avant-garde designer phases. Blue over the eyes, red on the lips. A blonde wig I had used as Marilyn Monroe last Halloween. To complete the ruse, I borrowed Mom's old Ford pickup truck for the day.

Dobb and Cazzie Cole lived in a trailer plopped on a dirty half acre of land on the outskirts of Cocke County, one of the most rural and dangerous places in Tennessee. It took me a little over four hours to make the drive from Leiper's Fork. As I pulled up to the isolated residence, I felt my heartbeat quicken. To get them to talk, I would have to play my part convincingly. That's what made me nervous. I was no actress. I had done exactly one play in school. A seventh-grade musical, where I had been cast as a flower. The teacher thought it would bring me out of my constant worry and sadness. I didn't think playing a flower would take away my greatest fear that, like my father, my mother or brother would suddenly be ripped away from me and I would be left all alone.

Still, I accepted the role since flowers don't speak and there were no lines. But my teacher informed me on the first day of rehearsal they do smile. My mother and brother showed up to watch my debut, where all I had to do was stand there and grin. Of course, I frowned the entire play and was replaced the next performance. All these years later, I hoped my inner thespian would bloom.

Despite the chilly mid-September weather, beads of sweat formed on my forehead as I walked from the truck up to the rusty trailer door and knocked. Immediately, kids started yelling. Not two seconds later, the door was flung open.

Dobb Cole was a massive man who had to duck under the doorframe. But something about his eyes put me at ease. They were soft. Kind. And despite his full, thick beard, I could tell he had a sweet face. Hiding behind him was a husky, sweet-eyed seven-year-old girl who looked just like him in the best possible way.

"Hello," Dobb said, politely. "Who are you?"

Uh-oh. I repeated his question silently. In all my commotion dressing for the character, I had forgotten to give myself a name. I must've thought about it too long, because his voice snapped me back to attention.

"Ma'am?"

I had to think quick, but my mind was blank. I couldn't even remember my *own* name. Then I saw a star. A metal star, rusted and brown, hanging from a frayed string directly over the front door.

"My name is St...Star...Stareene. I was just wonderin' if I could have a moment of your time. Maybe speak with you and your wife about something kinda personal."

The massive, gentle man turned back to the living room. "Cazzie! Could you come out here for a second, sweetheart?" He then turned back to me. "Stareene, huh?"

What a ridiculous name. I knew I'd blown it.

"It's pretty," Dobb said. "Real pretty."

I smiled with relief as Cazzie walked up with her hand on her son's shoulder. This child was skinnier and about two years older than the daughter. He was chewing the inside of his cheek.

"Yeah?" the angular, stern woman said to her husband.

"This here is Stareene. She says she needs to talk to us about somethin' personal."

Cazzie sized me up. "No," she said, then nodded for her big husband to follow her back inside.

My ruse was crash-landing after barely getting off the ground. I had to gain their sympathy. Now. I drew from my deepest wells of emotion and broke down in hacking sobs. It sounded more like I was hyperventilating than crying, but it was enough. It took me as much by surprise as it did the Coles.

"My husband's rottin' in jail, and he didn't do nothin'," I said, improvising between forced sniffles and rubbing my eyes. "I need him back home. I'm willin' to do anything. Please, can you help me?"

Dobb and Cazzie looked at the pitiful creature crying on their porch with apprehension. Curiosity trumped common sense as to why I was standing on their doorstep asking questions they'd rather not answer. Questions whose answers could end up sending Dobb back to jail. They took pity on the pathetic display, so they invited me in and shut the door.

"You ain't the cops, are you?" Cazzie said.

"No, ma'am," I said, laying on a thick drawl. "I'm just like you, trying to hold my family together." I surprised myself with how naturally I played the part. I was really on a roll.

She nodded me in, and we walked to the kitchen and sat around the square metal table. It was overcrowded with small ceramic figurines.

"Sorry to have to ask, but we had a fella visit from the daggum FBI," Dobb said. "It's put us a bit on edge."

"Yeah, and ruined our damn future, too," Cazzie added.

"Honey, that ain't her problem."

"I didn't say it was her problem, Dobb, but it's sure as hell ours." Cazzie turned to me and continued. "That damn FBI put him under subpoena to appear smack-dab in the middle of Dobb's first week of long-haul work. Can you believe that? Wouldn't even listen when I asked him to change the date."

"Long haul?" I said, confused.

"A damn miracle gets Dobb outta jail, and then he lucks into an actual decent-paying job as a distance trucker, benefits and all, but now he can't take it 'cause of this damn subpoena bullcrap. Excuse my French."

"Anywho…" Dobb said.

"Anywho, nothin'," Cazzie said. "After everything we been through, this family deserves a break. Hell, Dobb would be willin' to tell the law whatever they wanted to know if they'd change the date so he could take this job. As long as they promise not to stick him back inside."

"Anywho, Cazzie!" Dobb repeated, using a deeper voice which stopped his wife from talking. He turned to me and grinned. "How can we help you, Stareene?"

I had already forgotten my fake name and kept looking at Cazzie, waiting for her to continue.

"Stareene?" Dobb repeated.

"Oh, yes," I answered, hiding my mistake. "Well, it's about that miracle you mentioned earlier. I was hoping to figure out a way to get one for my husband."

Dobb and Cazzie both became very still.

"Look around, honey," she said. "It seem like we're workin' miracles?"

I followed her order and looked around. The trailer was old but clean. Sparse furniture made room for Cazzie's ceramics obsession and what seemed like thousands of figurines on every available shelf and flat area. Cats, dogs, boys and girls. Cars, bikes, bells, and angels. Wall-to-wall, ceiling to floor, ceramic figurines.

"Maybe not," I answered, as I fiddled with the corncob saltshaker in the middle of the table. "But my husband heard talk inside that you might know someone who does."

The Coles went quiet. Then the young girl crawled off her father's lap and onto mine. Shock colored my features, but it didn't hold a candle to the looks on the Coles' faces.

"Good lord," Cazzie said. "She's never gone to anyone before."

"Just that little puppy dog in the park that one time, remember?" Dobb said.

The girl wrapped her arms around my neck, then gave me the sweetest hug. They both sat there and watched, amazed.

"I'm D.J.," she said. "What's your name?"

"Ah, it's…Stareene. Who's your brother, there?"

The thin older boy just stared.

"He's called Colter," D.J. said. "He's mean."

"No, I ain't, dummy!"

"Hey, watch your mouth," Cazzie said, then looked to me and shrugged her shoulders.

"Kids," I said. "Whatcha gonna do?"

"You must be a momma?" she asked.

"No," I said, trying to move the child's arms from around my neck.

"You should be," Dobb said. "You'd be a dandy."

I knew he meant it as a compliment, but the whole scenario reminded me of failure and lies. Plus, the child was starting to squeeze my throat. I grabbed her arms hard enough to unlatch them. The girl frowned and hurried back to her father.

"Please. I can pay," I said, feeling guilty and hoping I hadn't blown my chance. "Whatever it takes."

Dobb stood and grabbed a pen and paper, but Cazzie stood and stopped him. She tried to take the paper and pen from his hand. He was too strong. She leaned close and whispered something in his ear. Dobb listened, nodded, then kissed his wife's cheek and rubbed his daughter's face. With that, he sat the paper on the metal table and wrote a phone number across it before handing it to me.

"Call that number," he said. "Tell him what you told us. Especially the part about payin'."

"Thank you," I said. "Thank you so much."

"Just don't mention Dobb's name," Cazzie said. "Whatever you do, don't do that."

I nodded and watched Dobb hold his wife's hand as he struggled to hold back his tears. "I'm just so thankful to be home," he said. "I hope you have the same luck we did."

As I watched the massive man struggle with his emotions, I felt guilty. My tears had been fake. Dobb Cole's were real.

CHAPTER THIRTY

Mack and I stared at the wrinkled piece of paper in the middle of the kitchen table. The number waiting to be dialed. He had been livid when I told him how I got it.

"You put your life in danger!" he said. "You thought it was a good idea to play dress-up and visit a convicted killer, by yourself, without telling me?"

I just stood there with a dumb look on my face. He had a point. I didn't know what to say.

"You can't call this number," he said.

"Why?"

"Tricking Dobb and Cazzie Cole is one thing, but that number's gonna take you to people who are much smarter. And much more dangerous."

"The Dixie Mafia?" I said with a laugh. "More like the *Hee-Haw* mafia. I knocked one of those rednecks on his ass. Plus, Dobb is as sweet as pie."

"These people aren't sweet. And they're not dumb. Believe me, I've seen what they can do to their enemies. If you call that number and start asking questions, that'll put you on top of the list."

"Well, if I don't, seems like nobody else will. And I don't have time to wait around for the FBI to grow a pair."

"What are you talking about?"

"Black keeps talking to the press, blaming me and the FBI for dragging his name through the mud without any evidence. Keeps calling Agent Beard out by name. He's tired of it."

"I don't blame him," Mack said.

"But if Dobb talks, that's another story."

"So, let's just say, for kicks, he does talk. Say he lays it all out and puts the Governor in the middle of it. Then you've got a firsthand account. That's enough to indict, right?"

"Maybe," I said. "Black's a crook, but he's still the Governor. And he's covered his tracks. Everybody's scared to death to look like fools. Or end up murdered."

I suddenly felt nauseous and stood up from the table.

"Are you okay?"

"Yeah. Just need a little fresh air."

I walked out the glass doors and stood on our back deck, looking in the direction of my childhood home. Memories of my father filled my mind. He had passed down to me a love for the law. Not because he forced it upon me, or steered me in any particular direction, but because I simply wanted to make him proud, and to me, as a young girl, becoming what he was, becoming a criminal-defense lawyer, would do that better than anything else could. Now, as a federal prosecutor, I was about as far away from that, and from him, as I'd ever been.

"Hello?" Mack said. "You still here?" His voice brought me back from the past. I blinked and turned to face him. He was holding my Vandy hoodie in his hands. "Put this on before you freeze."

After zipping up the jacket, I said, "Governor Black used me to kill two kids. I think he probably had his own Commissioner of Transportation killed, too."

"Why do you think I'm begging you to be careful?"

"I wonder what Dad would do if he were me?"

"I think he'd call," Mack said. "But you're not your dad. Sometimes I think you forget that."

"Sometimes, maybe," I said. "But not right now."

I walked to the table and grabbed the wrinkled paper with the number. Then I reached for my cell.

"Wait," Mack said. "Are you sure about this?"

I nodded.

"Well, then, use my work phone," he said. "It'll come up as unregistered. They won't know who you are."

"They'll know when they meet me."

The words struck him like a lightning bolt. Enough to pull back his phone. But I had already made up my mind. I took it from him, dialed the number, and listened as it rang.

"Yeah?" the man's voice said on the other end of the line.

"Hello?"

"Who is this?" he said. "How'd you get this number?"

The voice was deep, but unfamiliar.

"My name's, uhhh, Stareene..." Mack looked at me, confused. I had forgotten to tell him about my character. "Somebody I trust told me to call. Said you might be able to help my husband out of a certain kind of bind. I got the money to pay for it."

There was a silence that seemed to go on for eternity. "Hello?"

"Stareene?" the voice asked, suspiciously.

"Yeah."

"You know Barney's on Eighth Avenue South?"

"Know it? It's my favorite spot."

"Be there for lunch on Friday at 11. Wear something red. I'll find you."

"Red?" I said. "Like what?"

Click.

I handed the phone back to Mack, barely able to control my excitement.

"What?" he said.

"I'm in! I'm gonna take him down," I said. "I'm gonna take him all the way down."

Mack looked at me but kept quiet.

"What's the matter? Aren't you happy?"

"Are you?"

"Yes," I said. "A case like this, bringing a Governor down, that's all I've ever wanted. They'll know my name all over the country."

"Presley...Myers," he said.

"Come on, Mack. You know why."

"I'm proud of you, Presley. And I know your dad would be, too. But for the tenth time, please be careful."

I hugged him and yelled in excitement, but he nudged me back a few inches and became very serious. "What is it?" I said, feeling worried. "What's wrong?"

"Nothing," he said. "I just have one question."

I nervously waited on it, and finally, with a grin, he said, "Who the hell's Stareene?"

I wrapped my arms around his waist and stood on my tiptoes to whisper in his ear. "Come on to bed," I said, in the heavy Southern accent of the character. "And I'll introduce you."

CHAPTER THIRTY-ONE

That Friday I was at Barney's at 11:00 am, in full Stareene regalia. The blond wig, thick makeup, fake nails and lashes, low-cut top, and push-up bra. The most important part of the costume couldn't be seen. At least, I hoped not. It was a small wireless recording device that Mack had taken from the Sheriff's Department and taped under my cleavage.

It was a little early for the lunch rush, but there were still quite a few people eating. Most of them stared when I walked in and took a seat at the half-full communal table closest to the door. At the same time, Mack was sitting in an unmarked police pickup truck at the far end of the parking lot watching me through high-powered binoculars with a high-powered rifle resting across his lap. Knowing Mack was out there, ready to protect me, kept my heart rate down and the sweat off my forehead.

I almost told Dan and Larry about the meeting but decided against it. I don't know if it was pride, fear, or both, but I felt keeping it to just me and Mack would not only guarantee secrecy, but hopefully prevent anyone from getting hurt or killed.

If we could pull this off and get the man on tape arranging a prison release for pay, we would be well on our way to working up the chain to Governor Black. Still, I held my excitement and nerves in check as I waited for the man to show. I expected him to be late, but after the first hour passed without a sign, I began to worry. I waited. And waited. And waited. Eventually, after the second hour, I ordered food. Miss Ardean looked at me sideways when she served my hamburger steak. I could tell she was trying to place this strange woman. That made me feel even more confident about meeting the mystery man, who would probably know my face from the photo that accompanied the article in the *Tennessean*. Turned out it didn't matter. He never showed.

Back in Mack's truck, I called the number that Dobb Cole had given me at his trailer to set up the meeting.

It had been disconnected.

CHAPTER THIRTY-TWO

The next day I was sitting in Dan Smith's office with Agent Beard beside me. I had called the meeting at the last minute but hadn't told either man what it was about. Before they had a chance to ask, I slapped a manilla folder on Dan's desk.

"What's this?" he asked.

"That's Dobb Cole's file," I said. "And it's gonna help us take Black down."

"Who's Dobb Cole?" Dan asked.

"No one," Agent Beard answered, glaring at me.

"Dobb Cole is a career petty thief, who after losing his last job, decided to hold up a Gas-N-Bait in Cocke County for the cash in the register and a pound of bologna. On Dobb's way out, the clerk pulled a .20 gauge full of buckshot. Dobb had a .38 six shooter and got a round off first. Wounded the guy. He was serving a twelve-year stretch for attempted murder and armed robbery but was released after six months. Care to venture a guess by whom?"

"Governor Black," Dan Smith said, rubbing his temples.

"Bingo."

"Sir, we sent an agent out to see him last week," Beard said. "We subpoenaed him, but he's not gonna talk."

"If you change the date on the subpoena and let Dobb drive his truck, he will," I said.

"What truck?" Dan said.

"Sir. I, um… I read the agent's report," I said to Dan, lying. "Dobb got a job with a long-haul trucking company, but the subpoena date is keeping him from being able to take it."

"I'm sorry, sir," Beard said. "But I don't have the faintest idea what she's talking about."

"That's because you didn't read the report," I said, hoping I was right.

Beard's face turned bright red. I guess I was.

"So, you're telling me you think Cole will talk if we let him out of his Grand Jury appearance?" Dan asked.

"Not let him out," I said. "Just change the date. And give him our word we won't send him back to jail."

"We can't send him back to jail, Presley, no matter what he decides to do," Beard said. "He's been officially pardoned. Unless he commits another crime, he's free and clear whether he talks to us or not."

"That might be true," I said, "but Dobb doesn't have to know that. I don't think Mr. Cole is exactly an expert in the minutiae of jurisprudence."

Beard went quiet. He knew I had a point.

"What makes you so confident about Mr. Cole?" Dan asked.

"Because this job changes everything for him and his family. He wants to go straight."

"This is absolutely ridiculous," Beard said. "We're the FBI, not a placement agency—"

"Do it." Dan said.

"But, Dan, if this blows up, we'll be a laughingstock."

"Maybe. But if we don't get some indictments soon, we'll not only be a laughingstock, we'll be an embarrassment. Then the axes will start falling." Dan rolled his thumbs over each other, then continued. "Walk the line," he said, "but tell Mr. Cole what you need to tell him to get him on board."

Agent Beard swallowed his pride, nodded, and walked out of the room.

"Is this the best lead we have?" Dan asked.

"It's not just the best one," I said. "It's the only one."

CHAPTER THIRTY-THREE

Agent Beard was pacing outside the room where the 23-person Grand Jury was waiting to hear the testimony of Dobb Cole, who would verify that a criminal could, in fact, buy his way out of prison in the state of Tennessee.

On Dan Smith's orders, Beard had personally visited Dobb and Cazzie's trailer to let them pick their date to testify in order to allow him to accept his trucking job. The Coles were immediately suspicious of the buttoned-up agent and refused to let him inside without a warrant. Yelling through the closed door, Agent Beard proceeded to detail what would happen to Dobb if he didn't agree to testify against Governor Black.

The threat of going back to prison was enough for Cazzie to open the door. Once inside, Beard tried a different, softer approach, outlining the benefits of coming clean and helping the state of Tennessee put away its dangerous and corrupt leader. It all seemed to fall on deaf ears until Agent Beard spoke of the Coles' children. He talked of the family putting their rough past behind them and moving forward with a clean slate and new beginning. Starting with Dobb's long-haul trucking job.

When Agent Beard was finished, both Dobb and Cazzie wiped tears from their eyes and agreed to the terms. Cazzie offered to make him lunch, but the fried bologna sandwich didn't appeal to the by-the-book agent. She insisted, and when he took his first bite, he changed his mind and ate the entire thing before asking for another. The meeting had gone as well as it possibly could have, and Agent Beard left the trailer with a full belly and an unexpected fondness for Dobb and Cazzie Cole.

But now the day had come to testify, and Dobb was nearly two hours late. Beard was worried and irritable, and he was just about to walk out when his phone rang.

"Hello?"

"It's me."

"Damn it, Dobb! Where the hell are you?"

"If I go through with this, you know I'm gonna be in bad trouble."

Beard knew he had a point. But, as harsh as it was to admit, this was bigger than one man. This was about the corruption of the most powerful elected official in the state. "You have to honor your subpoena, Mr. Cole. You remember what I told you would happen if you don't, right?"

"How could I forget that?" he said. "I had nightmares about it."

"I don't blame you," Beard said, playing the good cop. "It would be horrible having to go back in and serve the rest of those twelve years after being so close to putting the past behind you. It'd crush those kids."

"It don't seem fair," Dobb said with a shaky voice. "Don't seem fair at all."

"So, what's it gonna be?" Beard asked, glancing at his watch.

"I was thinkin' that maybe you and me could meet somewheres a little more private and talk," Dobb said. "Away from the crowd… and the danger."

"What danger?" Beard asked. "Did someone threaten you?"

"Not exactly," Dobb said. "I'd just feel better keepin' it between me and you."

"I don't know—"

"Please, Mr. Beard," he said. "I could meet you tomorrow morning. Somewhere private, maybe? You could record it, and I'll answer whatever questions you ask. You think that maybe we could do it that way?"

Beard thought about the risk and reward. If Dobb's information created a direct link that moved them one rung up the ladder to Governor Black, it would be worth it. If he was just scheming to keep his trucking job without testifying, then Beard would be right where he was now. Nowhere. He mulled it over, and finally made his decision.

"All right, Mr. Cole. You got a deal."

CHAPTER THIRTY-FOUR

The next morning, freezing rain fell on the windshield of Agent Beard's blue Chevy sedan as the car idled in the secluded parking lot at Percy Warner Park. The sun had just risen and had not had time to warm the cold of the pre-dawn darkness. This was the same lot Beard had used to meet me for the first time. Today, though, I was inside the car, sitting in the passenger seat next to the quiet agent. I had tried several excuses to get out of being at the meeting, but Beard wouldn't take no for an answer. Still, I kept trying.

"I don't think I need to be here, Larry. He'll probably talk more if it's just you two."

"It's Lawrence," he said. "And I told you that I want a lawyer here just in case."

I had taken to calling him Larry most of the time, despite his protestations. "In case what?" I said. "You've got a gun."

"In case Mr. Cole gets cold feet later on and decides to scream coercion or abuse or whatever the hell else people scream these days after giving a confession they regret."

"But I should be back at the office going through files. I have a ton of work to do."

"Those files aren't going anywhere. And if this works out, we may not even need them."

I was chewing one of my fingernails.

"You might want to ease up on that, before you eat your thumb off," Beard said.

"I just don't think it's a good idea for me to be here."

"I don't understand you," he said. "You gave me hell when I wouldn't let you go to his house the first time, and now I have to pull you kicking and screaming to meet the man. You'd think I was standing you in front of a firing squad."

I wanted to tell him why I was so nervous. I wanted to tell him that when Dobb Cole sits in the Chevy and sees "Stareene," all would be lost. His confession. The firsthand witness. All of it gone. Hell, it would be the end of my career once the story of my acting stunt got back to Dan Smith.

"Larry, I gotta tell you something—"

"What the hell?" Larry said, interrupting me.

I followed his gaze, and to my surprise saw Dan Smith pulling up beside us in his black Tesla. My stomach dropped, and for some reason I felt tears welling in my eyes as I rolled down the window.

"Come on back to the office," he said. "You might be in danger."

"But, Dan," Agent Beard said, "this is going to be his grand-jury testimony. He has crucial information to share."

"Mr. Cole won't be sharing anything anymore," Dan Smith said. "His trailer caught fire last night. He's dead. Looks like his wife and children are, too."

I felt my body go numb. My vision tunneled, and the air around me began to vibrate with a dull roar. Four more people were dead. Two of them children.

I had their blood on my hands.

CHAPTER THIRTY-FIVE

During the ride with Agent Beard from Percy Warner Park to downtown Nashville, I had gone from numb to rage, and once we all arrived back at Dan's office, I was pacing back and forth like a caged animal between the two men.

"Black killed them!" I yelled. "He killed them all!"

"Calm down, Presley," Dan said.

"Dobb was going to cooperate, and they found out!"

"How are you so sure?" Agent Beard asked.

"Don't be thick, Larry," I said. "It's obvious."

Agent Beard seemed to agree with me. I sensed it and, for the first time, felt warmth toward the cold man.

"*It's obvious* isn't gonna cut it," Dan Smith said. "This is a sitting Governor. We need proof. Lots of it."

"This is absolutely ridiculous!" I said. "We've got a full-scale assault on this state's criminal justice system by the people who have sworn to uphold it. He's accepting bribes to set people free, and now he's killing them if they talk."

"We can't prove that in court," Dan said. "Without Dobb, we've got nothing."

"So, you're just gonna sit here and take it?" I said, before turning toward Agent Beard. "What about the big, bad FBI, Larry?"

He seemed hurt and shrugged his shoulders.

"He has no choice," Dan said. "Neither do I. We have strict guidelines to follow for these kinds of cases."

"Guidelines? Your guidelines are getting people killed!" I could tell my accusation made his blood boil, but he kept his composure.

"It's not my first rodeo," Dan said. "I know what'll bring a conviction and what won't."

"If we don't do this, nobody's going to," I said, looking at both men. "You think state authorities will take on their own governor? If you kill this investigation, we're essentially giving Black the green light to sell pardons with impunity. To kill anybody that gets in his way. Hell, he's already doing both while being investigated by the federal government. Imagine what's next if we cut and run. Is that what you call justice?"

"It's not justice," Dan said. "And I didn't say we're quitting. We just need to start over. We need another solid witness, or some sort of evidence that can't be explained away by a talented defense attorney, which is exactly what Black will have if this ever goes to court."

I had come too far to quit now. Even if it meant my job. Even if it meant my life. As Dan Smith leaned back in his chair, I reached in my pocket and pulled out a wrinkled piece of paper, then laid it on his desk.

"Dobb Cole gave that to me when I went to see him a few days ago."

Agent Beard turned to me. "You did what?"

"Went undercover," I said. "Makeup, sequins, wig… I went whole hog."

"Whose number is it?" Dan asked.

"I don't know. Dobb told me to call after I asked for help getting someone released."

"And?" Beard said, fuming.

"The guy who answered told me to meet him at Barney's."

"Where?" Beard said. "Meet who where?"

"I called the number and offered to pay for executive clemency for my husband," I said. "He set up a meeting at Barney's, but never showed."

"Why didn't you tell us?" Dan said. "You should've said something."

"I'm saying it now. What are you gonna do about it?"

Dan looked from Agent Beard to me. "Nothing," he said. "We're not going to do anything because it doesn't change anything."

"What are you talking about?" I said. "Dobb was released by an executive order, signed by Governor Black, after paying whoever's number that is."

"That still doesn't mean Black knew," Dan said. "It doesn't mean anything. Other than you kept important information from us. From this investigation."

It was silent for a few seconds, then Dan stood from his chair and walked around the desk. "You were never authorized to visit Mr. Cole," he said. "You were never authorized to contact a suspect without letting both Agent Beard and myself know beforehand. And you most certainly were not authorized to plan a clandestine meeting with that suspect."

"I thought—"

"Your actions could have compromised the entire investigation," Dan said. "You might have cost that family their lives."

He was right. There was nothing for me to say.

"You're not an investigative agent," Dan said. "And now, unfortunately, you're no longer an Assistant US Attorney either. I'm sorry, Presley, but I've gotta cut you loose."

I looked toward Agent Beard, hoping for some help. He seemed to empathize but stayed quiet.

Dan held out his hand for my badge and ID card. I unclipped the badge from my belt and the carabiner attached to my ID card from its spot on a belt loop, then handed them over. I walked out without a word.

Outside of Dan Smith's office, I hurried down the hall toward the elevator. I had expected disciplinary action for going behind their backs, but I hadn't expected to be fired.

"Presley, wait up!" Agent Beard shouted, as he chased me down the hallway. "Hold on!"

I ignored him and kept walking until I arrived at the elevator and pushed the down button. Beard hurried up beside me, huffing from the short sprint.

"You all right?" he asked.

"Fantastic," I said, with as much venom as I could muster. "Thanks for all the help in there."

"It's his department. His call."

"I guess that's what you meant about courage, huh?"

"Listen, I think you're right," he said, hiding his embarrassment. "I believe we can make this case, and I'm willing to stay with it. We can take him down."

"Oh, it's we now? That's just great," I said. "Usually, rats jump *off* a sinking ship."

"We might have some leaks in the hull, but I think we can keep sailing."

I was shocked. He had never shown any real emotion, and now he seemed desperate to stay involved. But what did it matter now, anyway? Dobb Cole was gone, and he wasn't coming back. There was nothing to investigate. Black and his murdering goons had won.

"You go right ahead, Larry. Have fun digging through that red tape."

"I'm the federal agent in charge," he said. "I am the red tape. Which means I can cut as much of it as I see fit."

Ding. The elevator opened, and I stepped inside. I was tired. I just wanted to go home.

"I believe in this investigation," he said, as the doors slid shut. "And I believe in you."

CHAPTER THIRTY-SIX

Mack had called me a few times since the meeting and left messages. Dan Smith had told him what happened and how sorry he was it worked out the way it did. I let each of his calls go to voicemail. I knew we would talk about it, eventually, and I knew Mack would understand, but right now I didn't want to talk. Right now, I wanted to drive.

A little over four hours later, I pulled onto Dobb and Cazzie's parcel of land, and parked in front of what was left of their trailer. The sun was dropping as I stepped inside the charcoaled shell. It was surreal to see the home that was once so filled with life reduced to ash and disfigured metal. I saw Cazzie's ceramic figurines on the remaining shelves, blackened and melted. I walked toward the kitchen where I had met the Coles, and, surprisingly, the metal table was still standing—discolored and bent, but it was still there, along with one of the chairs.

I sat down and took it all in. I thought about what might've been going through Dobb and Cazzie's mind as their world burned down around them. I wondered if they had put two and two together and figured out it was me, "Stareene," that had brought this hell upon them. Then I thought about the children. The young, snot-nosed girl that had come to me and refused to let me go. I dropped my head and wiped the tears away, and noticed something shiny on the ground, directly under the table. It was bright yellow and green, and stood out among the gray. I reached down and pulled it from the ashes. It was the corncob saltshaker. I wiped off the soot and shoved it in my front pocket when a hoarse, gravelly woman's voice made me jump.

"Who are you?"

I turned to see a worn young woman—still pretty despite early wrinkles—who looked about my age, with medium-length brown hair and big green eyes. She wore tight Levi's, and despite the cold had on a white, sleeveless T-shirt. She held a bottle of Miller High Life in one hand, and the nub of a cigarette in the other. It made sense. Her voice sounded like she'd smoked and drank from the time she left the womb until this very moment.

"My name's Presley Carter," I said. "I knew Dobb and Cazzie a little."

"Enough to steal from 'em, looks like."

I blushed, reached into my pocket for the saltshaker, and walked up to the suspicious woman. I reached the cob out to her, and she looked at it for a second, then took a drink of the beer and a drag of the cigarette. "Keep it," she said. "They ain't gonna be needin' to salt nothin' no more anyway." Then she held out her hand. "I'm Dobb's sister, Sheryl Lee. 'Cept it's Everett now, not Cole."

I shook her hand, then she turned toward her beat-up, rusted-out Chevy Van, stuck her thumb and pinkie in her mouth, and blew a high-pitched whistle. I covered my ears and watched a lean thirteen-year-old girl that was the spitting image of Sheryl Lee lead Dobb and Cazzie's two small kids out of the van. The sight of the children hit me like a train. I just stood there, staring, with my hands over my ears and my mouth hanging open.

"I thought they were dead," I finally said.

"Nah, they was with me. Dobb and Cazz was celebratin' their fourteenth anniversary and wanted a little romantic time together before he started haulin', so they dropped 'em off at my place for the night."

The teenager led the Cole kids up to Sheryl Lee, but when the young girl saw me up close, she yanked away from the older girl's hand and hugged my leg. She squeezed so tight I could feel my toes going numb.

"Stareene," she sobbed into my leg. "Stareene..."

Sheryl Lee heard it and looked at me suspiciously.

"Nickname," I said.

"'At's weird," Sheryl Lee said. "Neither one of 'em has said a word since I told 'em their momma and daddy wasn't comin' back."

The girl kept squeezing, but Sheryl Lee grabbed her arm and pulled her off. "We came for your bikes, so go get 'em," she said. The heartbroken girl stared at me a little longer, then followed her older brother toward a leaning metal shed off to the side of the trailer. The teenager followed, uninterested.

"That's a fancy outfit you got there," Sheryl Lee said. "What do you do for money, if you don't mind my askin'?"

"I'm a lawyer. Or used to be, I guess. Just got fired."

"Man, that sucks," she said. "I thought about doing that when I was young. That or some sort of pet doctor. I got knocked up early though, and that was that." She took a swig of beer, then continued. "Don't get me wrong, now, I love my kids and I'd do anything for 'em, but if a person was a hundred percent honest about it, they'd have to admit that nothing kills dreams quicker'n havin' babies. That's just facts."

Hearing that reminded me of Ruthie Mae's similar sentiment. Two very different women, preaching the same gospel. You can't have it all, Presley, I reminded myself. You can't have it all.

"I don't know what the hell I'm gonna do with 'em," Sheryl Lee said, watching the Cole kids riding their bikes toward the van. "I got two of my own, besides Lexi there. I work part-time on minimum and tips, and got a husband locked up 'til he's an old man… I know life ain't supposed to be easy, but son of a bitch, this is ridiculous."

Her face tightened and I could tell she was tired. I hadn't known this woman for more than ten minutes, but I already liked her. I also respected her. "I'm sorry," I said, feeling it was a hollow gesture.

She chuckled, killed her beer, and slung the bottle against a half-standing wall. "Sorry for what?" she said. "It ain't your fault."

CHAPTER THIRTY-SEVEN

I thought about Sheryl Lee Everett the entire four-hour ride home to Leiper's Fork. She had absolved me of any fault for her brother and sister-in-law's death, but she hadn't known the truth. Her life had been hard, and now, thanks to my decisions, had become harder still.

I called Mack when I first got on the road, and when he asked me where I'd been, I told him the truth. He said he didn't see the point, but that he understood. He also told me not to eat on the way back, because he had a surprise for me. As soon as I opened the garage door and walked into the house, I knew it was barbeque.

"That smells so good, honey," I said. "I'm starving."

"Good," he said and handed me a loaded plate.

I grabbed the dish of food with one hand and pulled him close with the other. I kissed his lips and meant it.

"You wanna talk about it?" he said.

I took a huge bite of pulled pork and shook my head. "What's the point? You already know."

"Dan said he never would've known about what you did if you hadn't pulled out the number. He said you were almost out the door."

"I thought it would save the investigation," I said. "But he didn't want to hear it. He just took my badge and sent me packing. There are four people dead we know about, and Black's gettin' off scot-free."

"Come on, now, you know better than that. Somebody that brazen is gonna get caught, eventually."

"Maybe," I said, "but it won't be me catching him, will it?" I took another bite. "And after how many others are killed? Hell, forget about the dead ones. What happens to their kids, their relatives that gotta pick up the pieces? It's almost worse for the families."

Mack finished his bite of pork and moved closer. "Speaking of family."

I stopped chewing.

"I know you're upset about how it all worked out, but you did everything you could do. I'm so damn proud of you, Press, but we can't let one case stop us from living our lives."

"Let me guess what's coming next," I said.

"And why not? We always said the only thing that was stopping us was time. Well, now we've got a little."

I suddenly lost my appetite.

"I mean, just think about it. You're in between jobs, we've got plenty of savings, my insurance is as good as it gets. This might be the perfect time for it."

I took his beer and damn near drank it all in one swallow.

"Okay," he said, impressed. "Is that a celebration chug?"

"I still can't have kids, so I don't see how it could be."

"You know I'm talking about adoption," he said. "Why do you have to be this way?"

"I'm not being any way. I just… I can't just give up on it. People are dead, Mack, and it's partly my fault. You want me to just forget about it all, adopt a couple kids, take 'em camping and fishing, be mother of the year, and act like none of it ever happened?"

"Yes," he said, without hesitation. "That's exactly what I want."

In that moment, I loved him more than ever. And in the exact same moment, I resented him just as much.

"Well, then," I said. "Maybe I'm not the right woman for you after all."

The comment took us both by surprise. I couldn't believe the words had left my mouth. But they had. The silence was deafening before Mack finally spoke.

"I need another beer," he said, then turned and walked to our stocked fridge in the garage.

The thought of losing him brought tears to my eyes and fear to my heart. After my father had been killed, my mother checked out on us. Years later, my brother left me. It was as if that one bullet hadn't stopped when it killed my father. Its destruction shattered my entire family. I was petrified of getting close to anyone. I worried myself sick that they would leave me or be hurt in some way for loving me. In Mack, I had finally found stability. He was steady and made me feel safe and protected. In some ways, he gave me my life back, and I had just dared him to throw it away.

I had to apologize. I had to tell him he was my everything. My life. He had been gone longer than normal, so

I walked to the garage to check what was keeping him. The door was cracked, and I reached out to walk through, but what I heard inside stopped me in my tracks.

It wasn't the first time I had heard Mack cry. There were plenty of nights where we both woke from our own nightmares in tears. But it was the first time knowing that what I'd done—or, more to the point, what I refused to do—was what had caused him so much pain.

CHAPTER THIRTY-EIGHT

The next morning, I woke up alone. Mack and I hadn't talked since the argument, and he slept in the guest room. After using the bathroom, I walked down the hall to apologize. When I opened the door, the bed was made, and he was gone.

When he returned that night, I told him I was sorry and I hadn't meant what I'd said. He accepted it and life went on. For the next few weeks, we ate dinner, watched television, and went to bed as usual. We smiled and hugged, passed each other in the hallway, worked out, and occasionally made love. On the surface, everything had returned to normal. But underneath, something didn't feel right. Something was off.

The days were hardest for me. Mack would leave for work before eight in the morning and not be home again until eight at night. I was lonely and worried about our marriage. I was embarrassed that I'd been fired, and I had no desire to go back to work. But sitting at home all day thinking about it was driving me crazy. I knew I needed something to focus on. To pursue. To solve. So, I returned to the search for my father's killer.

I would spend the better part of the mornings in my home office, poring through files and paper, searching for anything, digging for clues. It always turned out the same. I would find a promising lead, then, upon digging deeper, would learn that there was no connection between that particular criminal and my father. It was maddening, and sometimes pushed me to the verge of giving up. But I knew I never would. I would never stop looking.

The next day, I was digging through files when my phone rang. I quickly realized that I had left it on the kitchen counter, so I had to sprint across the house to reach it. It was Cheri at my Franklin office. I had told her to stay on at the US Attorney's Office, but she wouldn't have it. She immediately tendered her two-week notice. They let her go ahead and leave that day. She immediately renewed the lease on our Franklin office, which, luckily, had not been rented. We had a unit at one of those temperature-controlled storage facilities and stored everything from the office there. She spent her days getting our operation back up and running, on the phone while I licked my wounds and hunted for a ghost. My phone stopped ringing just as I picked it up, so I called back.

"You need to get down here," she said, in an odd tone.

"Why?" I said. "What's wrong?"

"Nothing, I don't think," she said. "But there's a woman here waiting to see you. I told her you were out all day, but she's refusing to leave. Says she knows you, personally. Looks kinda nervous, too. Or maybe scared."

"What's her name?" I said, curious.

"Um, she says her name is, um, Sheryl Lee Everett."

I nearly dropped the phone. I had thought of her constantly since our meeting, and now she was sitting in my office. Why?

"I'm on my way," I said. "Tell her I'll be right there."

CHAPTER THIRTY-NINE

When I walked into my office, Sheryl Lee was drinking a Dr Pepper on the waiting-room couch. Cheri was typing on her computer, stealing glances at the skittish woman.

"It's so nice to see you again, Mrs. Everett," I said, offering my hand. When she stood and shook it, her hand felt like she had just dipped it in a bucket of water. That, along with her continued glances out the window, made it obvious this woman was scared of something.

"Let's go on in my office," I said.

After shutting the door, I sat behind my desk and Sheryl Lee took the chair directly in front of me.

"How can I help you, Mrs. Everett?"

"Why does it say Presley Myers out front?" she said, shaking slightly. "You told me at Dobb's it was Carter."

"One's professional. The other's personal. It helps with privacy."

"Don't help too much," she said. "I found you in two minutes."

She was right. If somebody wanted to find me, they could find me. She sure had. "So, again, how can I be of help?"

"I don't know about all this now," she said. "My feet are gettin' colder by the second."

"Mrs. Everett, would you say we're in a setting where you could expect your communication to me is private, pertains to a legal matter, and there's intent on your part to establish an attorney-client relationship at some point?"

"Uh. Yeah. Why?"

"Then we've checked all the boxes to ensure whatever you came to tell me falls under attorney-client privilege," I said. "Nothing you say will ever leave this room."

"I just want my husband back home."

"I don't understand. I thought you told me at the trailer he was in prison for a long time?"

"He is. But I got a call the other night..." She stopped midsentence.

"Yes?"

"Never mind. I gotta go."

She stood, and so did I.

"It's obvious you're scared to death, Sheryl Lee. Why don't you just sit back down and take a breath."

"Screw a breath," she said. "I need a shot."

I knew it wasn't professional, but this woman needed a drink more than just about anyone I'd ever seen. So I stood, opened a drawer, pulled out a bottle of Jack Daniel's, and looked for a glass. I couldn't find one, so I handed her the whole thing.

"Go easy," I said.

She nodded, then drank a gulp of whiskey big enough to make me wince. She squeezed her face tight, shook her head, then handed the bottle back.

"Who was it that called you?" I said.

"Never said his name. Just that he could help me get John out of prison. If I was willing to pay."

I didn't need a name. I knew who was behind the call. Governor Black and his cronies were still at it, soliciting executive releases for cash. Even calling the sister of a man they'd likely murdered.

"How long's his sentence?"

"Fifteen years. He's just coming up on a year inside, so fourteen left."

"That's a helluva long time. Would you mind if I asked what he did?"

She stared at me, thinking it over. Finally, she nodded toward the bottle. I handed it to her, and she took another large swig.

"Where should I start?"

"At the beginning."

"Well, I was born in a small town in Oklahoma of about 3,500 nice people, and—"

"No, Sheryl," I said, cutting her off. "The beginning of this situation."

"Oh. Yeah," she said, before starting over. "Well, me and John was doin' fine. He had got out of a eight-year bid for armed robbery after three for good behavior. We was both working hard, but then I got pregnant with the twins, and added to Alexi, who's from my first no-good, son-of-a-bitchin' husband, we couldn't hardly make ends meet."

"Were you both working?"

"I was cleaning houses. John was on a construction crew."

"Construction's not bad pay."

"Shoulda been decent," she said. "They were lowballin' him, though, 'cause they knew he couldn't complain, bein' a felon and on probation and all. Except he did. It wasn't fair, and he told 'em so. They said he could either work for what they give him, or he could hit the bricks."

"Let me guess."

Sheryl Lee nodded. "After that, we were in trouble. So, John decided to do a little favor for a fella, and that's when the cops pulled him over and found the crystal."

"How much?"

"Enough for 'em to revoke John's parole and send him back to prison," she said. "I figured he'd get some years tacked on to the five left on his first stretch if he got convicted, but that damn petty judge added on an extra ten to 'send a message.' When he said it, I stood up right there in the middle of court and flipped him the bird. Said I had a message for him, too. Told him to sit and spin. That got me a week inside for contempt… was worth every second."

"And this anonymous man just called you out of the blue, offering to get John out for money?"

"Yep," she said. "About a week ago—no, exactly a week ago—I remember, 'cause it was the day I got the check."

"What check?"

"Well, turns out Dobb used some of his robbin' money to buy a little insurance on that double-wide. Them kids are supposed to get it, but since I'm their legal guardian now, it's gotta run through me."

"And you got the call the exact same day you received the money?"

Sheryl Lee nodded.

"Like a miracle," I said, sarcastically.

"More like a death sentence," she said. "Cazzie told me she got the exact same call offering to get Dobb out." She lit a cigarette with shaky hands. "Didn't end too good for them, so…" She was a tough woman, but she was struggling to hold it together. "I want John out more than anything in this world, but I'm scared to death I'm gonna end up cooked alive, too."

I didn't say so, but she was right to worry. These men were vicious and wouldn't hesitate to wipe her off the face of the earth. "Just out of curiosity, how much did you get from the insurance?"

"Thirty thousand bucks."

"Did you tell that to whoever called you?"

"I started to," she said, "but I figured if I kept it a secret, then maybe I could negotiate a cheaper price."

"Did you?"

She waited a few seconds before she answered. "He told me right off they don't negotiate. He said if I wanted John out, it'd cost me thirty thousand on the nose. Take it or leave it. I figured it wasn't no coincidence."

"Just so we're clear," I said. "Paying for John's release is a federal crime. You could end up in prison. Then what would your kids do?"

"Is there any way to get John out without me goin' to prison, and maybe take these murderin' sons-of-bitches down, too?" she said. "It'd be sorta nice to kill two birds with one stone… so to speak."

Maybe this was another shot for me to take Black down. I wanted it more than anything. I wanted him behind bars for killing Dustin and Emma, Dobb and Cazzie, and who knows how many others. But I couldn't put another life at risk. Especially this woman's life, with so many innocent people dependent on her.

"It's too dangerous," I said. "Too many people have already died trying to bring them down."

"That don't matter to me," she said. "Not if there's a chance I could get John out."

"I'm not going to put you in harm's way—"

"Is there a chance?" she said.

"Yes. There's always a chance, but we'd have to get it all on tape. You'd have to wear a wire. Are you willing to do that?"

"What are the chances you can get him out if I do?" she said. "I mean the odds?"

"I don't know."

"Just ballpark it," she said. "Your best guess."

"60-40."

"For?"

"Against."

"Jesus H. on a popsicle stick," she said. "At least you coulda lied a little and painted a rosier picture."

"It's too dangerous to lie," I said. "I need to know you understand the risks."

Sheryl Lee looked at me. I couldn't read her face. There was no way to tell what she was thinking. I felt the odds were too steep in the wrong direction for her to take such a risk, and I was content with that. To my surprise, a moment after I had that thought, Sheryl nodded.

"Hell with it," she said. "Let's do it."

After she left my office, I spent the rest of the day thinking of how best to proceed. Dan Smith had told me to find another good witness, and here one was. But I no longer worked for Dan Smith or the US Attorney's office. For me, that avenue was a dead end.

I needed someone else. Someone with the power and resources to revive the investigation. Someone who wanted Governor Black behind bars as much as I did.

I knew exactly who to call.

CHAPTER FORTY

It was another cold day at Percy Warner Park, but the unexpected sunshine had brought out the joggers, bikers, and hikers. But I wasn't watching them enjoying their exercise, I was watching Agent Beard walk from his Chevy sedan up to my Audi. He looked over his shoulder before opening the passenger door and sitting down. It was awkward, but there was business to discuss and little time to waste.

"Are you sure she's on board?"

"One hundred percent," I said. "She's rarin' to go."

"You haven't promised her anything, have you? Just because she's cooperating doesn't guarantee her husband's going to be released."

"She knows."

"Good."

I looked at Larry. He seemed different. He seemed conflicted. "What about you? You're sure you want to do this? You seem wishy-washy."

"I'm not wishy-washy. I'm just way out on a limb on this thing. Anything less than handing them Black on a silver platter could mean my job. Might anyway."

"So, why are you doing it?" I asked. "You don't have to, you know."

I was surprised to see him drop his head and get quiet. I was just about to say something when he started talking.

"I was engaged to be married a long time ago," he said. "Right when I was joining the bureau."

I was completely taken off guard by the confession but was more than happy to listen.

"I asked her to marry me, and she said yes," he continued. "I think that—no, I know—that day was the happiest day of my life."

"Can I meet her sometime?" I said. "I'd love to meet the woman who could put up with you."

He was quiet, and I knew I'd made a mistake.

"The second week on the job, I'm serving a warrant on a guy for distributing child pornography out of his mom's basement. A soft target, they told me. No history of violence. Well, it turns out 'they' were wrong, 'cause as soon as we pulled up and I stepped out of the car, he opens fire from his bedroom and gets me in the gut. Straight through my vest."

I sat there, stunned.

"I flatlined twice before they got me stable. Spent two weeks in ICU before I got back home. I could tell something had changed, but she wouldn't talk about it. Not until I asked her if she was ready to have kids… That's when she told me she couldn't bring a child into the world not knowing whether its father would make it home each night."

The story was hitting close to home.

"So, I told her I didn't need kids as long as I had her. As long as we were together, it was enough. That's when she said it wasn't only kids she was worried about. Said she couldn't live worried about it either. The next day, she left. And that was it. I've been on my own ever since."

"I'm sorry," I said. "I'm really sorry."

"You asked me why I want to do this?" he said. "Because I've given up everything else to do this work. The job's all I have left."

Maybe I had more in common with this stuffy agent than I thought. Hell, maybe someday we'd even become friends.

CHAPTER FORTY-ONE

The Faraway Inn sat in the middle of Trinity Lane in a run-down section of North Nashville, directly across from Biney Beals's original Fish Shack. The dilapidated one-story motel only had twelve rooms, and in room number eight, me, Agent Beard, and a terrified Sheryl Lee Everett prepared for our classified sting operation. Agent Beard had suggested we keep it from Dan Smith until we had evidence that was concrete and irrefutable. That way, hopefully, he would keep his anger to a minimum after he found out I had continued working the case after being fired. And, if nothing came from our work, Dan would be none the wiser. No harm, no foul.

Agent Beard tested the tiny recording device that Sheryl Lee had agreed to wear under the waistband of her blue jeans. He had gotten the device from the FBI office. It was very small, but if she were searched well enough, it would be discovered.

Sheryl Lee had gone through the same hoops as Emma Hodge to set up this meeting, and now she was going to meet the same disgusting man at Biney Beals's downtown Fish Shack. The same lowlife that had taken advantage of Emma — Chuck Haynes.

"Remember, Sheryl," I said. "If he tries to get you to the back room, don't go. Even if he threatens to kill the deal, just walk out. We'll find another way to get to them. Okay?"

Sheryl nodded, then retched. "My stomach's turnin' cartwheels."

"Take a breath," I told her. "And just stay out of the back room."

"Boy, I need me a joint," Sheryl said.

I could have used one myself.

Agent Beard finished attaching the small recorder under her waistband. "I hope you're kidding," he said. "You don't need to smoke marijuana right now, Mrs. Everett. You need a clear head. And besides, that stuff will kill you."

"Kill you?" she said. "What are you talking about? Pot relaxes you. It calms your nerves. Ask her," she said, nodding to me. "I bet she knows."

"That's what I hear," I said, half joking.

"Believe me, Agent Beard, you oughta try it," Sheryl Lee said. "Hell, every cop in the country should be *required* to take a toke."

"Well, that's not gonna happen," Beard said. "Sorry."

"Well, how 'bout some booze then?" Sheryl Lee said. "Shit, I'd kill for a cold beer right about now."

"No pot and no beer!" Agent Beard said.

Sheryl was shaking when I sat beside her. "I know it's hard, but I promise you, we'll be listening every second. If anything goes wrong, we'll be right there."

***

Sheryl walked out of the motel, crossed the street, and stepped to the front door of the one-room restaurant. A Closed sign hung on the door. She squinted and pressed her face closer to the glass, but the place was empty. She knocked hard three times and waited. It didn't take long for Chuck to appear behind the glass: fat and greasy with long stringy hair, and the rare face that looked worse with a smile. He pulled open the squeaky door.

"Howdy, there, Sheryl Lee, right on time."

"Thank you for meetin' me, Mr. Haynes. I really appreciate it."

"Oh, come on, now. Forget all that Mr. stuff. It's Chuck, darling. Just call me Chuck."

"Okay."

"So, sweetheart, what can I do for you today?"

"Well, like I said over the phone, I'd like you to help me and my husband out of a bind."

"What sort of a bind, honey?"

"I was told that you could help get him out of jail. For a price."

"Well, it seems you might've been misinformed. That would be illegal, now, wouldn't it?"

"I don't understand. Please, I'll do anything to get him home."

"Anything?" Chuck asked. "You sure about that?"

Sheryl nodded.

"Okay," he said. "What's in it for me?"

"I told you, I'll pay the money—"

"I ain't talkin' about money, honey. I've got a little something different in mind."

"What?" Sheryl asked.

"Why don't you come on back to my office and let's talk about it?"

Sheryl stared at the greasy, fat man. "I don't know if that's such a good idea."

"Suit yourself," Chuck said. "Have a nice life." He motioned for her to leave, then turned to walk away.

"Wait," Sheryl said. "I guess it wouldn't hurt none to talk."

"Wouldn't hurt none at all. Just let me lock the front door so nobody don't bother us." Chuck grabbed the keys and walked toward the front, brushing up against Sheryl as he passed. "Go on back behind the counter. Office is right there."

I ripped off my headphones and headed toward the door.

"Wait a second," Beard said.

"I'm not letting this happen again. I'll kill him first!"

"You go in there and Black and everybody else in the city's gonna know what we're doing."

"I don't give a damn!"

"Just wait a few more seconds. Sheryl's no kid. She might have a plan."

I thought about it. "You got ten," I said, then put my headphones back on and we both continued to listen.

SHERYL: So… What did you want to talk about?
CHUCK: You like snakes?
SHERYL: Shit, no. Who in the hell likes snakes?
CHUCK: Well, pretty lady, I'm afraid you're gonna have to learn to like 'em if you want to get your hubby out of the can.

(Sound of a zipper.)

SHERYL: What are you doing?

CHUCK: I'm introducing you to *my* pet snake… Now get on your knees.

I had my hands on the headphones, ready to toss them off and sprint across the street.

(Sheryl starts laughing)

I looked at Beard. Maybe she did have a plan.

CHUCK: What's so damn funny?

SHERYL: Nothing… I just… When you said *snake*, I pictured something… bigger. And longer.

CHUCK: You a smart-ass bitch, ain't ye? Start suckin' or start walkin'.

(Sheryl is heard kneeling, then a pause, then CHUCK screams)

SHERYL: I done told you I'll do anything to get my husband out of prison. That includes yanking your skinny little worm right offa your fat, greasy body.

(Chuck stops screaming, starts crying)

CHUCK: Please, let it go… It hurts…

SHERYL: Who do I need to talk to for help? I know you ain't runnin' nothin'.

CHUCK: Biney… Biney Beals… I'll set it up, I promise… Please…

SHERYL: Soon.

CHUCK: Okay, okay, okay…

SHERYL: Promise me, Chuck.

(Sheryl yanks, Chuck screams)

CHUCK: I promise, damn it!… I swear on my momma!…Please…

SHERYL: You've got my number... if you mention this to Mr. Beals, I'll make sure to tell 'em you almost let thirty grand walk out the door 'cause I wouldn't get your rocks off. Don't forget y'all came to me, not the other way around.

CHUCK: I swear to Jesus I won't say nothin'! Just let it go...

(Sheryl releases Chuck's member and stands.)

SHERYL: Good luck, Chuck. I'll be waitin' on the phone to ring.

(Chuck sobs. She walks out of the office and the front doorbell rings.)

Agent Beard and I sat in the motel room, stunned.

"I guess she had a plan after all," Beard said.

"To what?" I said. "Pull a Stretch Armstrong on his johnson?"

Agent Beard and I were both thinking of an answer to that question when the motel door opened, and Sheryl Lee walked in. Without a word, she casually strolled to the bathroom sink and washed her hands, before appearing in front of us with a smile on her face.

"Well?" she said. "Can I have a beer now?"

CHAPTER FORTY-TWO

The little honky-tonk was nearly empty when Sheryl and I walked in and took two stools at the bar. Agent Beard was invited along but had politely declined. Sheryl had the first beer gone within thirty seconds and immediately ordered round two. She was still buzzing with excitement from her dangerous encounter, and the extra energy seemed to keep her talking.

"Hell no, it wasn't planned," she said, answering my question. "I can't believe I just grabbed it like that. It was like my hand had a mind of its own."

"Took some balls," I said. "Literally."

"You think he'll keep his word and set it up?"

"We'll see," I said. "I would if I were him."

"I meant what I told him in there about doing anything to get John out of prison."

"Evidently," I said. "You must really love him."

"More'n anything."

"How'd y'all meet?"

Sheryl laughed and took a drink of beer. "Willie Nelson, believe it or not. Good ol' Papaw Stoner himself."

"How did he get involved?"

"You want the long or short version?"

"It depends."

"On what?"

"On how good you can tell a story."

Sheryl winked at me, then killed her second beer. "Well, I got knocked up at seventeen. I wanted the baby, but not the daddy. I'm from a tiny town in nowheresville Oklahoma. Real religious. My mother told me God wouldn't want me to keep the kid and leave its father. I took the bait and Momma signed the consent papers and called a pastor, and two hours before the baby came, I married the idiot. We had a white wedding, too."

"Really?" I said. "How?"

"Everybody had on hospital gowns."

I laughed as the pretty bartender sat down Sheryl's third beer. "That was Alexi?" I asked.

"'At was her. The thickest hair I'd ever seen. Raven black, too. Healthy as a horse. I divorced the daddy the day after that, then as soon as I was out of the hospital, me and her hit the road runnin' wilder'n a raped ape."

"How'd you end up here from Kansas?" I asked as I drained my first beer and motioned for a second.

"Oklahoma," she said, correcting me. "And I don't really know. I mean, Dobb and Cazz was already here, and they offered to help out with the baby, plus I just always loved country music, so I figured I'd head on down and see what was what. It wasn't no more'n a week before I scored a few tickets to a Willie show at the Fairgrounds. As soon as I saw his steel-guitar picker, I fell head over heels."

"Hold on, your husband was Willie Nelson's steel player?"

Sheryl laughed. "Shit, no."

"I'm confused."

"Well, Willie's man was pretty damn handsome, so I decided to sneak backstage and make friends, if you know what I mean. But I'd had a few tokes and a couple brews, so on the way over, I accidentally bumped into an ol' redneck and spilt his beer all over his boots."

"That was John?"

"That was him. And that was it."

"Instant?"

"Well, let's just say that when he turned around to let me have it, and I saw those baby blues, I forgot all about Willie's boy."

We both took long swigs.

"What about you?" Sheryl asked, nodding to my wedding ring. "Looks like somebody likes fixin' your recipe."

"I guess so."

"You guess?" she said, pointing at the diamond. "That ain't no 'I guess' rock."

I nodded, took another sip.

"Young'uns?" she asked.

"Nope."

"What the hell y'all waitin' on? If he's half as good lookin' as you, y'all's kids will be pretty as puppies."

"He's better lookin' than me," I said. "Pretty's not the problem."

"What is then?"

"Me, I guess. I'm dry as a bone."

"Well, there's about a million ways to get kids these days, if you really want 'em."

"It's complicated," I said. "There are extenuating circumstances."

"There's who?"

"Never mind."

"What?" Sheryl asked.

I shook my head.

"Come on, honey. Sometimes it helps to say it out loud. I promise you, whatever it is, I've either done it, had it happen to me, or heard of it happenin' to somebody else."

I took one last drink to finish the bottle, then turned to her. "My father was murdered," I said, shocked at how easy it was to say.

"Oh, honey…"

"I was twelve. Somebody walked in our house and shot him in his office. Point blank, in the head."

"They catch him?"

I shook my head. "Killed him, then vanished."

"I ain't no shrink or nothin'," she said, "but it don't take no psychologist to figure out that that more'n likely has something to do with you not wantin' kids."

"I'm almost as old now as my dad was when he died. All I can think about is what if I had a kid—kids—and something like that happened to me or Mack."

"I get it," Sheryl said. "Life is scary, and for a long time that's how I lived it. From dawn to dusk, scared as hell. But, after about the fiftieth shitstorm hit me, I finally figured out that me being scared ain't gonna stop whatever's supposed to happen from happening. So, now, I just get up in the morning, give all that fear the finger, and keep on truckin'. Ain't nothin' much changed, but I do feel a little bit better about things."

I finished my last sip of beer and stood from the stool. "I better be gettin' home," I said, then paid the entire tab and threw down an extra twenty in front of her. "Keep going if you want to, Sheryl Lee. You earned it."

CHAPTER FORTY-THREE

Governor Black was furious after learning Dan Smith had fired the nosy crusading lawyer. Black had paid a hefty sum to get Smith on his payroll, and he expected the man to follow orders. Black had OK'd the hiring of Presley Carter, making her an Assistant US Attorney. Before that, Governor Black had been mulling over different options to deal with the pain-in-the-ass woman. He had no qualms about killing her as long as it was done discreetly. In fact, he was close to giving the order when Dan Smith called and told him about the chance to hire her.

Black saw an opportunity. Here was a chance to keep an eye on the woman. To be privy to the strategies and tactics implemented by someone absolutely hell-bent on orchestrating his downfall.

But now Smith had fired her. And with her went his window into the mind of his main adversary. When he heard the news, Black seriously considered having Dan Smith killed, or at least fired. The more he thought about the situation, however, the more he found himself at peace with the decision. Smith hadn't closed the investigation. He had effectively removed its teeth. That could work in Black's favor.

Now, Dan Smith could appoint whomever he wanted to take point on the investigation. Lonnie Black needed to be on board with Smith's choice, so before making a decision, he called the Governor.

"You should lead it," Governor Black said.

"Me?" Smith answered. "I'm swamped as it is. I can't take that on."

"Exactly," Black said. "Just keep it open and let it slip into purgatory. Before long another story will break, and people will forget all about ol' Governor Black's scandal."

"And if they don't?" Dan Smith asked.

"Then you tell 'em you're working like a dog to dig up the truth. And you'll let 'em know as soon as you do."

"What about if the Feds start pressing?"

"The United States Justice Department has a lot on its plate," Black said. "Let me ask you something, how many times has Beard asked about me since you fired the Carter woman?"

"Well," Dan said, mulling it over. "None, now that I think about it."

"Exactly. I don't think they have any intention of carrying the torch on a witch hunt into a sitting Governor who's a member of the President's political party."

"I don't know," Smith said. "Agent Beard's not dumb. I doubt he'll just let this thing rest."

"Jesus, Dan, I wish I could say the same for you," Black said. "If Beard, or anybody else asks about it, you just tell 'em the investigation is ongoing, but that's all you can say at this time. If they keep pressing, tell them you've had to close rank because you suspect a mole in their office ... Now, do you need me to come over there and hold your pecker while you pee?"

"No, sir. I'll take care of it."

With that buttoned up, Black could get back to the business of running the state and collecting bribes for clemency and extortion without any interference. In fact, there was an inmate name written on a piece of paper resting on the table in front of him.

JOHN EVERETT

Even though Chuck Haynes was a white-trash flunky, he'd been a solid gatekeeper for deciding which inmates to move forward on. He had green-lighted this name for Beals, who had agreed to pass Everett's name up to Black. The money looked right to the Governor, but there was a big difference between this inmate and the others he'd dealt with in the past. Before signing off, he needed some legal advice.

"You sure it's smart to do this for Cole's sister?" Black asked his lawyer, Reginald Gray, when he arrived at his office.

"What do you mean?"

"Her brother just died in that awful fire," Black said. "You think she suspects anything other than the tragic accident that it was?"

"I don't," Gray said. "But even if she does, it doesn't make a bit of difference to us."

"How can you be so sure?"

"Because," Gray said. "Either she suspects something and is doing the deal, or she doesn't suspect something and is doing the deal. Even if she has suspicions, there's nothing to gain by rocking the boat. Her husband is rotting away in a cell, and you're the only one with the keys. Why would she jeopardize that?"

"And you're sure she's got the money?"

"I'm sure. She was Dobb's beneficiary."

"Who the hell puts insurance on a double-wide trailer?" Black said.

"Dobb Cole, evidently," Gray said, then opened his briefcase and pulled out an official clemency document. "Just need your signature to make it official."

Black looked the document over one last time. Then he pulled out his gold Montblanc and signed his name with a flourish.

CHAPTER FORTY-FOUR

"So, what, you just decided to go rogue without telling me?" Mack asked me, in the middle of dinner. I had just told him about the sting operation, and he was not happy. "Par for the course, I guess."

"Nobody's going rogue," I said. "But I have a woman who's been offered the chance to free her husband from prison for money. I'd be crazy not to take advantage of that."

"Who made her the offer?"

"We don't know exactly," I said. "Not yet at least."

"You shittin' me?"

I shook my head back and forth.

"Jesus. Have you told Dan?"

"Not yet," I said.

"Why not?"

"First, because I no longer work for Dan. Second, my informants have a history of winding up dead, and I'd like to prevent that from happening this time, if at all possible."

"But if you tell him, it could change his mind. He stands to gain as much as anyone from bringing Black down."

"That's why I'm gonna wait," I said. "Once I've got the case all wrapped up in a bow on a silver platter, then I'll let Agent Beard walk it into Dan's office. All he'll have to do is hand it over to Mattie Thompson and let her bring it home. Until then, nobody knows except me and Agent Beard. That way, Black and all his goons think nobody's watching. They're already gettin' lazy, now I want 'em to get cocky. That's how we'll catch them."

"And the FBI is behind this?"

"Sort of," I said.

"What does that mean? I thought you said Agent Beard was with you?"

"He is."

"Okay, so, usually if an FBI agent is running a sting, that means the FBI is behind it."

"Larry works for the FBI, and they're behind it," I said. "But he doesn't exactly have a cheering section."

"Larry?" he said.

"What? That's his name."

Mack shook his head.

"What?"

"You're walking a very thin, very dangerous line with this," he said. "I just hope you know what you're doing."

"Me, too," I said. "Me, too."

He looked at me for what seemed like forever, then said, "I'm tired, Presley. I think I'm gonna hit the hay." With that he kissed the top of my head and walked out of the room. I started to follow him, but as soon as I stood up, I heard the door to the guest room open and close.

CHAPTER FORTY-FIVE

Sheryl got the call in the middle of the night. It came from Chuck Haynes, who gave her Biney Beals's office address followed by a date and time to meet. She tried to ask a couple follow-up questions, but Chuck hung up immediately. Sheryl called to tell me the news, and I relayed it to Agent Beard.

Two days later, in the tenth-floor suite of the downtown Hyatt, Sheryl was ashen as she watched Agent Beard once again attach the tiny microphone inside her waistband. She was so nervous; she nearly smoked the entire cigarette hanging from her lips in one giant inhale.

"You okay?" I asked.

She wiped sweat from her forehead and nodded.

"Remember now," Agent Beard said. "Half the money now, half when you see John walk out of the prison gates."

"I know," Sheryl said. "You've said it a thousand times."

"I just want to make sure," Beard said. "And don't give him the fifteen until he gives you the clemency document. And make sure it has Black's signature—"

"I know," Sheryl said again. "You're about to drive me crazy."

I hugged her and led her to the door before Agent Beard said something that made her change her mind for good. "Come on, girl," I said, low enough so Larry didn't hear. "This meeting's one step closer to gettin' John back home."

Sheryl Lee walked out of the Hyatt at 1:33. Agent Beard and I watched from our high suite as she crossed Memorial Square and headed toward the Capitol for her meeting with Biney Beals. Just before she stepped inside the old, impressive building, she turned her head and stared up at the glass facade of the new hotel. She seemed to be looking right at us.

Once inside the Capitol, Sheryl Lee waited in line at the security station. Agent Beard had assured her the new, cutting-edge recording device she had stuck in her waistband would not be detected. But, as she moved up the line, little by little, she began to get nervous.

"Ma'am, please step forward," the fat security guard said.

Sheryl was so anxious she didn't answer. Just stepped through the metal detector and held her breath.

No beeps.

"Thank you very much," the guard said. "Enjoy your day at the Capitol."

Sheryl managed a nod and kept walking to the elevators. Beals's office was on the fourth floor. His secretary was gone, and he was waiting for her as she walked in.

"Well, look at you," Beals said, as he shook her hand. "Sheryl Lee Everett! You're as pretty as Chuck said you was."

Sheryl smiled and played along. "Nice fella."

"Oh, you ain't gotta lie to me, honey," he joked. "You already got the meetin'!"

He led her back to his office, and when she stepped inside, it looked to her like a shrine to Tennessee Vols football. Orange everywhere. Floor to ceiling. Sheryl thought it was ugly. She had never liked Tennessee Orange. Always reminded her of road crews picking up trash on the side of the highway. Biney Beals, on the other hand, was a fanatic. His favorite item of Volunteer football memorabilia sat proudly at the front of his desk. It was an authentic game-worn helmet signed by the program's most famous player, Peyton Manning, during his fourth and final season. He led the team to the conference championship and finished as the runner-up for the Heisman Trophy. Sheryl was interested since she had never touched a football helmet. She picked it up to look it over, but Beals quickly took it from her and placed it back on the desk.

"That one's special," he said. "Nobody touches the helmet but me."

"I get it. It's a cool office, though," she said, lying to the man's face.

"Can't beat that UT Orange," he said, as they both sat down. "Most beautiful color in the world."

"Besides green," Sheryl said. Then she did exactly what Agent Beard told her not to do. She reached in her purse and pulled out $15,000 in cash.

The move shocked even Biney, and he was on her in an instant. "Stand up," he said, as he walked around his desk.

"What's the problem?"

"Take off your boots," he ordered.

"What—"

"Take off the boots. Now!"

Sheryl nodded, dropped the money back in her purse, then pulled her boots off.

Biney picked them up and plunged his hand in each before turning them upside down and shaking them. While he was preoccupied, Sheryl quickly yanked the recording device from her waistband and stuck it down the front of her panties. She barely had it hidden when Biney dropped the boots and looked at her.

"Turn around," he said.

She did as she was told, and he rubbed his hands over her body, searching for a wire or microphone. His hands went from her shoulders, to her breasts, down her stomach, along her waistband, and, finally, between her legs. She slapped his hand away just before he grabbed her crotch.

"That's as far as you're going," she said. "I'm here for my husband, but I got a line."

Biney stared at her, reading her close. After a few seconds, he laughed and sat back down. "Can't be too careful," he said. "I'll take that money now."

"What about the release paper?"

Biney stared at Sheryl for a long time. "About that…"

"Where is it?" Sheryl said, starting to worry.

"Don't fret yourself, it's all signed and official. It's just not been dropped off yet."

"So, what are we supposed to do in the meantime?" Sheryl said. "I mean, about the money?"

"You give me the fifteen now, and I'll have the document for you tomorrow. Easy."

"See, there, that's what scares me," Sheryl said. "I can't just hand you half of everything I got in the world without some kind of guarantee John will see the light of day."

"That's what I'm saying to you," Biney said. "If I can't get him out, then the money goes back to you. In full."

Sheryl Lee thought that over. "All right," she said. "I got your word?"

"It's my bond," he said. "I really think we can help him."

With that, Sheryl Lee nodded and handed Biney the money. He wheeled his chair around, then took a knee in front of a small safe tucked under a credenza. He whirled the combination lock back and forth until the door opened, then stuck the cash on top of the signed release document with John Everett's name on one line and Governor Black's name on the other. He had every intention of handing the paper over when she walked in, but after seeing her in person, he decided to string her along another day. You never knew what could come of it.

After stuffing the money in the safe, Beals stood and walked close to Sheryl.

"I hope you'll pardon me for the impromptu feel-up."

"I get it." she said. "I'm paranoid, too."

"It wasn't too bad, though, was it?"

Sheryl held his gaze. "I'll be back tomorrow for the paper."

"You got it, honey," he said. Then he stared at her ass as she walked out of his office.

***

Sheryl Lee was nearly hyperventilating as she stormed into the Hyatt suite. "I'm sorry!" she yelled. "I know I wasn't supposed to give it to him without gettin' the document, but I thought I was gonna have a heart attack."

"Just calm down, Mrs. Everett," Agent Beard said.

"Calm down? He was an inch away from finding the recorder. If I hadn't moved it, it would've been over."

"Here, drink this," I said, after grabbing an airplane bottle of Vodka from the mini fridge. Agent Beard gave me a perturbed look, but I waved him off and handed Sheryl the tiny bottle. She killed it in one swallow.

"He was feelin' all over me," she said. "I swear I would've took off running, but I was so damn scared my feet wouldn't move... Oh, my Lord, he almost caught me..."

"Hey," I said, moving to sit beside the distraught woman. "Look on the bright side."

"What bright side?" she asked. "Tell me what's the bright side of giving that asshole half of my brother's insurance money for nothin'?"

"He took the money for the release," I said. "We got him taking the money."

CHAPTER FORTY-SIX

I was excited to tell Mack the good news when I walked in the house, but the sight of him packing a suitcase caught me by surprise. And scared me to death.

"What's goin' on?" I said.

"A triple murderer just climbed over a fifteen-foot fence at Riverbend. I'm gonna go find him and take him back."

"You?" I said. "Alone?"

"There's a team, but I'm O.I.C."

"Remind me, again?"

"Officer In Charge, Presley."

"Of course. Why can't you ever be 'Officer That Gives Orders from Home'?"

"I'm gonna be late."

He zipped his bag and walked out of the room. I followed him.

"Can I give you a ride?"

"I've gotta go right now."

"That's fine. I'm ready."

He stopped and looked at me. After a few moments, he nodded.

His office was only a fifteen-minute drive without traffic, so I was hoping for congestion. I wanted a little time to talk and hopefully repair some damage. Naturally, the freeway moved as fast as a Sunday morning. If I wanted to talk, it would have to be fast. While I thought of the right thing to say, Mack started.

"Willie Wetzel got shot two days ago."

"Shot?" I said. "My God, that's horrible. Is he okay?"

"He's gonna make it, but he's far from okay. Gonna have to learn how to walk again. A fifty-year-old man, ran triathlons, and now he can't even stand up. Can't play with his kids…"

"What happened?"

"Raid out in the boonies. Meth, of course."

"You were there?"

"I'm the boss. I'm always there."

"Why didn't you tell me?"

"I just did."

"Yeah," I answered. "On your way to a manhunt."

Another silence filled the car as I drove the empty interstate.

"Were you shot at, too?"

He didn't answer.

"Were you?"

"It's my job. You know that."

"Just because it's your job, doesn't mean I have to like it."

"Ditto," he said.

"What's that supposed to mean?"

"Never mind. I don't wanna fight."

"You sure about that?" I said. "You seem pretty damned set on picking one to me."

"Let's just drop it."

"No, I'm not gonna drop it. What the hell did you mean?"

He shook his head. "I just wish that you would put as much effort into us as you do the Governor."

"Um, I'm not the one going away to hunt down a psycho killer ready to shoot you the first chance he gets."

"I don't have a choice."

"And what, you think I do?"

"Look, I don't know how long this is gonna take, so please, can we not?"

"I'm not arguing," I said. "I'm talking to my husband about something important. Now, will you please answer my question?"

"All I'm saying is that after Wetzel got hit, it really made me think about things. It made me realize what's important. It made me realize how much I want a family."

"And what are we?"

"You know what I mean."

"Yeah, that makes perfect sense," I said. "Let me just drop you off, and I'll head on down to the adoption agency and pick up a few kids. They'll be washed and ready when you come back from your fun little mission. *If* you come back."

The silence was heavier now. More dangerous. After a few more miles, I pulled my car up to his office. He grabbed his bag from the floorboard and opened the passenger door.

"Hey," I said, grabbing his arm before going silent. I wanted to tell him I loved him and needed him, but for some reason I didn't say those things. For some reason, I didn't say a word.

I let go of his arm and watched him walk toward the front doors of the Sheriff's office. It wasn't an airport this time, but I knew that he would, at least, keep our goodbye tradition. As he stepped up to the doors, I waited for him to stop and turn, then smile and blow me a kiss.

But he didn't stop. He didn't turn. He didn't blow me a kiss.

He didn't even look back.

CHAPTER FORTY-SEVEN

The next day, Biney was again waiting for Sheryl Lee at his empty receptionist desk, where he shook her hand and led her back into his office.

"So," he said, "looks like you're gonna have yourself a very Merry Christmas after all."

"What do you mean?"

"I mean it looks like your boy's gonna be cut loose on Christmas Eve, if that's all right with you?"

"Really?" she said. "Christmas Eve? The kids will be in hog heaven."

Biney walked to his small safe, and after twirling the combination, reached in and pulled out the clemency document. He walked over to Sheryl Lee holding the sacred paper.

"Due to John's ability with his hands—plus the good time he's already pulled—it looks like the powers that be agree that he'd be of more use on the outside than in."

"Who's that?" Sheryl Lee said, trying to get him to say Black's name.

"Who's what?" Beals asked, not taking the bait.

Sheryl Lee was scared and decided not to push it. "Nothin'," she said. "I just don't know what to say. I don't know how to thank you."

She reached for the clemency document, but Biney pulled it away.

"Yeah, you do," he said, as he positioned himself between her and the door.

"He's almost home free, honey," he said. "Just consider this a little toll-booth before your last exit."

***

Back in the Hyatt Suite, I had already ripped off my headphones and started for the door. Sheryl Lee was smart and tough, but Biney Beals was no Chuck Haynes. He was dangerous. If he forced her to undress and found the recording device, she'd end up dead.

My sudden movement surprised Larry. He said something as I ran out, but I was too focused to hear what it was. I sprinted down the hall, took the elevator to the hotel lobby, then continued running out the front doors and toward the Federal Building. I knew if I barged in like a maniac, I would likely be stopped and detained. So, I stopped running, took a breath, and walked in the quiet lobby.

The security lines were nearly empty, and I stepped right through. Until I heard a beep. The Security Officer stopped me and told me to go back and double-check my pockets. In my frantic state, I had forgotten to remove my cell phone and watch. I hurried to place them both in a plastic bowl, stepped through again—this time successfully—and after grabbing my belongings, walked as fast as I could to the nearest bank of elevators and hit the up button.

Once the elevator door pinged and opened on the fourth floor, I realized I didn't know the direction of Beals's office. I was in a panic. Then I spotted a woman in a suit at the far end of the hallway.

"Biney Beals?" I shouted. It startled the woman. I smiled and waved, trying my best to seem professional despite being terrified of what was going on in the office I was trying to find. "I have a meeting with him, but I've never been here before!"

The annoyed woman pointed me in the right direction, and I took off like I was shot out of a cannon. The office, of course, was at the opposite end of the building from where I stood, and I was breathing hard as I hurried past the empty secretary station and swung open the wood door with Biney Beals's name mounted at the center in gold letters.

"Let her go!" I screamed, as I barged in the room. But what I saw was not what I expected. Sheryl Lee was calmly buttoning her blouse as Biney Beals sat on his leather couch watching her, a glass of whiskey in his hand. His black ostrich-skin boots on the floor next to him.

"Who the hell are you?" Beals asked. I was surprised at the question. I expected him to recognize me immediately. Relieved, I looked to Sheryl, who silently pleaded with me to stay quiet. I followed her eyes to the signed clemency document on the chair in front of her.

"You know this woman?" Beals asked her. No answer. "Hey, I'm talking to you!"

Sheryl had a decision to make, and she made it. "No," she said. "I've never seen her before in my life."

I didn't know what was happening now or what had happened before, but I followed her lead. "I'm so sorry," I said. "My husband's office is on this floor, but I must've gotten turned around. The son of a bitch is cheatin' on me with his secretary, and I thought I'd catch 'em red-handed."

Beals looked from me to Sheryl, then back to me again. He smiled, stood up, and suddenly grabbed a fistful of Sheryl's hair. She cried out from the pain as he yanked her close to him, his thick forearm collapsing her windpipe.

"I know who you are now," he said. "You got five seconds to tell me what's going on, or your friend here's going nighty-night for good."

I could see panic in Sheryl Lee's eyes, but I could also see sadness. If I told Beals the truth, we would have to arrest him. Once he was arrested, our operation would be exposed. The Governor would feign ignorance and place the entirety of the blame on Beals. And, worst of all for Sheryl Lee, her husband would lose all hope of being released.

Even with all that at stake, I had to try to save her. Maybe telling him what he wanted to hear would keep her alive long enough for me to think of a way out. Any way out. So, I opened my mouth to tell him the truth.

"Let the woman go and step back!"

The deep voice was familiar.

"Don't make me say it again! LET HER GO AND STEP BACK!"

I turned to the source and saw Agent Beard standing in the doorway, gun drawn and pointing straight at

Biney Beals, who didn't look as tough as he had just a few seconds earlier.

"I didn't do anything wrong!" Beals shouted. "I just follow orders!"

"Then you don't have anything to worry about," Agent Beard said. "Just let her go, and we'll figure it all out."

"You think it's that easy?" Beals said. "You think he'd let me live if I talked to you? Are you that stupid?"

"I'm FBI. I can protect you."

"From Lonnie?" Beals laughed hard after saying the name. "Tell that to Dobb and Cazzie Cole."

I couldn't believe what I was hearing. Beals was admitting that Lonnie Black, the Governor of Tennessee, had been responsible, however indirectly, for multiple murders. And we had it on tape.

"They didn't have the resources I have at my disposal," Agent Beard said. "We could put you in the protection program. He'd never find you."

"He's got eyes and ears everywhere," Biney said. "You have no idea how deep this goes."

Did Black have a mole in the bureau, I wondered? While I was running through names in my head, there was a flash of movement. It was Sheryl Lee rushing toward Agent Beard, out of control. Beals had pushed her, and she was moving fast. Sheryl crashed into Larry, knocking him off balance long enough for Biney to grab Peyton Manning's helmet, turn it upside down, and grab the nine-millimeter handgun that was taped inside. Agent Beard slung Sheryl off of him and right into me. The force took us both to the ground.

"Don't do it," Beard yelled. "Put it—"

POP! POP! POP! POP!

Biney fired shots and Agent Beard returned fire as Sheryl and I scrambled for cover. It was over in an instant. My ears were ringing, and my nose was filled with acrid smoke. Sheryl Lee was hunched in a ball, her arms hugging her head and her knees pulled to her chin. After another few moments of silence, I peeked out from behind a chair that had been overturned in the struggle.

I saw Biney Beals first. He was splayed out on the floor, blood pooling around him. The white football helmet was in front of him, smeared with red streaks. He was dead. Then I saw Agent Beard. He was lying on his side with his back to me. He wasn't moving, so I crawled to him. His left arm was covering his face, and my hand was shaking when I reached out to move it. When I saw his face, I knew. His eyes were open wide, like he had seen something too big to take in. Too beautiful to believe.

Whatever it was, I hoped it gave him some comfort as he left this world.

CHAPTER FORTY-EIGHT

Before Agent Beard followed me to Biney Beals's office, he had called for backup. Within five minutes of the fatal shots, the FBI had the building locked down and surrounded. News vans and helicopters swarmed.

To protect Sheryl Lee and me, and to avoid any information being leaked, the FBI took us to their field office on Elm Hill Pike. As we were driven away, I saw Agent Beard's body, covered in a blood-soaked white sheet, being wheeled away on a gurney. He had lost his life to save mine. He had risked everything to bring Black and his criminal administration to justice. And he had done it because he believed in my crusade. Because he believed in me.

On the drive to the field office, I tried to call Mack over and over again. He didn't answer. I was sad, but not surprised. He had warned me that if the chase for the escaped inmate went deep into the woods, his cell reception would suffer. It had only been a day since I'd heard from him, but I kept calling, hoping he would pick up. All I wanted was to hear his voice. To tell him I was sorry. That I loved him. I left five voice messages, urging him to call me back. I tried to keep my composure, not wanting to scare him, but it was useless. I broke down crying each time.

After arriving at the FBI's nondescript Field Office, an agent gave Sheryl and me a bottle of water and a bag of cookies from the vending machine. Then we were told to wait. I tried to get more information, but they refused. As they left, Sheryl stopped one of the agents and said, "I tossed the recorder in the trashcan outside Biney's office. And my nephew's fifteen grand should be in his safe. You might want to send somebody to go get 'em." The agent looked shocked but nodded as he left.

"Did you toss it before or after you… you know?"

"Before," she said. "Otherwise, I'd be dead under a bloody sheet, too."

My stomach knotted. That meant we probably had nothing recorded that directly implicated Governor Black. The media onslaught resulting from the deaths of Agent Beard and Biney Beals would surely bring massive scrutiny to the Governor and his administration, which meant I doubted there ever would be direct evidence. Even Lonnie Black wouldn't be brazen enough to keep releasing inmates for money with all the new media attention.

It had all been a waste. All the death and destruction. The case, the truth, Larry Beard. All gone. For nothing.

"You think I'm awful, don't you?"

Sheryl's question brought me out of my haze and caught me off guard.

"What do you mean?"

"I ain't never had nothing in my life worth holding on to 'til my kids and Johnny," she said in a whisper. "I knew I'd never get out of there with that paper unless I did what he wanted me to do. So, I made up my mind to do it."

My head pounded and my stomach cramped.

"It was just sex," she said. "He just got my body for a few minutes. If that's what it was gonna take to get John out, then so be it. I just closed my eyes and went to someplace nice and peaceful... I went to Christmas morning."

I held back tears, then held her hand. "I don't think you're awful at all," I said. "I think you're a damn superhero."

An hour later, Agent Beard's boss, Special Agent Jock Haskins, walked in. He was a tall, handsome black man that looked to be older than Larry. He had a soothing voice that calmed me as he spoke. He asked both Sheryl and me about what had happened and wrote it all down in a notebook.

I told him my version, then Sheryl told hers. Then she asked him about the money and recording device. Haskins told her the recorder was there, but the money was missing. The horrible incident Sheryl went through with Biney hadn't brought tears to her eyes. Finding out she had lost half of her niece and nephew's inheritance did.

"But you're still going after Black, though, right?" I said. "You think the tape will be enough to put him away?"

"I wouldn't hold my breath."

"Did you listen to the whole thing?" I asked.

"I did," Haskins said. "And what I heard was a career criminal admitting to extorting a desperate woman for money and sex, with no specific mentioning whatsoever of Governor Black."

"Beals implicated Black in multiple killings right in front of us," I said. "He said Black gave the orders!"

"Maybe you're right," he said. "Maybe he said all that. But it's not on the recording, which means it's he said/she said. Which means it won't hold up in federal court."

Sheryl Lee and I kept quiet. For very different reasons.

"Agent Beard's passing is a tragedy," Haskins said, "but that doesn't change the fact that he lied to the agency."

I looked up, confused.

"He failed to mention he was working with two civilians," Haskins said, holding back his anger. "I could bring you both up on charges for interfering with a federal investigation."

I was terrified, but Sheryl Lee seemed oblivious to the threat.

"It was my idea," I said. "I forced him. I forced Mrs. Everett, too. If you're gonna charge anybody, charge me."

"I'm not going to charge anyone," he said. "I just wanted you to know what I could've done."

"So, you're gonna keep going after Black?" I asked.

"Did you not just hear what I said about having nothing on tape to directly implicate him?"

"But we both heard Beals say that Black ordered those murders," I said, nodding to Sheryl Lee. "We can testify."

"Again," Haskins said, "that would be hearsay. I don't know about Dan Smith and the US Attorney's office, but The Federal Bureau of Investigation does not make a habit of taking cases to court on hearsay."

"But—"

"You're both free to go," he said, interrupting me. "I'd hurry up if I were you, before I change my mind."

With that, he walked out of the room.

"Does that mean John's not gettin' out?" Sheryl Lee said to me, her voice trembling.

"Sheryl—"

"Is he gettin' out or not?"

"No," I answered. "He's not."

"You lied to me... You and Agent Beard both used me, and you both lied."

"I told you there were no guarantees—"

"I trusted you," she said. "I thought we was friends."

"We are, Sheryl. If there's anything I can do for you, night or day, I'm here."

Silence.

"Sheryl...? Sheryl Lee..."

"I don't think so, Presley," she finally said. "You've done just about enough."

CHAPTER FORTY-NINE

It was midnight and I couldn't sleep. Another day had passed without talking to Mack. It was the longest we'd ever gone without speaking, and I missed hearing his voice. I had tried him all night, but each call went straight to voicemail. He was gone, chasing God knows who through God knows what. I needed someone to talk to, but there was no one. My mother was home, but when I called her, she told me she was watching a movie with her new boyfriend. She asked if it was an emergency. It was, of course, but I told her it wasn't and hung up the phone.

Later that night, around eleven, I was half-drunk in front of the television when I thought I heard the doorbell ring. I shrugged it off as nothing and kept watching. The second ring got my attention. The third, fourth, and fifth rings got me scared.

"Who is it?" I yelled. "It's almost midnight."

"It's Deputy Sheriff Kemp, Presley. I'm sorry for disturbing you. Can I come in, please?"

I immediately knew something was wrong. I opened the door and saw Kris Kemp, Mack's second-in-command. His camouflage fatigues covered in mud and blood. His eyes red and watery.

"Where's Mack?" I said, in a steady, calm voice that surprised me.

"I'm sorry to have to tell you this, Presley, but Mack's been shot."

I had expected something terrible, and there it was. Still, I didn't cry, scream, or collapse. I just asked another question. "Is he dead?"

"No," Kris said. "But he's in surgery."

"Come in," I said, before walking toward the kitchen. "Would you like coffee?"

"Don't go to any trouble. I'm here to take you to the hospital if you want to go."

"It's no trouble at all," I answered, turning on the kettle. "Sit down, you must be worn out." As he sat, I opened a cabinet and took out two coffee cups. On the way to sit them on the counter, I dropped one. It was Mack's.

"Let me help you," Kris said.

"No!" I yelled, bending down to pick up the pieces. "Don't touch him!"

I picked up one piece, then another and another, until I had the broken cup in my hands. I walked to the trash can and stepped on the lever that flipped open the lid and dumped the broken pieces into the trash. That's when I collapsed.

After crying myself dry and taking a shower, Deputy Kemp drove me to the hospital. On the way, he told me about the manhunt and what had transpired. He went into every detail, but I didn't listen. It didn't matter to me. All that mattered right now was seeing Mack, talking to him, touching him.

"Did you hear me, Presley?" Kemp said, bringing me out of my daze.

"What?"

"Mack saved lives tonight," he said. "A lot of them."

I nodded but stayed quiet. After we pulled into the hospital parking lot, Kemp walked me to the waiting room, where the team of officers who had been on the manhunt with Mack were standing. They were filthy and smelled like wild animals, and every one of them had been crying. They were his brothers. His family. The big, strong men were skittish as I passed them to sit on a hard waiting-room chair. We all waited in silence for what seemed like an eternity before a young surgeon in blood-stained scrubs stepped up to me.

"Are you Mrs. Carter?" he said, in some sort of Northern accent.

I nodded.

"I'm Doctor Satterwhite," he said. "Your husband is very strong."

"So, he's gonna be okay?"

"He's alive, but he's not out of the woods. The next few days will be crucial."

"Can I see him?"

"He's still under anesthesia and has a little help breathing," Satterwhite said, "but I think a loving voice would be as beneficial as anything right now."

I couldn't feel my feet touching the ground as I walked toward Mack's room. When I saw him lying there, it took my breath away. He looked twenty pounds lighter. I had just seen him walk through the doors at the Sheriff's Office, healthy as a horse. I was shocked at how quickly a body could change. Atrophy. Disappear. It was horrifying.

All those thoughts fell away when I stared at the ventilator, its tube snaking from the metal and plastic machine across the white linen, up between Mack's broad shoulders, and finally, crawling down his throat. I stepped closer to the bed and held Mack's hand. It was cold, so I pulled his blanket up to his chin.

"Hey, you," I whispered. "I hear you're a hero…"

My throat seized up, so I stopped talking and laid my head on his chest and felt the rise and fall. My tears soaked his hospital gown. Why hadn't I said all the things I wanted to say that day at the Sheriff's Office? Now the words were gone. Lost in a fog of regret and despair.

CHAPTER FIFTY

I woke up early and sore in Mack's bedside chair. But when I looked at him, the pain disappeared, and my heart skipped a beat. The ventilator tube was gone. Mack was now breathing on his own. I was on my way to find a nurse to ask about the good sign when Mack's face appeared on the television hanging from the ceiling near the far wall. The daring manhunt and eventual capture were national news, and it seemed the media outlets couldn't get enough of Mack's rugged good looks.

It didn't take long for the room to be filled with cards, flowers, food, and well-wishers. My mother brought me a change of clothes, a toothbrush, and biscuits and gravy from Hardee's. She was escorted by her new boyfriend, but he stayed in the hallway. I caught a glimpse of the tall man wearing sunglasses and immediately disliked him.

Mack's father even made an appearance. I stepped out while the stoic man visited his unconscious son for the first time in over a decade. It was quick, but I saw him wipe his eyes as he hurried from the room toward the elevator without speaking to me.

An hour later, my former boss and Mack's good friend, Dan Smith, walked through the door. "Hello, Presley," he said. "I didn't know whether to visit or not."

"Don't be silly," I said. "Come on in."

"How're you doing? I mean, besides…"

"Better," I said. "I swear, I think he knows I'm here. The doctor says no, but…"

"What the hell do doctors know?"

An awkward silence fell after that, until I broke it. "You want any food? I've got enough to choke a goat." He shook his head, but I could tell he had something to say. "What is it?" I said. "Stop staring at the wall and spit it out."

"It's just… I feel horrible about what happened between us."

"Don't," I said. "I deserved to be let go. You did the right thing."

He gave a weak nod. "I keep thinking if I hadn't done it, maybe Agent Beard might still be here."

I nodded, feeling the tears welling.

"There's something else," he said, looking at the floor.

"That doesn't sound good."

"Well, I spoke to Senior Agent Haskins today," he said. "And, unfortunately, we both agree it would be best to move on from the investigation."

The news hurt, but it didn't surprise me. Haskins had already said as much to me at the FBI office. He also told both Sheryl Lee and me not to mention the fact we were involved in the sting operation. He said it was the only way he could guarantee our safety.

"I'm sorry," Dan said. "I know how hard you worked on it."

I wanted to argue for the case to continue being built. I wanted to tell him how close we had been to having a full confession implicating Governor Black on tape. I wanted to sing Agent Beard's praises, to tell him how Larry saved my life and Sheryl Lee's, too. But I did what Agent Haskins had advised me to do. I stayed quiet and nodded.

"Well, another reason I stopped by Presley—other than to check on Mack, of course—was to offer you your job back. If you'd be interested in having it back, that is."

"Really?" I said, shocked. "Why?"

"Because, even though you made a couple rookie mistakes, I think you're one of the gutsiest, most passionate attorneys I've ever met. We've got some important cases coming down the pipe that could really build the right young lawyer's reputation. Maybe even make her famous."

I stood from the chair and stepped to within inches of the honorable United States Attorney. I looked him in the eye, stuck out my hand, and said, "I appreciate the offer, Dan. I truly do. I'm sure some young lawyer will enjoy the perks from prosecuting those cases." Then I walked to Mack and grabbed his hand. "It's just not gonna be me."

"Of course," he said. "If you change your mind, your office will be waiting for you."

Dan smiled and patted my shoulder. "Be careful out there, Presley," he said. "You got lucky with Gibson that day on the street, but you just never know how long that luck will last."

I nodded my appreciation for his concern, then watched Mack's friend walk out of the room. He was a good man.

That night, I fell asleep in the hard chair beside Mack's bed again. I dreamed that he was awake and talking to me. Whispering in my ear. But when I woke to adjust myself in the chair, I realized the voice was no dream.

"Presley," Mack said. "Wake up." His voice was low, but strong.

"Mack?" I said, still thinking I was dreaming.

He smiled and nodded. "When did you start snoring?"

I was overcome with gratitude. "You're awake… I can't believe you're awake."

He took a deep breath and let it go. "Of course, I'm awake. How could I sleep with you sawing logs like that?"

I began weeping as I wrapped my arms around him. "I'm so sorry," I said. "You were right about everything."

He winced in pain and shifted a few inches. "I don't know about that. I'm the one with a bullet hole in me, not you." With that, he saw my face change expression. "What is it? What happened?"

"It's Agent Beard," I said. "… Beals shot him… He's gone."

"Where were you?"

"Right beside him."

"Biney got away?"

I shook my head. "Larry killed him. Saved my life doing it."

A silence formed as Mack adjusted again. "What about Black?"

It took a second, but I shook my head again. "It's over."

"I'm sorry, Presley."

"It doesn't matter," I said. "I've been thinking about what you said about family. Kids and stuff."

"Press—"

"No, listen to me. I think you're right. I think it's time we bit the bullet... So to speak."

"When I was in the woods chasing that fool up and down the river, you know what I thought about the most?"

I shook my head for the third time.

"Us. I thought about me and you. How when I saw you that first time, I knew I'd eat glass just to know your name. Just to hold your hand."

He scratched an itch around a bandage, then reached out to interlace his fingers with mine. "Everything else has been beyond my wildest dreams. And, you know, I've had my share... But on that last night in the woods, right before the shooting started, it came to me..." He choked up and I squeezed his hand tighter.

"What?"

"My life started with you," he said. "You're all I've ever wanted... And if I'm lucky enough to end it with you, and I mean *just* you, then that's about as lucky as a man can get."

CHAPTER FIFTY-ONE

With Mack awake and out of danger, I finally left his side and went home. I needed a shower and a good night's rest. After drying my hair and lotioning my body, I turned on the television and lay on the bed. It was noon the next day before I woke. And when I did, a familiar voice opened my eyes. I squinted to see Governor Lonnie Black standing on the front lawn of the Governor's mansion, making a statement. I sat tall and turned up the volume:

> *"I am stunned and deeply saddened by the tragic death of my former friend and associate, Biney Beals. I considered him a brother. He was family. But, like many family members, you can't always see the red flags directly in front of you. You are blinded by your devotion to that person. Your hope for that person. Your love for that person. Which is why it hurts me so deeply to have to reveal my friend's dark side. It seems he was using his position in my administration to conduct illegal and dangerous business, without my knowledge, for his personal and financial gain. We have learned that Mr. Beals was laundering drug money through his restaurants, extorting women for sexual favors, and*

promising executive clemency to prisoners for money, working alongside a long-time business associate of his by the name of Charles "Chuck" Haynes. He was even going so far as to forge my signature on official documents. We were in the middle of an investigation of Mr. Beals when he was shot and killed by an FBI Agent who was also investigating him. Tragically, that agent was also killed. Upon hearing this terrible news, I immediately ordered officers to question Chuck Haynes about his role in these nefarious dealings. Mr. Haynes then pulled out a handgun and opened fire at the officers. Miraculously, no law-enforcement officers were injured, but Mr. Haynes was struck by several rounds and was pronounced dead at the scene. It is with great sadness that I have to confront these revelations about Mr. Beals, my former friend. But, friend or family, old or young, rich or poor, I will not abide anyone who breaks the law. You elected me to uphold the law, and that is what I have proudly done and continue to do. So, sleep peacefully tonight knowing you are safe and secure. And that your Governor is always looking out for you. God bless you, and God bless the great state of Tennessee."

I turned off the television and sat quietly. He had cheated, threatened, stolen, and killed relentlessly since taking office, and he had gotten away with it. I knew there would be more dangerous criminals released. More crimes committed. More money made. And there was nothing anyone could do about it. I had tried, over and over again, and failed. The game was over. I had lost. It was time to move on, so that's what I decided to do.

CHAPTER FIFTY-TWO

Defying all expectations except mine, Mack was out of the hospital and doing rehab in just over a week. Two bullets had been blocked by his vest, but a third had slipped through. It ripped straight through his left pectoral muscle and made a clean exit out of his upper back. The bullet missed his heart by a quarter inch.

With Mack on his way to recovery, I wanted to start my own rehabilitation. First, I decided to change my firm's focus. I would no longer be just a high-profile criminal defense attorney. Instead, I would become a version of a public defender. I would defend those I felt needed it most, even if I was paid the least. Which meant I would be buying less expensive shoes, but, hopefully, sleeping better at night. When I mentioned it to Mack, he was supportive. His six-figure salary was guaranteed, and his insurance was spectacular. But, more than that, he was happy that I was happy.

The second change needed paint. My office sign hung by a gold chain from the front porch awning and read:

Presley Myers, Attorney at Law

I removed the plaque and called the company who made it. They picked it up and had it back to me in two days. I made Mack come with me to the office under the guise of a free lunch afterward at Barney's. When I pulled up, he figured something was going on when he noticed a towel draped over the new sign. I had asked Cheri to cover it for me so that I could have a big reveal. After a count of three, I yanked off the towel and there it was:

Presley Carter, Attorney, Defender of the Public

"What do you think?" I said to Mack, hoping for the best.

He stepped closer to the sign and pushed it with his good arm. As it swung back and forth, he turned to me and said, "Got a pretty nice ring to it."

I could tell he was thrilled. But he must've been hungry, too, because he stepped closer to me and whispered, "Does this mean we can't afford to eat at Barney's anymore?"

We were both full and happy as we pulled out of Barney's, so it surprised me when Mack asked me to make a left on Division Street and pull in at Frugal MacDoogal's liquor store. MacDoogal's was an institution in this part of the city known as Pie Town, and Mack and I had spent our fair share of money in the place.

"I say we've earned some bubbly," he said. "What do you say about some Champagne?"

"I say hell yeah, is what I say."

As I was about to turn into the parking lot, Mack and I noticed a few police cruisers with their lights flashing.

They had a man handcuffed and were leading him from the store toward one of the cruisers.

"Keep drivin'," Mack said. "There's gotta be another package store on up."

I pressed the gas, and we headed east further down Division, eventually passing Vine Street, then Sixth Avenue South. Once we were past Lafayette Street, we decided to call it and hop on I-40 and pick up something closer to home. A block before I turned onto the freeway, Mack got excited.

"Booze ahoy!" he said, pointing at a small liquor store tucked into a nondescript strip mall. I pulled in and parked in front of the store. A simple sign above the door read Suleyman's Fine Wine and Spirits.

"I'll be right back," Mack said.

"You sure you're up for it?"

"Once we get this champagne in us, I'll be up for more than this," he said. Then he gave me a soft, long kiss before walking inside the store. While he was gone, I fantasized about being with him. After all these years, he still gave me butterflies. I was going to speed on the way home.

A few seconds later, a black Cadillac pulled up beside me. A man in all black stepped out of the car and walked toward the liquor store. Before he went in, he turned around and looked from side to side. I recognized him immediately. It was the man who threatened me with a gun in front of my office. The man I had knocked to the ground. He pulled the door open at the same time Mack walked out and held it without making eye contact. As Mack walked to the car, the man disappeared inside.

"It's him," I said to Mack as he carefully sat in the passenger seat.

"Who?" he said, confused.

"Gibson," I said. "Zeke Gibson."

Mack became very serious. "Where?"

I looked at the liquor-store door and saw Gibson walking back out, now carrying a manila envelope toward his black car.

"Right there," I said. "Right freaking there."

My mind was racing as Mack and I followed Gibson through the working-class streets of Antioch in southwest Nashville toward the manicured, old-monied West Nashville suburb of Oak Hill. I had a feeling I knew where we were headed, but it was still shocking when we arrived. I parked a block away, and we watched Gibson's car disappear inside the gates of the one house I never wanted to see again. I was looking at the house that gave shelter to the most corrupt, most powerful man in the state.

I was looking at the Governor's mansion.

PART III

CHAPTER FIFTY-THREE

Mack and I sat at the dining-room table. We had both racked our brains trying to figure out why Zeke Gibson would be carrying a suspicious envelope out of the liquor store. Was the store a front for another illegal operation? Was Gibson operating a side hustle without Governor Black's knowledge or approval? Or did Black have something to do with it? There was no way to know for sure. At least not in our kitchen.

The next morning at dawn, Mack and I were parked at the far end of the strip mall, waiting for the Suleymans to arrive for work. At 8:30, an old gray Toyota Camry pulled into the lot a few spaces to the left of the front door. An olive-skinned, heavy-set man with a shaved head and face walked from the Camry to the liquor store. After finding the right key, he opened the door and walked inside.

"That's the man who helped me yesterday," Mack said. "That's gotta be Suleyman."

The night before, I had Googled the name. It was Kurdish, which made sense. The last ten years had brought a giant influx of Kurdish immigrants into Nashville. So many, in fact, the city had become home to the largest Kurdish population in the United States.

This man's outfit didn't match the images I had seen online of the traditional dress associated with Kurdish culture. He wore jeans, white tennis shoes, and a navy-blue Tennessee Titans hoodie.

"Drive up a little closer, so I can get the plate number," Mack said.

It took less than five minutes for Mack to get a hit on the plate. The car was registered to Fuad Suleyman. Suleyman was, indeed, a Kurdish immigrant who arrived in Nashville with his wife and two young children four years earlier after helping US troops in Iraq as a translator. For the last year, Fuad had owned and operated Suleyman's Fine Wine and Spirits. Another phone call to the Davidson County Clerk's office revealed the Suleyman's liquor license was up to date, aboveboard, and legal. Still, there was a nagging feeling in the pit of my stomach that something wasn't right. We decided to observe the place until Suleyman left for the day.

"It'll be a stakeout," I said. "Just like the movies."

"Give it another eight hours," he said, "then talk to me about the movies."

He was right. I quickly learned stakeouts were not fun. Time crawled by like molasses sliding slowly out of the bottle. We ate breakfast, lunch, and dinner in the car. We talked some, but we mostly kept an eye on the people pouring in and out of the busy establishment. I hoped to see Zeke Gibson again, but he never showed up. Finally, after ten hours of sitting, watching, and waiting, Fuad Suleyman walked out, locked the door, then strolled toward his Toyota. I opened my car door and made a beeline to meet him next to his vehicle.

"Hi," I said while showing him my warmest smile. "My name's Presley Carter. I was wondering if I could have a quick word?"

Skepticism oozed from the man, but I also detected a hint of fear. "I don't want any," he said, before a coughing spurt stopped him. Eventually, he continued his thought. "…I don't want any trouble, please. I bother no one."

"I'm not here to cause trouble," I said, trying to get it out before he shut his car door. "I'm actually hoping I might be able to help you. If you are interested in help."

"No, thank you very much," the man said, then slammed the driver's side door.

I stepped close to his closed window and shouted, "There was a man who visited with you yesterday. A man dressed in black who left holding an envelope. Is he a friend of yours?"

"Friend?" he said, angrily. "He is no friend."

"I'm a lawyer," I said. "A defense attorney, actually, and if you happen to need anything, for any reason, I think I can help." I pulled out my business card and held it toward the glass. He stared at it for an unusual amount of time before turning away and starting his engine.

"No!" the man shouted. "I want no trouble!"

I quickly stuffed the card in between the window and doorframe, just as he reversed out of the parking space and sped out of the lot. I didn't know if my gut was right or wrong. I could've been barking up the wrong tree, but I had to admit it felt good to at least be barking again.

Now, I wanted to hunt. It was time to get back to being the wolf.

CHAPTER FIFTY-FOUR

There was no real evidence of a crime, but Mack and I both agreed there was too much smoke not to be fire. The way Suleyman had reacted to the idea of Gibson being a friend only served to bolster my instincts that something was off. But what was it?

"What about Dan?" Mack said. "Do you think he could help you dig a little deeper?"

I thought about Dan Smith. He seemed genuinely sorry for firing me, and I felt he would, at least, listen to my ideas. And if he agreed with my suspicion, maybe he would put someone on it.

"He could," I said. "Hell, he offered me my job back when he came to visit you in the hospital."

"He's a good guy," Mack said. "He likes me but thinks the world of you."

"I don't think I told you, but even after I turned the job down, he was still looking after me like a big brother," I said. "Told me to be careful. Said just 'cause I got lucky with Gibson once, doesn't mean I will again…"

I wanted to keep talking, but my mouth wouldn't move. I was stunned still and quiet. It couldn't be, could it? No, not him. Not US Attorney Dan Smith. The more

I tried to convince myself it wasn't true, the surer I became.

"What's wrong with you?" Mack said. "You look like you've seen a ghost."

"Did you tell anyone Gibson threatened me in front of my office?"

"I may have mentioned someone threatening you to some guys at the office, but I didn't mention any names. Why?"

"Larry kept it close to the vest, too. He didn't want anyone knowing he and I were associating at the time."

"Why does any of this matter?"

"He didn't know," I finally said, still searching my mind for facts.

"Know what?"

"There's no way he could've known… No way…"

Mack was getting frustrated. "What are you talking about?"

"There was no way for Dan to know about Gibson threatening me in front of my office unless one of four people told him. Me. Larry. You… Or Gibson."

CHAPTER FIFTY-FIVE

I once again found myself in the Kefauver Building in downtown Nashville sitting across from Dan Smith. I tried to hide my nerves as I filled him in about seeing Zeke Gibson at the Suleyman liquor store, and how he left the store with an envelope he then delivered to the Governor's mansion. Dan seemed shocked, but he listened attentively. He nodded while I spoke and took detailed notes.

"That's very interesting, Presley," he said. "What do you think's going on?"

"Well," I said, "I was hoping *you* might have some ideas regarding that question."

"It could be a number of things, or nothing at all," he said. "The trouble is, with only hearsay and no hard evidence, we're right back in the executive clemency boat. Which, as you know, just sunk."

"Well, that's the thing," I said. "If you meant what you said at the hospital, and my office here is still waiting on me… I'm ready to move back in and get to work."

He stared at me for what seemed like eternity, not blinking, but with an awkward smile on his face. "Well," he said, "are you sure you wanna go through all that again? I mean, Mack's probably gonna want you around the house to lend a hand for the next couple months, right?"

"Are you kidding?" I said. "He was ready for me to get outta the house after day one."

Dan let out a pained chuckle, then rubbed his temples in slow circles.

"I don't know, Presley—"

"I promise to keep quiet, keep my head down, and do my job," I said. "No more unsanctioned crusades. I give you my word."

Again, he stared at me for a long moment without blinking. I could tell his brain was spinning at warp speed, trying to figure a way out. But the fact remained he had made me the job offer, and I was here in front of him, taking him up on it. Finally, he blinked.

"Okay," he said. "If you're sure."

"I'm gonna start right now," I said. "Thank you, Dan!" I clapped, and when I did my watch flew off my wrist and landed on the floor. "Whoops!" I said, as I knelt to pick up the timepiece. "I gotta fix this clasp. It's the second time this week." Without waiting for a response, I hurried toward the door, but his voice stopped me before I was gone.

"What are the chances?" he said.

I turned to him and was taken aback. His face had gone pale, and he looked ill.

"What are the chances of what?"

"That you'd run into Gibson at Suleyman's. Out of all the liquor stores in Nashville, I mean."

I thought about it. He was right. The odds were astronomical.

"A million to one," I finally said. "A million to one."

CHAPTER FIFTY-SIX

It was a little after three in the morning when the hooded man stepped from the shadows and up to the power box on the side of Presley Carter's house. He took out a small pair of pliers, and after locating the wire he needed, snipped it in two. There was no hesitation in his movements. No doubts. He had done this too many times to count and felt as comfortable in this situation as most people felt walking their dogs. The only worry he had before arriving was that the alarm would be wireless. That would require much more patience, skill, and risk. He could've done it, but he was happy he didn't have to.

The house sat on a good-sized piece of property, and the nearest neighbor looked to be at least a quarter mile down the road. Even with that distance, the man felt jittery and exposed on the porch, so he worked fast to pick the lock. After no more than thirty seconds, the lock clicked, and the man gently pushed the front door inward. No alarm. No dog. No surprise. He hadn't expected one.

The black-clad man stepped lightly through the living room as he pulled out a Beretta M9A3 with a silencer attached to the end of the barrel. Only the light beams of a bright moon slipped through the blinds as he reached the Carters' room. The man never liked to be unsure of where his target or targets were located, so he had spent the evening doing reconnaissance, ranging the property, and assessing the house patiently through high-powered binoculars. His targets had gone to bed several hours ago.

The Carter bedroom door was ajar a few inches. He had always been lucky when it came to killing, he thought as he gently eased the door open far enough to enter. It was a frigid night and the couple had completely covered themselves with blankets. It was impossible to tell the lawyer wife from her sheriff husband, but it didn't matter. He could distinctly see the outlines of their bodies since his eyes had long-since adjusted to the darkness. The man cocked the Beretta's hammer and squeezed three rapid rounds into the center mass of both Mack and Presley Carter.

He moved in close to finish the executions with a bullet to the forehead of each of his victims. He leaned close and pulled the covers back from the still bodies.

"What the…"

Lying there were two life-sized silicone dolls, harmlessly staring up at the ceiling with sinister smiles on their eerie faces.

Instantly, the man was tackled from behind. He heard his gun clatter heavily across the floor as bodies pinned him facedown and rained blows into his back and ribs. After what seemed like an eternity, his arms were yanked behind his back and plastic ties fitted around his wrists, all while orders were barked for him to stop fighting, stay still, and shut up.

After he was secured, the camouflaged officers pulled him to his feet. He watched, befuddled, as the man he thought he had just killed walked up to him and spoke.

"Zeke Gibson, I'm Sheriff Mack Carter. You're under arrest for breaking and entering, illegal firearm possession by a felon, and two counts of attempted first-degree murder."

CHAPTER FIFTY-SEVEN

The operation was planned and executed perfectly. Mack had laid everything out to the last detail. I rode with him to the station, then watched as a couple deputies hauled Zeke Gibson into an interrogation room at the Williamson County Sheriff's Office. He didn't say a word, other than to ask for his lawyer. Two deputies led Gibson to a telephone. Less than five minutes later, the same deputies guided Gibson back into the cramped room and seated him at a small plastic table. Mack and I followed and took the seats opposite him. My presence was against protocol, but none of Mack's deputies were inclined to object. Truth be told, I knew the dos and don'ts of a well-executed interrogation better than they did.

Gibson's demeanor had changed. Some of the arrogance that typically colored his features had been replaced by dejectedness.

"What's wrong, Zeke?" Mack asked. "Get some bad news?"

Gibson kept quiet.

"Let me see if I can guess how the call went," Mack said. "I'm guessing you dialed an attorney by the name of

Reginald Gray who just happens to be the sole counsel of the Governor of Tennessee, who just happens to be your boss. And I'm guessing you felt pretty good about it, too. But when ol' Reggie picked up, he wasn't quite as nice as you expected him to be?" Mack leaned closer. "Am I warm so far?"

No answer, so he continued. "Well, I'm guessing after you told him you'd been caught red-handed doing what the Governor or somebody close to the Governor put you up to, dear old Reggie told you he was sorry, but there was just nothin' he could do for you on this one. He probably said he wished it was different, but the best thing for you to do from here on in would be to lose his number." Mack smiled. "How close did I get?"

Gibson kept quiet. Of course, Mack had monitored the entire call. The practice of recording and logging each and every phone call coming in or going out of the jail was legal, and the practice was stated on several signs posted near the bank of telephones both in English and in Spanish. Mack found the notice made no difference when inmates were scared. Many would talk openly, desperate to find a way out of their current situation. The lack of discipline always backfired. Just as it had this time for Zeke Gibson.

Mack was getting nowhere with the man, so I decided it was time to intervene. I put on my best smile.

"You need anything to eat or drink?" I said to the man who had just tried to kill my husband. And me.

No answer.

"I don't know why," I continued, "but I can't help but feel bad for you, Mr. Gibson."

BLOOD IS BLACK

He looked up, confused, but stayed silent.

"I mean, Lonnie Black used you," I said. "And now that you're no use to him anymore, I'd bet money he's gonna forget you're breathin'."

No answer, but I could see Gibson was hearing my words.

"The Governor isn't coming to save you. His lawyer isn't coming to save you," I said. "I'm your only hope. You talk to me, give me what I need, and I'll see what I can do to make this a prettier picture for you… How 'bout it, Zeke?"

Gibson looked back up at me. His face was softer than it had been. More desperate. Even scared. I couldn't help but feel a little sorry for the man.

"Lonnie Black would kill his momma to save his own skin," I said. "So, what do you think that means for you?"

I paused for dramatic effect. Gibson held my gaze for a few seconds, then slid his eyes over to the cinderblock wall.

"It's your decision," I said, "but I'd watch my back if I were you. Hell, I'd watch my back, front, and both sides." I turned to Mack and gave him a quick nod. He took the hint, and we both rose from our seats. Just as we were about to reach the door, Zeke's voice stopped us.

"How can you help me?" he said.

"Depends," I said. "What do you want?"

Gibson sat back and thought about it, then he said, "Seein' my wife and my cat would be a pretty good place to start."

CHAPTER FIFTY-EIGHT

I called Dan Smith to schedule a meeting to go over some new developments in the Black case. There was a long silence, then he stuttered as he warned me he had a very busy day and would only have a few minutes to spare. I assured him that was all I would need.

"What can I do for you, Presley?" he said, after I walked in and took a seat in the same chair as my previous meeting. "Don't tell me you've already built the case."

"No, not yet," I said, laughing. "Not against the Governor, at least."

He looked at me oddly. "Who then?" he said.

"You."

"Wh-what do you mean?"

"I missed it when you came to the hospital," I said. "I guess I was sorta preoccupied with other things, so when you said it, it went right over my head. But then it hit me when I was telling Mack what a nice guy you are. How you warned me to be careful with men like Gibson. How lucky I had been when he came after me the first time."

"I don't understand," he said. "What does this have to do with Governor Black?"

"I never told you that story," I said. "Mack didn't either. I doubt very seriously Beard did. And that leaves the only other person who knew about it— Zeke Gibson."

"I don't know what you're talking about," he said. "You must've mentioned it when—"

"You're on Black's payroll," I said. "Right? And after Mack came to see you about hiring me, you called the Governor and asked him what you should do. Am I right?"

No answer.

"I hear the Governor was over the moon to have the one person who wanted him arrested more than anyone else in the state under his thumb," I said. "Black told you to give me the job and keep tabs. Which you did. Which led to the deaths of Dobb and Cazzie Cole, and the attempted murder of an assistant US Attorney and her Sheriff husband. That's me and Mack if you were wondering."

"Presley, I tried to warn you," he said. "That's why I told you to be careful. That's why I didn't want you to come back. Don't punish me for that. There's more to it than you know."

"I know quite a bit, Dan," I said. Then I stood up and turned over my chair before peeling off the tiny recording device that I had placed the day before after "accidentally" dropping my watch.

"Thanks to this little gem, I know you called Zeke Gibson and told him everything I told you about the Suleymans as soon as I left this office yesterday. I know you told him that if he knew what was good for him, he'd 'take care' of me as soon as possible. I also know that after advising him to do all that, you gave him my home address."

Before he could answer, we heard a commotion outside his door. He didn't expect it. I did.

"But you don't have an appointment!" his secretary said feebly as Mack and his armed deputies walked into the room.

"It's time to go, Dan," Mack said. "But you knew that already."

"Black had… there were pictures… it would've killed my wife and son if they ever saw them," Dan said. "I didn't have a choice, Mack. I swear to God."

"Stand up and let's go."

"We know Black was extorting the Suleymans," I said. "We also know he was using you and Gibson, and god knows who else, to do his dirty work for him."

Dan suddenly became quiet and still. Like a statue.

"I'm not gonna ask you again," Mack said.

"Take the stand and testify against him," I said. "Do something good here, Dan. You're not a monster. I know that. I know you're not like Lonnie Black."

Dan stayed quiet, but he nodded. Then he pulled open his middle desk drawer.

"Stop!" Mack yelled, as he pulled his weapon from its holster. "Let me see your hands!"

Dan partially complied and raised one of them. His right hand, which held a .357 magnum. He pointed it at his temple.

"Don't!" I shouted, but it was too late.

Dan Smith pulled the trigger and blew his brains all over the Tennessee flag that hung from a copper pole next to his desk.

CHAPTER FIFTY-NINE

Using the address Zeke Gibson had given him, Mack and I rode to Fuad and Diyari Suleyman's brick apartment complex in La Vergne, a working-class community fifteen minutes from downtown Nashville.

Knowing the history of violence usually tied to Black's associates, Mack was armed with his Glock 9 handgun and a high-powered deer rifle. He also insisted I wear a bullet-proof vest under my jacket. It was a hot day for mid-October, and I felt sweat pooling under my heavy flak jacket as I walked to the Suleymans' apartment. I barely finished knocking before a small child, around seven years old and wearing glasses, yanked open the door. The smell of unusual food filled my nose. Exotic spices and flavors wafted over me as I noticed her father and mother along with another, younger child who was strapped in a wheelchair with her head slung to the side. Besides the wheelchair-bound girl, all were sitting around an old folding table on metal folding chairs. The walls were bare except for the US and Tennessee flags that hung side by side flanking a large framed photo of the sixteenth President of the United States, Abraham Lincoln.

The only furniture I could see besides the table was one small couch, one small recliner, and one small light.

"Hi!" the little girl said.

"Hello," I answered. "My name's Presley. Would it be okay if I spoke to your parents?"

"Um, we're eating, so if you want to come back after then—"

"Yad, come back to the table," her father said as he approached the door.

"You can have some food if you want to," the little girl said to me as her father nudged her away.

"How can I help…" he said, but immediately stopped when he recognized me. "You? How did you find our home?"

"Please, I'm not here to harm you."

"I told you before, we do not want trouble," he said, before turning his head to cough. "Now, please, go away and leave us alone." He looked back to his wife, who had already walked up behind him.

"Zeke Gibson and Governor Lonnie Black," I said. They both froze, so I continued. "I know what they're doing to you, and I want to stop them from doing it. I just need your help."

The young girl in the wheelchair began coughing and moaning. The sounds were jarring, but the woman reacted by rote. She walked to her daughter, adjusted a few straps and buckles, then held up a sippy cup to her open, wet lips. The sounds stopped. After the woman kissed the girl's head she returned to the door and stepped in front of her husband. "Please excuse our rude. Come in, please."

After a quick nod to Mack in the car, I stepped into the small, barren apartment, and the man shut the door. As the seven-year-old played dolls with her handicapped sister, I sat on the small couch beside Mrs. Suleyman while her husband pulled up a metal chair.

"I am Diyari," she said. "This is my husband, Fuad. And those are our daughters, Yad and Shad."

"Names are no important now," Fuad said. "Our life is very… uh… no stable. If I help you, can you take care of that?"

"That's why I'm here," I said. "But you have to tell me what's going on for me to do something about it."

"The store is all we have. It pays for apartment. It pays for food." He turned toward his young, disabled daughter. "My dear Shad has many needs for health that are very expensive."

"Governor Black and Zeke Gibson are making that more difficult for you?" I said.

"I thought you say you know what is happening?" Fuad said.

"I think I do. But I need to hear it from you."

There was a long moment of silence. Mr. and Mrs. Suleyman looked to each other, then to their children. Finally, the lean woman grabbed her husband's hand and nodded. After another few seconds, the man turned to me.

"Zordari," he said. *"Mer santaje min dike."*

"I don't—"

Diyari slapped her husband's leg, and he immediately returned to English. "We are being extorted by the Governor," he said. "Blackmail. What you can do to stop it?"

"Well," I said. "That depends."

"On what?"

"On how truthfully you answer my next question."

Fuad looked to his wife, then back to me. "Ask me anything you like," he said. "I will tell truth."

"Have you ever, at any time, taken money illegally from your store or used the profits for any illegal activities?"

"No," Fuad answered. "I would never do such a thing."

"Think about it," I said. "It would be easy to find out for sure."

"I do not have to think about it. I know truth. I never do illegal with store money."

His wife suddenly leaned close and whispered in his ear. It took a long time, but when she was finished, Fuad's face was slack.

"It's best to tell me now," I said. "What is it?"

"To get license for store to open," Fuad said. "For me to have the, um, liquor license, I agree to pay a fee to Governor Black. Plus, fifteen percentage of total sales in every month."

"Graft," I said, immediately realizing the word would be lost on them. "You paid Governor Black an illegal fee for a liquor license to open your store, then fifteen percent of your total monthly sales?"

"I no pay Black," Fuad said. "I pay Zeke Gibson."

"But all the money goes to Governor Black," Diyari said. "All of it in cash."

Fuad nodded, coughed. It was deep and guttural.

"Are you okay?" I said. "That doesn't sound good."

"Every year," Diyari said. "He get sick like this every year at this time. He work himself into a grave."

Diyari looked to her small children playing together, and she started to cry.

"We did because of desperate," she said. "It is not our way to be criminal, but Mr. Zeke say we never get license if we not pay. We did not know what else we could do."

"Well, it's a good thing I'm here, then," I said. "Because I do."

For the next hour, Fuad Suleyman told me everything about the liquor-license deal with Governor Black. When I asked him to produce direct evidence he had paid money to the Governor, he stood and walked to his bedroom, disappeared inside for a moment, then returned with an orange Nike shoebox. It was full of bank statements, money transfers, and ATM receipts that showed the Suleyman's monthly kickbacks to Black via Zeke Gibson, and the original bank withdrawal receipt for $20,000 the Suleymans paid to obtain the liquor license and the exclusive rights to keep other stores from opening in the area. Then Fuad pulled out a handwritten note on official stationary from the governor's office. I read it aloud:

Dear Mr. and Mrs. Suleyman,
Allow me to welcome you and your family to our great country and this beautiful city. You are now a part of the great state of Tennessee, and as such, I now consider you my friends. And I always take care of my friends. Please find your license enclosed and enjoy your store. I know you will make it a great success. Warmest regards, L.B.

Fuad took the receipt for the original $20,000 and handed it to me. "Look at date on that one," he said. "It matches date on card."

He was right. The same date appeared on the money withdrawal and the note. I felt a surge of energy. This was more than a gut feeling. This was evidence.

"Do you know anyone else who's doing this?" I asked. "Anyone else who is paying the governor for anything? It would help tremendously in building the case."

They both became quiet, and after a look to each other, shook their heads no. I didn't believe them, but I didn't want to push. Not right now.

"Is there anything else you think I should see? Or know?"

Fuad thought it over, shook his head, then coughed a couple times. Out of the blue, Diyari said, "My toes. Tell her about my toes."

I looked at Fuad.

"After we pay for license, I didn't understand how payment worked for the fifteen percent of profits the following month. I think that twenty thousand apply to this total. I was wrong." He stopped talking and hung his head.

"Mr. Suleyman?" I said.

After silent encouragement from his wife, he continued, "Mr. Zeke show up at store. He say that not the case and if I don't pay money right then, he would break my wife's toes."

"Her toes?" I repeated.

"Yes," he said. "Every one. Then he say he would move to the fingers. Then to her neck."

CHAPTER SIXTY

After Dan Smith's suicide, Mattie Thompson was appointed as a temporary replacement. She was smart and fully capable of handling the position. She was also under a massive microscope. Which was why I was nervous when we sat down to discuss the new case. As she listened to me relay the Suleymans' first-hand accounts, Mattie scoured through their shoebox full of evidence.

"Is this all?" she finally said.

"That and Zeke Gibson," I said. "He's agreed to testify against Black." I held that ace in the hole hoping it would persuade her to issue an arrest warrant.

She kept quiet, her face unreadable.

"We don't have enough for probable cause," she said. "Much less to convince a grand jury."

My heart sank, but I pushed on the gas.

"Gibson will testify that Black ordered him to threaten the Suleymans into paying him for the license directly," I said. "Under the Hobbs Act, that's extortion. Two to ten years and a $5,000 fine."

"Presley, I'm sorry, but—"

"He'll also testify the Governor told him to 'Wave a gun around and make sure the towel-heads know we're serious.' That adds special circumstances of force, violence, and fear, which tacks on the Federal Hate Crime Prevention Act, specifically Code 241, Conspiracy Against Rights. With both charges combined, that pushes the minimum to twenty and the max to life."

She kept quiet and rolled her thumbs over each other.

"Mattie?" I finally said. "I can convict him. I promise you; I can win."

Her thumbs suddenly stopped moving, and she looked me in the eye. "You can't win a fight with no opponent," she said. "I'm not gonna draw up an Affidavit for an arrest warrant for the Governor of our state without first knowing we can get an indictment."

"So let me take it to a grand jury," I said. "If they bring back a No Bill, I'll let it go. But if they bring an indictment, you have to promise me you'll let me take first chair and burn his ass down."

Mattie Thompson went quiet again. This time for a full minute. I know because I watched the second hand make a full circle on the wall clock over her left shoulder. The same clock that kept time behind Dan Smith.

"Do it."

CHAPTER SIXTY-ONE

The grand jury took less than an hour to hand down an indictment once the evidence against the Governor of Tennessee was presented.

News vans and reporters filled the streets outside the gilded gates of the Governor's mansion. Enraged citizens, both for and against the Governor, jabbed signs in the air and yelled chants. But no one saw or captured the money shot: the sight of Lonnie Black being led out of the front door in handcuffs. His wife and both daughters were in tears as he was led away from the home and stuffed into the back seat of a black minivan with tinted windows. Their reaction surprised him and gave him an unexpected feeling of relief. Maybe it wasn't just the money they loved. Maybe his wife and kids really did love *him* after all. Maybe he had been wrong about that.

For his part, Lonnie Black stayed calm. He assured his family there had been a terrible mistake and he would be home before dinner. As the blacked-out van pulled through the front gate and out onto the street, the reporters swarmed with outstretched microphones, yelling questions to the moving vehicle as it began its journey to the Metro-Davidson County Detention Facility.

Lonnie Black's jail cell was better than he imagined. It was clean, bright, and the cot was covered with a soft cushion that would let him sleep. Or at least let him try. When he had seen the police cars pulling up to the mansion, he called his lawyer, Reginald Gray. Gray immediately went to work, calling in every last favor he had in the Nashville judicial system. It paid off, as he was able to arrange a preliminary hearing for Black the very next day. Now there was nothing for Lonnie Black to do but wait. Wait and think.

His first thoughts drifted to his childhood and his father. Little Lonnie, at age nine, had visited his father at this very jail. His daddy was a small-time hood. Most of the time he worked hard doing honest jobs, but he struggled to resist the temptation of an illegal scheme every now and again. More often than not, he wound up caught and arrested. Which meant Little Lonnie and his mother would have to come up with bail for his father, or if that wasn't an option, simply visit him whenever they could. Lonnie was embarrassed about it. His friends knew and teased him. Until he laid them out with a rock or a Pepsi bottle. It had made him tough. It had also pushed him to try and be better than his father. To be successful. To have money.

Yet here he was. In the same jail his daddy had been a guest of so many times. But Lonnie Black was no small-time hood. He was the most powerful man in the state of Tennessee. Little Lonnie had surpassed his father in that respect, at least. Still, here he sat accused of multiple felonies, which, if he were convicted, meant serious time. Even without the murders, he figured at least twenty years.

So much for outrunning your heritage, he thought.

CHAPTER SIXTY-TWO

Governor Black's arraignment was to be held in the US Courthouse Annex which was connected to the Kefauver building. The annex had been built in 1974, allowing the federal government to house all of its agencies and proceedings in one centralized location.

While driving to the arraignment, I felt pretty good about my case. I had a mountain of circumstantial evidence, some direct evidence, a firsthand witness, and I had motive. Gibson was the key. He was Black's bagman and the connective tissue that attached Governor Black to the extortion of the Suleymans. Still, even with the specter of life in prison hanging over his head if he didn't cooperate, I wasn't completely sure I could trust his testimony. How deep did his loyalty to Black run?

The news of Black's arrest exploded within the news media. Enough to force Mattie Thompson to hold a press conference outside our office entrance at the Kefauver Building, where she fielded questions from local reporters and national affiliates. Which was why I wasn't surprised when I pulled up and saw the mass of news trucks and vans parked in a public lot across the street from the federal parking garage. Lonnie Black protesters and supporters were jabbing signs in the air proclaiming both his innocence and guilt. All this for an arraignment, I thought. I had expected press, but this was another level. This case wasn't just a statewide news story. It had gone national.

After parking in the three-story garage reserved for federal employees, I used the service elevator to arrive at the sixth floor, where the courtrooms were located. When the ding sounded and the doors slid apart, I stepped out to a completely empty hallway. I was shocked. I was used to the criminal proceedings at the Birch building, where hallways would be bustling with lawyers, police officers, jurors, and spectators. Today, though, in this place, there was only me. Me and an eerie silence.

"Presley!"

The voice came out of nowhere and made me jump. I turned and saw Mattie Thompson walking toward me.

"You ready to roll?"

"Is it always like this?" I said. "Where is everyone?"

"There are usually some folks milling about, but they cleared the docket for today," she said. "They didn't want any trouble, so the Governor's got it all to himself."

"Wait a minute," I said. "What are you doing here?"

"Well, good morning to you, too."

"Sorry, that didn't come out right. I just wasn't expecting you."

"I started thinking last night about possible traps," she said. "Reggie Gray's not a rock star, but he's not bad, either. If he wanted to try and disqualify you on conflict of interest, he'd have a pretty good leg to stand on."

"I'm ready for it," I said, pulling out a bound stack of legal documents. "I have precedent."

She laughed and shook her head. "I shoulda known," she said. "You're running point, but I'll serve as second chair. I'll be right there with you."

Her reputation was on the line; of course she wanted to be in the courtroom. I smiled and nodded my head.

"Let's go get him, counselor," she said.

The US magistrate assigned to Governor Black's arraignment was Cynthia Mucci, a soft-spoken, spectacled woman in her early sixties with long, silver hair. Her voice was gentle, but there was a hard, practical edge to how she conducted her courtroom which came from several years of serving in the US Army. She was known to despise the media. So, it was no surprise to see the courtroom empty of the madness that was happening outside. No cameras, no reporters, no protestors. As I sat at the prosecution table, the only people I saw in the room were Lonnie Black's wife and two daughters, who sat in the front row, directly behind the defense table where Governor Black's lawyer, the slick, Armani-suited Reginald Gray, was seated. Along the far wall there were five Metro police officers, and flanking the back door, a handful of Davidson County Sheriff's deputies outfitted in green camouflage and long-sleeved green T-shirts covered with green bullet-proof vests. It wasn't normal for state agencies to be present during federal proceedings, but the feds had called in the cavalry for the governor.

I was arranging my papers on the table when I started to hear small gasps and soft cries coming from the direction of the Black family. I looked up and saw why. Three more green-clad deputies were escorting the handcuffed Governor into the courtroom. Black nodded and blew a kiss to his family before being placed in a bloodred leather chair behind the defense table to the side of the room.

A few seconds later, the judge glided in.

"All rise," the squeaky-voiced bailiff said. "Court's now in session. The Honorable Cynthia Mucci presiding. Please be seated."

"Okay," Mucci said, "we're here for the arraignment of Lonnie Ray Black. Could counsel on both sides state their names for the record, please."

"Good morning, Your Honor. Reginald K. Gray, on behalf of the Governor of Tennessee, Lonnie R. Black."

"Presley Carter, Judge," I said. "For the People of the United States."

"Alright, Governor Black," Mucci said. "You've been charged under the Hobbs Act with extortion with special circumstances. That's a class D felony, punishable by a minimum of 20 years and up to a life sentence, with a fine of—"

"Your Honor," Gray interrupted, "we'll waive the reading of the formal indictment at this time. We have been provided a copy by the prosecution and have reviewed it with Governor Black. He is aware of the charges he's facing."

"Where do you stand on entering a plea, Mr. Gray?"

"We plead not guilty on all charges."

"Any objection, Mrs. Carter?"

"None, Your Honor."

"All right, so if you're waiving a formal reading and entering a plea of not guilty to all charges, I'll enter the not guilty on Mr. Black's behalf," Mucci said. "I'll set a date on the calendar call for... hmm..."

"Your Honor," I said. "I would argue due to the grave importance and implications of this case, a speedy trial would be best for all Tennesseans."

Mucci's military background made her cynical, so she regarded me with suspicion. Then she turned her gaze toward the defense. "What do you say, Mr. Gray?"

Reginald Gray locked eyes with Lonnie Black before answering. "No objection, Your Honor. The sooner we can get the Governor back to work, the better."

"Okay, then," Mucci said. "I'll schedule jury selection for 10:00 a.m. Monday morning. Does that work for everyone?"

Both Gray and I agreed.

"Okay," Mucci said. "Bond."

***

In federal cases, the terms of a defendant's bond are determined by the US magistrate after reading a report compiled by the court's pretrial services and hearing arguments from counsel. Mucci had read the report prior to the arraignment. Governor Black was to be a free man. At least until a verdict was rendered.

I didn't think he was a flight risk, but I was concerned for Mack and me, the Suleyman family, and believe it or not, for my star witness, Zeke Gibson. I argued that a court-ordered ankle monitor would allow me and my witnesses to rest easier. Mucci disagreed, then reminded me of the zoo waiting outside. Her feeling was that they would be a thousand times more effective keeping tabs on Governor Black. Maybe she was right. Once the Governor was out, the media would more than likely stick to him like glue. At least, I hoped so.

Reginald Gray had countered my no-bond argument with a sob story about Black's family and how the media frenzy would be too much for them to bear on their own. He then argued Black was far too noticeable to flee but would happily hand over his passport. I had strenuously objected to every point, but, to my surprise, the unsentimental judge took the bait and let him walk. I immediately called to warn the Suleymans—and Gibson, who Mack had released from custody pending his cooperation with my case.

There was one bright spot, however. Reggie Gray hadn't tried to disqualify me on conflict of interest. I was surprised. If I had been in his shoes, it would've been the first order of business. Mattie Thompson had been right. Gray was good, but not great. If she knew that, I wondered if Black did, too.

I didn't want to think anymore. I just wanted to go home. I pulled out of the garage, past the news crews and zealots, and headed toward Leiper's Fork. Mack was waiting with dinner ready and a glass of red wine. As we ate, I told him the juicy details of the day. Then we went to bed early.

But not before Mack loaded a .38 revolver and stuffed it under the mattress on my side of the bed.

CHAPTER SIXTY-THREE

I had the weekend to study my case, practice my arguments, and ready myself for the jury selection. I worked every waking moment on both Saturday and Sunday. Preparation had always been one of my strengths, but I wanted to make sure I had dotted all the i's and crossed all the t's. I needed advice from someone I respected. Someone that had already argued momentous, career-defining cases. Someone who had already done what I was about to do. And, most importantly, someone who had won those battles.

Jury selection wasn't scheduled to start until 10:00 a.m., so I made sure to arrive at Ruthie Mae Potter's office at 9:00. I knew she usually arrived to work at least two hours earlier than that, so I didn't bother calling. Walking through the front door, I was immediately greeted by Brittany, Ruthie's receptionist. I had visited the office dozens, maybe hundreds of times over the years, but today felt different.

"Is Ruthie Mae in?"

"Ummm… May I ask what this is regarding?"

"Regarding?"

"Yes. Ms. Potter is extremely busy and isn't taking any phone calls."

"Well, since I'm not calling, that's fortunate for me," I said. "I'm right here. Visiting."

"No visitors today," Brittany said, getting more nervous by the second. "I'll be happy to take a message."

I was in a hurry, and the whole interaction was starting to feel bizarre, so I walked past the receptionist desk, through the dividing door toward Ruthie's office.

"Hey!" Brittany yelled in a squeaky voice, "You can't just walk in there!"

I was already through the glass dividers and opening Ruthie's shut door by the time the blonde caught up. When I stepped into the room, my heart stopped. At least it felt that way. I couldn't breathe. I couldn't move. I couldn't fathom what I was seeing.

"I'm very sorry, Ms. Potter," Brittany said. "She won't listen."

"It's fine, sweetie," Ruthie Mae said. "Go on back out front." Then she looked at me and smiled. "Hello, Presley. I believe you know Governor Black."

Surely there was an explanation. There had to be a misunderstanding. This couldn't be what I thought it was.

"What the hell are you doing here?" I said to the smiling politician.

"Presley—" Ruthie said, before Black cut her off.

"Remember when we first met, Mrs. Carter? The day you stormed into the mansion with a search warrant. You offered me a piece of advice that day before your men ransacked my home and found nothing. Do you remember what it was that you said?"

I was too angry to think. Too angry to talk. Too angry to blink.

"I guess not. Well, you advised me that day to hire the best defense attorney I could find. I thought it might be the right time to heed your advice."

He nodded at Ruthie Mae. "I feel much better now that I have you as an advocate, Ms. Potter. I'm confident we can bring this witch hunt to heel, so I can get on with what's most important to me. Helping the good people of Tennessee."

"That's gonna be tough once I put your corrupt ass behind bars," I said. "You're not gonna slip outta this one, Governor."

"I guess we'll see, won't we, Mrs. Carter?" With that, he walked out the door, leaving me and my mentor facing each other.

"How could you do this?" I said. "Do you know what that man's done? What he tried to do to me and Mack?"

"I know what you've accused him of doing."

"And you can still bring yourself to represent him?"

"The best lawyer I've ever known told me once that 'Every man, woman, and child deserves a proper defense if they find themselves charged with a crime. We're all guaranteed the right to counsel, and the defense lawyer should be zealous and meet a high standard.' Can you guess who said that?"

I didn't have to guess. "My father would never represent a man like that," I said. "He'd die first."

"I wouldn't be so sure. In fact, maybe that's exactly the sort of thing that got him killed."

The comment buckled my knees. "What are you talking about?" I said. "What does that mean?"

"It doesn't mean anything. We just don't know for sure, do we?"

"Tell me what you mean!" I yelled. "Tell me right now!"

Brittany reappeared at the door, holding a cell phone. "Ms. Potter, should I call the police?"

Ruthie locked eyes with me, then shook her head. "No, Brittany. There's no need for police. Presley was just leaving."

Ruthie walked around her desk and sat in her thousand-dollar chair, then slid on her bifocals, fired up a cigarette, and opened a file.

"You have no idea what you're getting into," I said.

She looked up, shrugged her shoulders, then held up the folder. "That's why I need to study up. We have jurors to select, Presley. I'll see you in court. May the best woman win."

It took every ounce of strength in my body not to jump over her fancy desk and use all the warrior skills I'd learned from Mack to beat her to a pulp.

Instead, I turned and walked out of the room. The fight had already started.

***

The blonde secretary closed Ruthie Mae's door and returned to her desk. Once alone, Ruthie dropped the folder and picked up her phone, then dialed a number from memory. After three rings, an old woman answered.

"Momma?" Ruthie said. "I've got some good news."

"I like good news, baby," her mother said in a shaky, sweet voice. "What is it?"

"I think I can get Leon out."

"He's got a life sentence, honey, how you gonna do that?"

Ruthie Mae wiped the tear running down her cheek. "Very carefully, momma," she said. "Very carefully."

CHAPTER SIXTY-FOUR

The windows of the Governor's Smoky Mountain chalet were glowing with warm yellow light as a thick trail of smoke rose from the stone chimney. It was so isolated that the chalet seemed to float in the middle of a black void, suspended in air, untouched by earth or sky. It was a freezing cold night in the woods high above Gatlinburg, but the turmoil inside the Governor's mind burned hot. The fortress of men he spent years building around himself was crumbling: Chuck Haynes, dead. Biney Beals, dead. Dan Smith, dead. Zeke Gibson, arrested. He had no choice. It was time to scorch the earth and limit the damage.

Governor Black and his lawyer, Reggie Gray, walked from the upstairs living room down into the basement and shut the door. Immediately, Gray walked to the left side of a floor-to-ceiling bookcase and pushed. The entire wall slid to the right, revealing a hidden door. He opened it, and out walked Zeke Gibson.

This meeting was part of a contingency plan that Black, Gibson, and Reginald Gray had worked out as soon as Black was elected Governor. The men knew that they would be committing serious crimes, and there was a high probability that someone would be arrested before the end of Black's term. It was a solid plan that had been triggered the moment Gibson was arrested for the attempted murder of Presley and Mack Carter.

So far, it had all worked like a charm. From Gibson's first phone call to Reggie at the jail the night of his arrest, to his confession and subsequent agreement to snitch on Lonnie Black, all the way to this meeting in the Governor's secluded cabin. The players had performed their parts to perfection.

"You sure you weren't followed?" the Governor said.

"No way in hell," Gibson answered.

"And the wife?"

"She don't ask no questions, Lon," he said. "You know that."

The two men sat on the sofa while Reggie served them whiskey on the rocks. "Hadn't had a chance to tell you," Gibson said after taking a long sip, "but I appreciate the hell out of you floatin' the missus that cash last week. The family'd be hurtin' about now if you hadn't."

"You know I take care of my friends," Black said. "Always have, always will."

Black sat on top of a desk and looked at the man. "Is everything still running smooth?"

"Smooth as this liquor," Gibson answered. "That Carter woman thinks I'm gonna get on the stand and sing like Dolly. It's almost insultin' how easy she thinks I'd flip."

"What'd she offer you?"

"Freedom," Gibson said. "Said if I'd tell 'em everything, I wouldn't have no problems. Said I'd be golden."

"It's a good deal," Black said.

"Yeah," Gibson said. "For a rat."

"So, you haven't told them anything?"

"No," Gibson said. "Besides what we agreed on."

"Good," Black said.

"I just wished I would've killed her in that parking lot," Gibson said. "Woulda saved us all a lot of trouble."

"I'm afraid you're right on that one," Black agreed.

"It ain't too late," Gibson said. "I'm goin' inside anyway. It'd be like a freebie."

"No," Reggie Gray said, before checking with Black for his approval. "I'm afraid we've missed our opportunity on Mrs. Carter."

"At least for now," Black added.

"Yes," Gray said. "For now."

Black was annoyed with Gray. He had done a decent job at the arraignment, but Black expected more. He damn sure paid him for more. Black couldn't say more of *what* exactly, just… more. He hoped the Potter woman was worth the expense and the risk. When she offered to represent him for free in exchange for executive clemency for her stepbrother, he was skeptical. But when she told him what it would cost to hire her straight up, it didn't take long for him to decide to help ol' Leon.

In contrast, Lonnie loved Zeke Gibson like a brother. He was loyal and trustworthy. He'd do anything for him. "Even though you'll have to pull a few years before I can get you out," Black told Gibson, "I give you my word I'll take care of your people while you're in, and I'll make it worth your while when you're out."

"What about them big-mouth camel-jockeys?" Gibson said, referring to the Suleymans.

Governor Black smiled but shook his head. "I have another plan for them."

Gibson nodded, then he watched Governor Black do the same toward Reggie Gray. Gray walked to a safe in the corner, pulled out a small leather satchel, and handed it to Gibson.

"That's a hundred thousand," Black said. "If you keep your mouth shut, you'll get a hundred more once you walk out."

Gibson smiled.

"Alright," Black said. "I'll see you on the stand." He shook Zeke's hand, then watched Reggie lead him to the secret door.

The posh lawyer didn't recognize the high-pitched whizzing sound that rushed past his right ear. It was over so quickly, Reggie thought he had imagined it. Until he turned and saw Zeke Gibson's lifeless body facedown on the floor. There were five bullet holes in his heavy winter jacket that formed a rough circle in the middle of his back.

"There's a bag of lime and a shovel out in the garage," Black said, as he wiped off the silenced handgun and walked it to his lawyer. "Bury this with him under the garden," he said. "And when I come back up here, he better be deep."

Lonnie Black walked to his car and drove away. As he made his way back to Nashville, he felt a mixture of emotions. Zeke Gibson was a good man who had been loyal, and Black knew Gibson would've stayed quiet behind bars. He also knew that there was no way he could've ever pardoned him. Not after the failed attempted murder of a Sheriff and his high-profile lawyer wife who had spent the better part of the last year trying to bring Lonnie down. It was too risky. The only other choice was to let him rot his life away in a cell. Zeke would rather die, Lonnie thought. It was tragic, but he couldn't help but feel he had done right by the man given the circumstances.

Leota, his beloved wife, would never know what happened to him. But, one day down the road, maybe after Governor Black had left office, she would open the mailbox and find an unmarked package. Inside she would see the money Lonnie had promised her husband. Enough money to change Leota and her family's life. Zeke Gibson had been a good friend. And Lonnie Black took care of his friends.

***

Back at the cabin, Reggie Gray held the murder weapon as he stood over Zeke Gibson's body. Gray was trembling as he stared at the man on the floor. Gibson hadn't even had time to remove his thick winter jacket. Reggie always knew working for Black was dangerous, but he'd never seen it this up close and bloody. Now he was part of it. The job paid well and allowed him to provide his wife and daughters the kind of life he only dreamed of as a child in the foster system. But it came with a cost, and now was his time to pay. He took the gun and stuffed it in his jacket pocket. Then he reached down for Gibson's ankles. He suddenly screamed and jumped back away from the body. Gibson's left foot had twitched. He was almost certain of it.

"Zeke?" he said softly. "Can you hear me?" Nothing. "ZEKE!" he screamed. "ZEEEEEKE!!!" No movement and no response. The man was dead. So, again, Gray grabbed his ankles and started dragging. As he pulled the body, Reggie thought about a show he'd inadvertently come upon late one night. It was about rattlesnake hunters. He remembered them saying they had to be careful even after the snake's head was cut off. Even without the body, the head could stay alive for close to two hours. The jaw could still close. The fangs could still kill. Lucky Zeke Gibson wasn't a snake, he thought.

CHAPTER SIXTY-FIVE

H. Clue Morgenson, a cantankerous 68-year-old dinosaur, was the judge assigned to preside over Governor Black's trial. He may have been gruff and unpleasant, but he was known locally as a pillar of honesty and integrity. At the start of court on Monday, Ruthie Mae asked for a continuance. Her request was granted given she had been retained as Lonnie Black's council less than 72 hours previously. Though it was well-known Morgenson and Ruthie Mae didn't like each other, he gave her eight weeks to prepare for trial.

Ruthie Mae actually tried to have the charges against Black tossed altogether, arguing that the governor's office, under the Hobbs statute, could not be considered a criminal enterprise.

In a quickly convened private counsel with Morgenson, Ruthie and I sat across from the judge as he looked over Ruthie's motion. "Lot of finely dressed nonsense here, Ruthie," Morgenson said. "But I respect the attempt. No dice. The Governor's going to trial."

I had gone over the charges and knew they were solid. Especially my witnesses. I wasn't worried about the charges being dropped, but I was very concerned about Ruthie arguing for my dismissal due to conflict of interest. Reggie had missed the opportunity, but unlike him, Ruthie was the best money could buy. I waited for that hammer to fall, but it never did.

Following the meeting, I left discreetly through the back door. Ruthie Mae, on the other hand, began phoning journalists the second we adjourned the private meeting in Morgenson's chambers. In less than twenty minutes, she had conjured a circus by calling for a press conference two hours later at the Governor's mansion.

With Ruthie Mae and his perfect family at his side, Governor Black stepped to the microphone in front of at least five hundred people and what seemed like just as many cameras and microphones.

"I'm surprised to be going to trial," Black started. "I've done nothing wrong. My only crime, if you can call it that, is caring too much for the people of Tennessee. The prosecution has based their entire case on a disgruntled former employee and a local package-store owner, a Kurdish immigrant looking to cash in on hot-button political issues when he sensed blood in the water. The US Attorney's Office has no ground to stand on, and this rogue lawyer, Presley Carter, has repeatedly hounded my family and me with trumped-up accusations that border on harassment. I have no idea what I could have done to become the target of her dangerous crusade. Still, I will pray for her and for her husband—who I consider to be a hero for serving on the police force and protecting us all at the risk of his own life. I do this because it is what Jesus would do. Thank you all for being here. God bless you. And God Bless the great state of Tennessee."

CHAPTER SIXTY-SIX

The following Monday morning, Mack and I woke up before the sun. It wasn't because we were well rested, unfortunately. My phone wouldn't stop ringing. Reporters, producers at news stations, website bloggers, and everyone in between had gotten ahold of my work cell number and seemed to be coordinating an assault on what little sleep was left to us. After taking a few of the calls, I politely gave a final "no comment" and turned off my ringer.

Regardless of the rude awakening, I was both excited and anxious for the first day of court. The night before, Mack had helped me go over my opening statement and gave me advice on my game plan. We still needed to pick the jury, and that usually took a few days, but you just never knew. If we happened to find them quickly, I wanted to be ready.

I had spoken to the Suleymans several times over the past two days. Most of that time was spent readying Fuad for trial, and even though he was nervous and scared, I knew his authenticity would shine through once he took the stand. He wasn't charismatic, but anyone with half a brain could tell the man was being truthful.

His testimony would match the bank statements and withdrawal receipts that documented the Suleyman's monthly payments to Black's "political action committee," which Zeke Gibson would then testify was a shell corporation for Lonnie Black's personal financial gain.

I hadn't spoken with Zeke Gibson since he signed his sworn statement that Governor Black was the mastermind and ringleader of a vast extortion ring that had targeted the Suleymans. To get the confession, I had agreed to drop all charges against Gibson, and Mack agreed to release him to his family. It worked. In exchange for immunity, Gibson would testify that the immigrant family was forced to pay the Governor a consistent portion of their profits for fear of bodily harm, including death.

We had both pushed for a confession connecting Governor Black to the assassination attempt in addition to the murders of Dobb and Cazzie Cole, Dustin Jackson, and Emma Hodge. He swore it was Dan Smith, and not the Governor, who had given him the order to kill Mack and me, and he knew nothing about the other deaths. Mack and I both strongly suspected he was lying, but Smith was dead. We didn't have any evidence to directly tie Black to the other murders, so we eventually eased off.

It was infuriating. I wanted justice for all of them. I wanted Lonnie Black to pay for the lives he ended directly or indirectly. But I knew better than most that life isn't fair. Still, I took some solace in the knowledge the crimes we were accusing Governor Black of committing were felonies. Not on the level of felony murder, but serious enough to likely put the Governor of Tennessee behind bars until he died of old age—if I could convince a jury of fellow Tennesseans to convict the most powerful, beloved man in the state.

After breakfast, I climbed into my Audi A7 for the commute from Leiper's Fork into downtown Nashville. Mack had wanted to go with me, but as a witness, he couldn't be in the courtroom until I was ready to put him on the stand. Today's sole purpose would be picking the jury.

As I drove up to the Kefauver building, I expected a crowd, but I was shocked by what I actually saw. The mass of people had doubled. News crews and their vans, supporters, protestors, and pedestrian onlookers had descended in droves. I drove at a crawl past the mob to avoid hitting anyone or anyone hitting me, until finally arriving at the gate outside the federal garage.

The peace and quiet of the private lot were a welcome change, but it didn't last long. After parking and grabbing my box of evidence and paperwork, I walked into the building toward the elevators. Just before I pressed the up button, a thin, freckle-faced woman with red hair and green eyes hopped out from a nearby alcove where she had tucked herself away. Her sudden appearance startled me until I saw her cameraman and microphone. She had somehow slipped through security, and judging by her cover-model features and body, it had probably been easy.

"What is your plan of attack, Mrs. Carter?" she asked. "Are you intimidated to face off against the great and powerful Ruthie Mae Potter?"

"No comment," I said, as I pushed the elevator button.

"She was a mentor of yours, was she not?" the young, aggressive reporter said. "Ms. Potter was a last-minute replacement. Why do you think she would take on a trial of this magnitude with so little preparation time? Do you think she considers you a worthy opponent?"

"You'd have to ask her," I said, as the elevator door dinged and opened.

"But I'm asking you," the reporter said, with an irritated tone. She tried to step onto the elevator, but I blocked her. She tried left, then right, but I mirrored her movements like a hockey goalie. She paused, her frustration growing. She was weighing the pros and cons of forcing her way onto this elevator with me. We locked eyes, and finally she relented.

She must have seen a wolf's eyes glaring back at her.

CHAPTER SIXTY-SEVEN

"Sequestered," I said to Judge Morgenson after Ruthie Mae and I had selected the jury for Governor Black's trial. It had been a slow selection process over the past three days, with Ruthie and I both using our peremptory challenges for cause. But now we had our twelve jury members, six women and six men along with six alternates. I wanted them sealed off from the ever-growing media frenzy.

"I object," Ruthie said. "These people aren't machines. They have families and lives outside of this proceeding. I don't want them locked up in a hotel room with no link to the outside world." She was a master of media and spin and wanted the jury members exposed to every last bit of it.

"I wonder why," I said.

"I'm not sure what she's implying, Your Honor, but—"

"Save it, Ms. Potter," Morgenson said. "I agree with Mrs. Carter. The jury will be sequestered for the duration of the trial."

We both nodded.

"Okay then," Morgenson said, "opening statements after lunch."

He must've been famished, because he was off the stand and in his chambers before Ruthie Mae and I had a chance to grab our coats. As I turned to leave, Ruthie started laughing. It was a cocky laugh, and it made me turn back. "What's so funny?" I said.

"You know you're only here because I want you here, right?"

"You and the justice system of the United States," I said.

"Do you really think I couldn't have had you off this case in a second for conflict of interest?" she said. "Hell, you're listed as one of the victims of the man you're prosecuting. That's as easy for me as a lay-up for LeBron James."

"Then why am I here, Ruthie? If it's so easy, why didn't you do it?"

She slid her arms into her camel-colored cashmere overcoat and answered me as she passed. "Because, dear Presley, I enjoy a little competition," she said. "You know that."

It was meant to shake my confidence, and it did. But not as much as her parting shot as she walked through the back doors. "And I do mean a little!"

I skipped lunch and stayed in the courtroom trying to give myself an edge, any edge to win. It was hard to focus with the noise and commotion coming from the media setting up microphones and cameras in their designated section at the back of the paneled room. I had expected a quiet, closed courtroom similar to the arraignment, but the typically reserved and ultra-private Morgenson had opened the court proceedings to any and all media that applied for a pass.

When I scanned the room, I noticed familiar letters: CBS, NBC, ABC, CNN, FOX. It went on and on. I even noticed the pushy red-headed reporter from the garage smearing on a fresh coat of red lipstick. And there was a documentarian who had schmoozed his way into the courtroom by assuring Judge Morgenson he would be a major focus in the final cut of the film. I hoped the documentary would have a happy ending for Fuad Suleyman, the US Attorney's office, and for me. I checked my watch. Lunch was nearly over.

I took a deep breath. The calm was ending. The storm was upon us.

CHAPTER SIXTY-EIGHT

"Greed and power," I said, standing in front of the assembled jury and the packed courtroom. "Those two words perfectly sum up the political life and career of Governor Lonnie Black."

"Objection, Your Honor!" Ruthie Mae said. "Will this court allow the first words out of the prosecutor's mouth to be inflammatory and prejudiced? It's an opening statement, not a character assassination."

"Overruled," Morgenson said immediately, before he nodded to me. "Please, continue, Mrs. Carter."

"But Judge—"

"Overruled, Ms. Potter," Morgenson repeated. "There's only one chef in this kitchen, and we are going to cook this turkey on my timer, using my recipe, and no one else's. Do you understand?"

"Yes, Your Honor."

I had a moment of admiration for the grumpy old man until I noticed him sneak a look to the long-haired documentarian at the back of the room and wink. The director seemed happy with the Judge's performance. We were all playing our parts.

"Thank you, Your Honor," I said, before stepping closer to the jury box. "If you'll forgive me, ladies and gentlemen, I think I'll stick with the Judge's cooking metaphor and say that greed and power are a combustible mix of ingredients. And when you throw in a large measure of sociopathic tendencies, that mix becomes deadly. And in our Governor's case, those ingredients led him to commit the crime of federal extortion by ordering his close friend and associate, Zeke Gibson, to threaten Mr. Fuad Suleyman with bodily damage if he didn't agree to pay the Governor $20,000 for a liquor-license application. An application, if filed through legal channels, that normally costs three hundred dollars. In addition, the Suleymans were ordered, under threat, to pay Governor Black 15 percent of their store's monthly profits. Those two crimes, ladies and gentlemen of the jury, amount to Federal extortion. Both Class D felonies, and both carry with them a sentence of up to 10 years in prison and a $5,000 fine. And, with Mr. Black instructing Mr. Gibson to use racial slurs, intimidation with a firearm, and the threat of deportation if the victim didn't pay, the Governor also violated the Federal Hate Crime Prevention Act, 18 US Code 249, which carries with it a sentence of a minimum of 20 years and a maximum of life in prison, which the United States will be seeking."

After rattling off the legal jargon associated with the charges, I wanted to connect with the men and woman of the jury on a deeper level. So, I told them not to worry. Even though the trial might seem overwhelming and confusing right now, I would lay out, piece by piece, the people's case against the Governor until it was as easy to understand as one plus one equals two. I assured them that after they had seen all the evidence and heard from all the witnesses, the logical solution would be simple.

"Lonnie Black, the Governor of our state, is guilty of all charges," I said. "One plus one equals two."

Ruthie Mae busted out of the gate. Being scolded by Morgenson had lit a fire under her, and she came out hot.

"This man sitting in this chair is a miracle," she said, pointing at Lonnie Black. "And I mean a real-deal miracle, not one sold on a late-night infomercial or a roadside stand. How else do you explain a poor, abused, dyslexic country boy, who, through sheer will, was able to rise above his station in life to become the Governor of the great state of Tennessee?" She might as well have been downstage center at the Andrew Jackson Hall, performing a one-woman show.

"This man knows what it's like to go to bed hungry," she said. "He knows what it's like to go without electricity when you can't pay the bill, and what it's like to share a bed with your siblings because there's only one room for all five kids."

She walked to the Governor and rested her hand on his shoulder, then nodded to his crying wife and children sitting behind him in the front row. "This man is not a criminal. And the prosecution doesn't have one shred of real evidence to prove that he is. Just a bunch of hearsay and speculation, smoke and mirrors, parlor tricks, and sleight of hand to confuse you and make you forget that the case against my client is, without a doubt, *the weakest case I've ever seen*! That is a fact. Another fact you might care to know: Lonnie Black is a faithful, loving husband

and a sweet, doting father. He doesn't have a mean bone in his body. He's beloved by family and friends, business associates, and fellow church parishioners, whom you will hear from on the stand in short order. He's a man of God. He's our Governor, our leader, and our protector. That's why he went into politics in the first place. Not for money, or fame, or power. He simply wanted to help. He wanted to ensure that each and every Tennessean avoided the hurt and pain of his own childhood. Now, the prosecution used a math problem to prove her point of guilt. 'One plus one equals two.' Well, I'm not going to use a math book for my proof of innocence. Instead, I'm going straight to the Good Book."

"Objection, Your Honor," I said. "This is a court of law, not a Sunday school service." Objections were rare during opening statements as a matter of professional courtesy, but I wanted to return the favor.

"Judge, I'm simply quoting a passage from one of the greatest pieces of writing ever recorded," Ruthie said.

"Overruled," Morgenson said. "As long as it's used to make a point and not a Believer, then I don't see the harm in hearing some scripture."

I nodded and sat back down, while Ruthie walked to the jury. She stood as close as she could get without leaning on the bar and spoke from memory.

"Matthew 5:11," she said, with gravitas. "Blessed are you when others revile you, and persecute you, and utter all kinds of evil against you...*falsely*!"

As I watched her work, I had to admit she was the best storyteller I'd ever seen. Whatever Lonnie Black was paying her, I thought, it wasn't nearly enough.

CHAPTER SIXTY-NINE

The first few days of trial were full of character witnesses. I called to the stand a long list of men and women who had previously worked for and with Black and who swore under oath he had forced them into supplying services at a steep discount, even for free, solely to benefit his own business interests. And, most importantly, they swore he had threatened them with bodily harm if they refused to comply. My most effective character witness was a sixty-year-old man with a sweet face and dirty fingernails, who was a former employee of Lonnie Black.

"State your name, please."

"Rufus McGee."

"What did you do for the Governor?"

"Mechanic at his dealership," Rufus said. "Long before he got to be Governor."

"Was Lonnie Black a good boss?"

"No."

"Can you go into detail, please?"

"He's a liar."

"Objection!" Ruthie Mae yelled.

"Overruled," Morgenson said. "Mrs. Carter is asking for his opinion. He's entitled to have one."

"Go on," I said.

"Well, it's simple," he said. "He told me he'd pay me thirty an hour if I'd leave my old job and come work for him. Then that first-month paycheck shows up, and I'm gettin' fifteen instead. Which was less than what I was makin' at my old place. Well, I go to him and tell him about it, expecting him to take care of the mistake."

"Did he?" I said.

"He didn't take care of nothin'. He told me he didn't remember no conversation like that and to suck it up, and if I didn't, he'd sic Zeke Gibson on me to make it so I can't use my hands so good."

"So, Mr. Gibson worked for Lonnie Black even back then?"

"He's been around him as long as I can remember."

"And what did you do about the pay shortage?"

"I sucked it up," Rufus said. "Figured makin' fifteen with good hands was better'n makin' zero with ten broke fingers."

On and on it went. I called character witnesses, then Ruthie Mae did her best to shoot holes in their testimony. She was effective on some, not on others. Overall, I felt I'd done what I'd set out to do: establish Governor Black's pattern of immoral, criminal, and occasionally violent behavior.

Then it was Ruthie Mae's turn. She called her own long line of character witnesses who swore under oath that the Governor was a God-fearing, honest man. The most effective to my mind, even more than Black's own wife, was his personal maid—a Latino woman who had immigrated to Tennessee from Mexico a decade earlier.

"Good afternoon," Ruthie Mae said. "Will you please state your name for everyone?"

"Rosalba Barrera."

"And what do you do for the Governor?"

"I do many things," she said. "Cook. Clean. Iron. Dust. Fold—"

"I'm sure you could keep going, Mrs. Barrera, but I think it's clear how hard you work."

"Yes."

"And how long have you done this work for Governor Black?"

"As long as I been in this country," she said. "Ten year."

"Would you call Governor Black a good boss?"

"*Si, muy bueno.*"

"In English, please, Mrs. Barrera."

"Sorry. Yes. He is wonderful boss."

"Wonderful?" Ruthie Mae asked. "Please, I think we would all like to hear why you consider Governor Black a wonderful boss."

"He look over me and my family," she said. "Always. Since the very first day."

"Could you give us specific examples of what you call 'looking over you and your family'?"

"Specific?"

"What kinds of things does he do for you?"

"He give me bonus money every holiday," she said. "*Mucho dinero…* Sorry. He give me much extra money on my birthday, and my children's birthday. All five of them… Also, on Thanksgiving and Christmas. He even pay for our turkey and the Christmas tree. He do this every year. All ten of them."

"So, you consider Governor Black to be a good boss AND a good man?" Ruthie Mae asked.

Rosalba Barrera started crying before Ruthie finished the question. "Oh, yes," she said through tears. "He is the best man I have ever known. He is an angel."

Like Ruthie, I poked holes in some witnesses, but not others. I decided to leave Mrs. Barrera alone. I believed her. And so did the jury. But that didn't change anything. Being decent to one person does not an angel make.

CHAPTER SEVENTY

It was Wednesday. The day I had planned to call Fuad Suleyman to the witness stand. As I drove past the ever-growing circus outside the courtroom and parked in the garage, however, my gut felt off. I had a bad feeling, but I pushed it down. There was no time for feelings. It was time to go to work.

When the elevator opened and I walked down the hallway toward the courtroom, I was met by two court deputies. Their faces were grim, and I knew whatever they had to tell me was bad news.

"Mrs. Carter, are you all right?" Morgenson said to me as I sat motionless, contemplating what the deputies had just told me.

My mind snapped back to the present. I was holding down vomit and felt faint. "Ahh, Your Honor, I would like to ask for a recess, please."

Ruthie Mae perked up, sensing possible blood in the water.

"What seems to be the issue, Mrs. Carter?"

I thought of ten lies in two seconds, but none of them were better than the truth. "I've just been informed by court deputies that my witness, Mr. Fuad Suleyman, has gone missing, Judge. I request a recess to find him and bring him into court."

"Do you know where he is?" Morgenson asked.

"No."

"So how do you expect to find him?"

"I'm not sure, Judge. I have some ideas."

Morgenson thought it over. "How long would you need, Mrs. Carter?"

"A day should be enough time."

"Objection, Your Honor!" Ruthie Mae said. "The prosecution wants to put the trial behind schedule an entire day simply because they can't keep track of their witness?"

"I'll give you until after lunch, but I'm not sacrificing a full day to a wild goose chase," Morgenson said. "Court's adjourned until one o'clock."

"It's hard to win a chess match," Governor Black said to me as he walked past with his family, heading toward the door. "Especially when you've been playing checkers."

I had roughly three hours to find Fuad and get him to court. I raced to the garage, jumped in my Audi, and floored it past the excited crowd outside the courthouse, then weaved in and out of traffic heading toward the Suleymans' Antioch apartment. I called Fuad over and over on the way, but there was no answer. I didn't know if they were there, but it was worth a try. After running two red lights and a stop sign, I screeched to a halt in the parking lot and sprinted to their door. I knocked hard, over and over, yelling their names. But there was no answer. I looked to the parking lot to spot Fuad's car, but there was no silver Camry. I pounded and pounded until my knuckles were sore. Nothing.

I turned to walk away, but behind the door, faintly, I heard familiar moans. It was Shad, their disabled daughter. Then I heard Diyari shushing her. They were home.

"Mrs. Suleyman, I know you're in there!" I said. "Please, I'm begging you, just open the door and talk to me. Please. I don't know what happened, but if you'll just talk to me, I promise I'll listen!"

Diyari opened the door. I saw both her daughters behind her, staring at me. I also noticed another familiar face, much older, staring at me from a picture frame on the wall—Abraham Lincoln.

"Are you okay?" Diyari asked, jolting me out of my trance.

"What happened?" I said.

She scanned the yard and parking lot over my shoulder.

"Come in. I don't feel safe out here."

I walked in, and she shut the door. The kids followed their mother as Diyari led me to the small couch. "Where's Fuad?" I asked. "I really need to speak to Fuad."

"You told me you would listen," she said. "Was it a lie?"

I shook my head back and forth. After that, she walked to her bedroom and brought out a half-full black trash bag and sat it in front of me. "Look," she said.

I opened the bag and lowered my head. Inside, there were stacks and stacks of banded money. It was odd to see that much at one time, and I caught myself holding my breath. "Whose is this?" I said.

"Ours," she said. "It is everything extra we ever pay the Governor. Even the twenty thousand bribe we pay for store license."

"Who gave it to you?"

She shrugged. "Fuad woke early this morning to drive to courthouse and found this in backseat. It also had note." Diyari reached in the bag and pulled out an unlined white piece of paper with three foreign words written in the middle.

"Bi Asti Bicin," I said, butchering the pronunciation. "What is that?"

"It is Kurdish saying. Whoever write it does not know language too good, but it means… to go in peace."

It was at that moment I realized the Governor was right. I had been playing checkers to his chess. Black, or someone working for him, had given the Suleymans the two things they'd always wanted him to facilitate. The two things that would keep them quiet and out of court. Their money and their business.

"I'm begging you, Mrs. Suleyman, please, may I at least see your husband? I've risked my life and my career on this case. All I want is sixty seconds."

Diyari shook her head, unwilling to talk.

"She's a nice lady, momma," Yad, the seven-year-old, said as she left her sister and walked to her mother. "Sixty seconds isn't very long at all. That's only one minute. I think Daddy wouldn't mind seeing Mrs. Carter for one little minute."

Diyari placed her hand on the child's face and gently rubbed. Then she turned and locked eyes with me, before shouting out, "Fuad!"

CHAPTER SEVENTY-ONE

A tile in the ceiling suddenly moved out of place, revealing a crawl space right above my head. I took a step back as Diyari set up a stepladder under the square opening. Then I watched as a pair of legs dangled in midair before the feet found purchase on the ladder's top step. Fuad Suleyman climbed down the metal steps, dusted the front of his shirt with his hands, and smiled at me.

"Black tea?" he said.

I didn't have time for tea, but I nodded, hoping it would help get him to court. He led me to the small kitchen and motioned for me to sit at the table. My foot twitched up and down from nerves.

"Mr. Suleyman?"

"I'm sorry," he said, setting two cups on the table. "Very, very sorry. But the most important thing to me is my family, Mrs. Carter. I have to take care of them, and this is how I can do that best."

"But you're under a subpoena, Mr. Suleyman. You are required by law to appear in court. If not, you will go to jail."

"I told Diyari you would understand," he said. "I guess I was wrong."

"I do understand," I said. "I understand that Governor Black gave you back all your money and let you keep your store. I understand you got what you wanted. But what about the next family that comes to this country and gets taken advantage of? What if they're not as lucky as your family? What if they don't get their money back, or their license, or whatever it is that would make them whole? This case is about more than just your family. It's about holding the people in power accountable so the next family doesn't have to suffer the way yours did. But, more than anything else, Mr. Suleyman, this is about justice."

"I love my country, and I love my people," he said. "But they cannot take care of my family. What if Governor Black is found innocent? Even if Zeke Gibson no longer hassles us, what will stop the Governor from sending another man to take from me, or worse, kill me?"

"I can promise you he's not going to be found innocent," I said. "He's guilty, and I'll prove it. I'm going to win."

Fuad took a sip of tea. "You can promise that?"

"Yes," I said. "One hundred percent."

"No one can do that. I have heard of too many trials in this country to believe you."

He was right, I couldn't promise a guilty verdict. Not with certainty.

"You don't trust me, but you trust Black to keep his word?" I said. "The man who started this whole thing?"

"He has no reason to lie," Fuad said. "If I remain quiet, he will leave us alone. And my family will have a store to take care of us. Maybe for generations. But if I testify against him…"

I saw movement at the kitchen door out of the corner of my eye, and when I looked up, I saw Yad, his seven-year-old daughter, peeking out from behind the wall. As soon as our eyes met, she was gone.

"I need you on the stand, Mr. Suleyman," I said. "You gave me your word."

He placed his rough hand on mine and softly patted my knuckles. "You are right," he said. "And if you say so, I will go. But I ask you to consider one thing."

I waited as he coughed and took a breath.

"Consider how important this case is to you, then consider how important I am to my wife. My daughters. If you lose this case, it will be hard for you. I understand that. But, if they lose their father, can you imagine how they will feel? What their lives will become?" He paused to let his words sink in. "Can you imagine their pain?"

I didn't have to imagine. I'd been living with it for as long as I could remember. I'd felt that pain ever since my father was murdered. I knew letting Fuad Suleyman off the hook would be a huge blow to my case. But I couldn't stop seeing those innocent brown eyes of Fuad's young daughter peeking out from behind the kitchen door. Her father was her hero. To his wife and kids, Fuad was the bravest man on earth. An indestructible protector. I knew exactly how important he was to his wife and daughters because that was how important my father was to me.

I didn't have a choice back then. I couldn't save my dad. But, maybe now, I could help save theirs. There was no guarantee, but my hands would be clean. So would my conscience. I nodded to Mr. Suleyman, then stood and walked toward the front door, passing his wife and daughters as I went.

"I'll tell the judge I couldn't find you," I said. "But I wouldn't stay here. I'd go to a hotel, or to a friend's. At least until the trial's over."

"Thank you!" he said, as I opened the door. "And may God bless you."

I walked out of the small apartment feeling nauseous. I had just voluntarily lost one of my two star witnesses, which more than likely had cut my odds of convicting the Governor by fifty percent.

My only saving grace was Zeke Gibson. With him on the stand, I could still win. It would be enough. It had to be.

CHAPTER SEVENTY-TWO

I was an hour late returning to court from the Suleyman's apartment, and Judge Morgenson was livid. After calling both Ruthie and me to chambers, the explosion began.

"I move for a mistrial!" Ruthie Mae said, after hearing that Fuad would not be appearing as a witness for the prosecution. "Mrs. Carter's entire case is predicated on Mr. Suleyman's testimony supposedly connecting the Governor to a rogue extortion enterprise. The state had scant evidence even before losing Mr. Suleyman, Judge, but now it doesn't even have enough to convict Governor Black of jaywalking."

Morgenson paused and thought. "You do have more to your case than just Mr. Suleyman, I assume, Mrs. Carter?"

"Absolutely," I said, hiding my dread. "As I mentioned in opening, I've got Zeke Gibson. The Governor's right-hand man for over thirty years. He knows everything."

"But, Judge," Ruthie blurted out, "how can she call Mr. Gibson if—"

Morgenson looked to Ruthie and waited for her to finish. So did I.

"Well?" he said. "How can she call Mr. Gibson if what?"

We both waited for her answer, but it never came. She just swallowed and shook her head.

"Gibson better be worth it," the judge said. "I'm just about out of patience, Mrs. Carter. I'll see you two back here tomorrow morning."

As soon as I was out of chambers, I hustled to my Audi and sped toward Gibson's house. On the way, I called Mack to have him meet me. I wanted him to keep an eye on the house until the deputies showed up the next morning to escort Zeke to court. I sped down I-65 on my way to Gibson's home in Shackle Island, a rural suburb about twenty-five minutes from the courthouse, and I kept noticing the same light-blue sedan moving in and out of traffic, following me. When I made the final turn onto Gibson's street, the car kept driving past. Maybe they just lived in the neighborhood. Maybe not. There was no time to figure it out right now. I pulled up behind Mack's cruiser and hurried to the driver's side window.

"Thank you for doing this," I said. "I'll just feel better if you're here watching for the night."

"Of course," Mack said. "You want me to walk up with you?"

I shook my head. "He's squirrelly enough as it is."

He nodded, and I turned toward the Gibson house.

My first knock went unanswered. So did the second and third. Two cars were parked in the driveway, so I kept knocking. Finally, I heard locks clicking and chains jangling, then the door opened. The woman who answered looked hollow and pale. I pegged her to be in her late fifties. She was wearing a housecoat and slippers and held a fat tabby in her arms.

"Yes?" she said, weakly.

"Hello, ma'am," I said. "My name's Presley Carter. I'm an Assistant US Attorney handling the case against Governor Black. I'm sure your husband's had a few choice words for me over the past few days."

She kept quiet and oddly still.

"Ma'am?"

Her arms went slack, and the cat hit the floor running. Then her knees buckled, and she hit the floor, too. I tried to catch her, but it was too late. I immediately motioned for Mack, but he was already on his way.

Ten minutes later, the thin, tough woman was sitting at her kitchen table drinking coffee Mack had made. She had refused an ambulance and threatened to kick us out of her house if we sent for one. I agreed and waited patiently for her to speak. I nearly fell out of my chair when she did.

"What?" I said, not believing what I'd just heard.

"I said I haven't seen nor heard from him in over a week," she repeated. "We ain't never gone longer'n a few hours without talking to each other in more than forty years."

"You didn't call the police and report a missing person?" Mack asked.

She stared daggers through him. "I don't trust cops," she said.

"It's okay," I said. "He's not just a cop. He's my husband. And a good man."

She dropped her head and fought hard to keep from crying. "As long as he's here, I got nothing to say."

I turned to Mack. "I'll meet you at home," I said.

"You sure?"

I nodded, and he walked out of the room, leaving me and the woman alone.

"Please, Mrs. Gibson," I said. "You can trust me. You can tell me anything, and I'll never mention your name. I give you my word. It's the only way we'll have a chance to find Zeke and get him back home safe."

She stopped sipping her coffee mid-drink and stared at me. "Safe?" she said. "Back home?"

"Yes."

"Zeke's dead," she said, wiping tears from her cheeks. "He's gone forever. Lonnie Black is evil. Pure evil."

"The Governor killed your husband, Mrs. Gibson?" I said. "You know that for sure?"

She looked at me and sniffed, then her face turned hard. There was no longer sadness in her eyes. Now, there was only one emotion on her face—anger.

"Why don't you go on and get the hell out of my house," she said. "And don't come back, neither."

"Mrs. Gibson, I need to know if you're sure something has happened to your husband! Please, it's very important."

The woman calmly stood and walked to her pantry, then pulled open a drawer and grabbed a .22 pistol. She pointed at me and said, "Get... I ain't gonna ask again."

As I hurried out of the home, I suddenly felt nauseous. Both of my star witnesses were gone. And so was my case. I hurried to the chokeberry bushes at the edge of the front yard and vomited. Once my stomach was empty, I stood and walked across the street to my car. As soon as I opened the driver's side door, I felt an arm wrap around my chest and a thick hand pressed a cloth over my nose and mouth. The scent of disinfectant flooded my senses. I fought with all my strength, but with each muffled scream, my body felt weaker and weaker. I was being dragged away from my car and across the street. The last thing I remember before passing out was seeing a gloved hand open the passenger-side door of a sedan. I remember because the car's color stood out.

It was light blue.

CHAPTER SEVENTY-THREE

Mack Carter waited three hours before he completely panicked. He had called his wife over and over during that time, but each try went directly to voicemail. Finally, he drove back to the Gibson house hoping Presley was still talking to the distraught woman and had simply turned her phone off for privacy. When he saw her Audi parked out front, he knocked on Gibson's door. He lost hope when the irritable woman told him his wife had left hours ago, then slammed the door in his face.

He could feel himself spinning out of control, his mind racing and skidding, hopping back and forth from terror to shame, from guilt to rage. He suddenly realized how fragile sanity could be.

Gathering himself, Mack called in a missing person's report, then logged Presley's personal information into the National Crime Information Center Missing Person File. Starting the NCIC search would alert all law enforcement to Presley's disappearance. It would, with some stroke of luck, increase the odds that someone in law enforcement might see her. A beat cop, a detective having lunch, or even a meter maid might come into contact with her. It was a long shot. He knew it, but it didn't matter.

Mack knew there was no time to waste. From experience—terrible experience—he knew that if Presley wasn't found in the first 48 to 72 hours, she would most likely never be found. At least not found alive.

Mack and a large group of his deputies drove around Nashville all night looking for any sign of Presley. They all knew it would take a miracle to find one woman in the big city, but they looked nonetheless. They searched until sunrise with no sign of his wife. No miracle to be found. There had been no reported sightings from the Missing Person filing. After the all-night search the others went home. Not Mack. He kept driving, kept looking, kept searching.

His worst fear had finally come true. Presley had pushed too hard. She had gotten too close. And now, the danger he had worried would find her during the investigation had come home to roost.

He had left his wife at the Gibson house against his better judgment, and now she was nowhere to be found.

Presley had vanished into thin air.

CHAPTER SEVENTY-FOUR

The courtroom was packed with cameras and spectators, court deputies and bailiffs, Ruthie Mae Potter, Lonnie Black, Judge Morgenson, and the jury. Everyone was present and ready, excluding the prosecuting attorney. Everyone except Presley Carter.

"Has anyone in the court seen or heard from Mrs. Carter this morning?" Morgenson said. "Anyone at all?"

Silence.

Finally, fed up with waiting and sensing a chance to end the trial, Ruthie Mae Potter stood and addressed the judge.

"Move for dismissal, Your Honor! This conduct is as egregious and unprofessional as any I've experienced in over forty years of practicing law. To keep the court waiting like this, with not only no sign of Mr. Gibson, the prosecution's star witness, but with *no sign of the actual prosecutor*! Mrs. Carter has turned this case into an absolute circus. But maybe that's why she has decided to leave us all here waiting for her like fools. She has no case, and she knew it. I think that instead of facing reality and dismissing the case against my client like a professional,

Mrs. Carter decided to quit. To cut and run. It's actually beyond unprofessional, Your Honor. It's criminal."

Judge Morgenson's face was now crimson red.

"Even if Mrs. Carter was here," Ruthie continued, "she has no witnesses that can connect Governor Black, in any way, to any of the alleged crimes. Can we please put this embarrassment behind us and release our Governor back to his family and let him resume his job of—"

"THE PEOPLE CALL MR. ZEKE GIBSON TO THE STAND, YOUR HONOR!"

The familiar, confident voice turned every head in the court to the back of the room, where they saw two figures standing in the doorway: Zeke Gibson and Presley Carter.

CHAPTER SEVENTY-FIVE

After I entered the courtroom, Judge Morgenson immediately called for a short recess so he could meet with us in chambers. His rage simmered, bubbling just underneath the surface as I explained what had happened over the past 18 hours. By the time I finished, he looked like a volcano ready to blow. At least I was no longer the target of the coming eruption, I thought. We resumed the proceedings shortly after I finished explaining myself.

"Good morning, Mr. Gibson," I said, as I approached the stand. "How are you feeling this morning."

"I'm good," he said, before turning to Governor Black. "Alive."

I turned to watch the Governor's reaction and saw bewilderment. The man he had supposedly shot and killed was now sitting in the witness box.

"That's good to hear, Mr. Gibson," I said, after turning back to the stand. "Would there be a reason why you might not be here, alive, but instead, buried six feet under a garden with five bullets in your back?"

"Objection, Your Honor!" Ruthie Mae shouted. "This is not a murder trial! The Governor is not charged with killing Mr. Gibson!"

"Well, obviously not," I said to Ruthie, "since he's sitting right here in front us."

The audience and the jury laughed, until Morgenson banged his gavel. "Order," he said. "Order in the court. This is not a comedy club, this is a court of law, Mrs. Carter." He turned his gaze to Ruthie Mae. "Objection overruled, Ms. Potter. Answer the question, sir."

"Because that man right there shot me five times in the back, fully intendin' to kill me," Gibson said, pointing at Governor Black as he spoke.

I looked again to Lonnie Black. "Thank you, sir. As to Ms. Potter's assertion that this isn't a murder trial, I beg to differ. Due to extreme and unforeseen circumstances," I said. "I'm requesting, through the Racketeer Influenced and Corrupt Organizations Act, that the court add three counts of murder and three counts of attempted murder to the existing charges, along with an additional twenty-two counts of federal extortion for executive clemencies."

I wondered if the Governor still thought I was playing checkers.

"Objection!" Ruthie Mae yelled.

"On what grounds?" Morgenson said.

"On… the grounds that the state has… no… evidence to support these… imaginary and completely fabricated claims!"

"What about it, Mrs. Carter?" Morgenson said. "The additional extortion charges are one thing, but it would take an extraordinary set of circumstances for me to consider adding murder charges."

"Would the weapon, bullets, and a full audio recording of the attempted killing of Mr. Gibson satisfy the court?" I said. "Along with his firsthand testimony connecting the Governor to the others, of course."

The entire room gasped when I asked the question, including Ruthie Mae. After submitting the weapon, bullets, and the tape as exhibits into evidence, I scanned the room and felt a sense of pride. Until the back doors opened, and Mack walked in.

When he saw me, he stopped in his tracks and covered his mouth with his right hand. I couldn't tell from the distance whether he was relieved or enraged. I would find out soon enough, I thought.

"Objection, Your Honor," Ruthie said. "None of this new 'evidence' has been presented to the defense," she said. "I move to strike the ridiculous request and get on with the trail at hand."

"That's what I'm trying to do right now, Your Honor," I said. "The evidence is here, and I've presented it to the court as quickly as I received it. The people respectfully ask Your Honor to include the additional charges and let us get on with trying the case."

Suddenly, the chaos of the moment was gone. Replaced by silence. The courtroom was now quiet as a library. All eyes, including mine, were watching Judge Morgenson. He held the case in his hands.

"I'll allow it," he said. "Proceed with the witness, Mrs. Carter."

"Thank you, Your Honor," I said, before stepping closer to the witness. "Mr. Gibson, could you please tell the court how many people the Governor has ordered you to kill?"

"Hearsay!" Ruthie said.

"Overruled," Morgenson barked. "He's a firsthand witness, counselor. Proceed, Mr. Gibson."

"Well, first there was Whitey," he said.

"I'm sorry to stop you," I said. "But can you state the full names of the people the Governor ordered you to murder or attempted to murder himself, please."

"Um… sure, if I can remember 'em all, that is." He shifted in his seat and counted on his fingers as he listed the dead bodies. "First was Whitey Cornett. Lonnie didn't pull the trigger, mind you, so I'm not sure if that counts."

I started to explain to Gibson that through the RICO statute, Lonnie Black could be convicted for not only the murder he attempted himself, but for all the other murders he *ordered* as well. Instead, I simply answered his question.

"It counts," I said.

"Well, then, I can tell you for sure he *ordered* me to kill ol' Whitey Cornett for being so reckless with how he handled Dustin and Emma. In fact, the Governor was standin' right behind me when I shot Whitey in the head while he was takin' a leak at Lonnie's cabin. He helped me roll him up in a carpet and throw him in my truck, too. Nashville's finest pulled him out of the Cumberland River a while ago. If you check the bullets against my gun, you'll see they match."

The courtroom gasped again, then murmured loudly. "Quiet," Morgenson said as he banged the gavel.

"I promise I'll clear you all out of here if I have to say it again!"

I saw the Judge look to the documentarian in the back of the room. The man was smiling and nodding, pointing his camera directly at the bench.

"Go on, Mr. Gibson," I said.

"Okay, um, so as far as the others he ordered me and Biney to kill, there's Dobb and Cazzie Cole. It was Lonnie's idea to torch their trailer, too."

"Is that all?" I asked.

"That's all for who he ordered killed that are actually dead, as far as I know. But, as far as the ones he ordered killed but are still alive?" He paused. "Well, that's easy. That's you and your husband."

I caught a quick glimpse of Mack but was careful not to linger.

"Can you give us the details of that night, please?"

"Sure, as far as you and your hubby goes, Lonnie told me to stake out your house until I felt comfortable, then break in and shoot you both in the head."

"And can you please tell the jury how that turned out?"

"Not too good," he said, nodding at me, then to Mack in the back row. "You're both still breathin'."

"And what about you?" I said. "The Governor shot you in the back with five bullets."

"He sure did," Gibson said, staring at Lonnie Black.

"Well," I said. "Can you tell the court about that, please?"

CHAPTER SEVENTY-SIX

As I stood in front of the witness stand waiting for Zeke Gibson to tell his story, I thought of the day before. Of being taken by this same man and tossed in his car. Upon my waking, he had immediately reassured me that he meant no harm. To prove it, he handed me a gun, grip first, and told me to shoot him if I felt threatened. I never did. Instead, we spent the rest of the day on an abandoned road that dead-ended near Percy Priest Lake, half an hour outside the city. He spilled his guts, confessing everything he had done for Black and everything he knew Black had done firsthand. Every crime he could remember, including the murders.

We waited until daybreak before driving back into Nashville, where we stopped at several banks. Each time, Gibson would return to the car with copies of prison release forms and the extortion money the Governor charged the convicts for the favor. As the Governor's power of attorney, Gibson had every key, combination, and code needed to obtain the crucial evidence that would, hopefully, put Black behind bars. Finally, Gibson opened the glove compartment and showed me the gun Lonnie Black had used to shoot him in the back. He also told me where Reginald Gray, Black's terrified lawyer, was hiding.

"Ummm," Gibson said from the stand, knocking me out of my daydream. "Where should I start?"

"From the beginning, please," I said. "Just start at the beginning."

"Okey-dokey," he said. "After I messed up killing you and the Sheriff and ended up behind bars, I knew exactly what to do. We had always had an emergency plan, from the first day Lonnie took office. We knew we'd be breaking all kinds of laws and figured one of us would be caught before it was all over with. So, when your husband gave me my one phone call at the jail that night, I knew exactly who to call and what to say. I knew the call'd be recorded, so the hardest part of the whole thing was acting like I didn't."

"What was the plan?" I said.

"The plan was that whoever it was that got pinched would put up a fight for a while, then play scared of doing the time, maybe throw in how much they wanted to protect their family or whatever, then agree to rat out their buddies on the stand in exchange for goin' free." Gibson glanced over at Lonnie Black, who looked to still be uncertain that the man he shot was sitting on the stand testifying.

"So why are you sitting here as a witness for the prosecution?"

Gibson turned back to me. "You," he said.

"Can you be more specific for the jury?"

"That night at the jail," he said, "when you came and talked to me, I had just tried to kill you and your husband. I'd just broke into your house and unloaded a full clip of rounds into two dummies that I thought were you and him, and here you were actually concerned for my well-being. I ain't ever experienced anything like that before. I know I ain't got it in me, that's for sure. But you warned me anyway. Told me a man like Black would turn on his own mother if it meant saving his skin. I acted like I was listening, but it went in one ear and out the other. Me and Lonnie went back ages. We were best friends. Closer, even. And, besides, he always swore he'd take care of me, no matter what. So, I just nodded long enough to make the deal and get out. Just long enough to get on the stand and suddenly forget everything I promised you I'd say."

"So, what happened?"

"I've already told you all this," he said. "Do I have to say it again?"

"I'm afraid so. It's important."

Zeke Gibson fidgeted and cleared his throat. "Well," he said, "after we made our deal and you got me out of jail, I got a call to meet Lonnie at his cabin. That got me thinkin' about what you said that night about watching my back, and it started to make a whole lot more sense. He'd ordered me to kill a man there myself, after all, so I knew it was the perfect place to get rid of somebody who no longer served a purpose. And, well, the more I thought about it, the harder it was for me to come up with what my purpose was anymore."

"So, what did you do?"

"I put on a bullet-proof vest under my sweater and drove up to the cabin."

"Then what happened?"

Gibson turned to the jury and told them of the secret meeting at the Governor's cabin in the mountains above Gatlinburg; the hush money being offered, which Black guaranteed with a handshake—a hundred thousand up front, another hundred thousand after Zeke's release from prison. He detailed what it felt like to be shot in the back five times, the bullets slamming into the Kevlar, nearly knocking him unconscious. Holding back the unimaginable pain. The shock of still being alive. The willpower to keep his eyes closed and stay silent as he was dragged over carpet, then cement, then grass, and finally plopped down on cold dirt. He told the jury about the fear he felt as he squinted his eyes open and saw Reggie Gray five feet in front of him, digging his grave in the dead garden. The high-pitched scream the puny lawyer made when he turned to see Zeke standing right behind him, alive. How he kept calling him a rattlesnake. Over and over, a rattlesnake, ready to strike. How he decided to take mercy on the pitiful man, but only if Gray kept the secret. Gibson then detailed the petrified attorney nodding and soiling his pant leg. He told the men and women of the jury how he laid low until the right time. How he followed me to his own home and took me off the street before his wife or any of his neighbors noticed him or his rented car. He spoke about our night and day together. Gathering documents, dirty money. The gun that was supposed to have killed him.

I knew we had enough, but I wanted to ask one more question. This one was for Mack.

"Lastly, if you would, can you please tell the court why you were so adamant about secrecy? You even swore me to secrecy yesterday. Please tell us: Why?"

Zeke Gibson looked directly at Governor Black before speaking. "Because Lonnie Black is always watching. He's always listening. If he found out I was still alive and meeting with you, or that either one of us had told what we know to someone else, we wouldn't be in this courtroom today. We'd be in the morgue. If we were lucky."

"Objection!" Ruthie Mae screamed. "That's opinion, not fact! That's a cold-blooded killer trying to save his skin!"

"That's true," Gibson said. "But at least I ain't never tried to kill my best friend."

Judge Morgenson shook his head back and forth, then waved Ruthie down with his right hand. She sat down without a fight.

"Thank you, Mr. Gibson," I said, then walked back to my chair and took a seat.

It was unnaturally quiet in the courtroom, until Morgenson spoke.

"Ms. Potter, it's your witness."

Ruthie sat motionless, staring down at the notes on her table. It was strange to see the powerful woman so vulnerable.

"Ms. Potter, you're up. Ms. Potter? Ms. Potter?"

CHAPTER SEVENTY-SEVEN

Ruthie finally stood and cross-examined Zeke Gibson. She used every bit of her skill and experience as one of the best defenders in the country, but it didn't matter. She tried to smear his already horrid reputation and call into question his motivations. No matter how hard she fought, she couldn't get rid of the evidence: the gun which was sure to come back covered in Black's fingerprints; the audio recording of Black shooting Gibson, then instructing his lawyer to bury him in the garden; Gibson's eye-witness testimony; the twenty-two illegal commutation documents signed by the Governor; on and on it went. Finally, after realizing Zeke Gibson was bulletproof, literally *and* figuratively, Ruthie wrapped up her questioning and sat down.

Closing arguments were just a formality.

It took less than an hour for the jury to return a verdict. The jury foreman, or more accurately, forewoman, handed the bailiff a folded piece of paper, then watched as the hefty man walked it to Judge Morgenson. After silently reading the paper, Morgenson handed it back to the bailiff, who then took it to the clerk. Finally, the clerk read the verdict.

"On the charge of violating the Federal Civil Rights Conspiracy Act, we the jury find the defendant guilty."

I was shocked. Without Fuad Suleyman's testimony, I thought the Governor would beat the original charge of extorting an immigrant through fear of bodily harm. I was wrong.

Then she read the new charges, starting with illegal executive clemency. One by one, after all twenty-two, she said the same word: "Guilty."

Then came the murder and attempted murder charges. My heart was racing, and there was an electric energy in the courtroom. Six counts were read, and six verdicts were given:

"Guilty as charged."

The courtroom audience gasped. Most were happy, but Black's family broke down and cried. Lonnie Black sat grim and expressionless, with Ruthie beside him, stunned. Even though it would be another thirty days before the sentencing hearing, her client, the Governor of Tennessee, was going to die in prison.

As Black's wife and kids wept, two Bailiffs started toward him. I noticed a change in his posture. His back bowed and his head dropped. His hands clinched and started to shake. Then, in a split second, the Governor exploded out of his chair and lunged at me, both of his hands reaching for my neck.

"I'm gonna kill you, bitch!"

My instincts and Mack's training kicked in as I stepped to the side and swatted his arms with my right hand, before coming around hard with a left cross. My knuckles hit flush against his top row of teeth, and I felt a crunch. The punch knocked him back across my body, and I threw a right overhand that landed solidly against the left side of his nose. That did it. He was down, bleeding and sobbing. He was also missing his two front teeth.

"I warned you before, if you came anywhere near me, you'd be picking your pearly whites up off the floor," I said.

He rubbed his tongue over the bleeding gum where his two front teeth used to be, as the Bailiffs cuffed him and dragged him out of the courtroom, screaming and crying.

He was a broken, bleeding man, but I felt no sympathy. He had done this to himself. He had weaponized his position as the most powerful man in the state and used that power to steal, terrorize, and murder. Now he was going to pay for it for the rest of his life.

After a last disappointed look to Ruthie Mae, I felt a hand wrap around my arm. I turned to see Mack. He nodded toward a side exit, then led me through it. We used the service elevator and walked to my car in the garage. Neither of us had said a word, and now, in the vacuum-sealed parking lot, the silence became deafening. He opened the passenger door for me, then walked around and sat behind the wheel. We both stared straight ahead in silence.

"I'm sorry I didn't call," I finally said. "I didn't know if the phone was bugged, or the house, or if I was being followed, or what."

He kept quiet, staring at the steering wheel.

"I wanted to tell you; I swear it. I wanted to tell you more than anything. I was just... I didn't want to put you in danger."

He stayed quiet, and I was getting nervous. Could my deceit have broken our bond? Our marriage?

"Please, Mack," I said. "Say some—"

He quickly leaned over and wrapped his arms around me. He hugged me so tight I could barely breath, but I didn't care. His body against mine, holding me for dear life, said more than all the words in the world. I didn't need words to know what that hug meant.

It meant he forgave me.

It meant he was proud of me.

It meant he loved me.

CHAPTER SEVENTY-EIGHT

My phone started ringing at five the next morning and didn't stop all day. Each call I answered was from a reporter or news agency, all wanting a quote from the prosecutor who took down the Governor of Tennessee. There were even a few calls from national TV talk shows. I had just won the biggest case of my life, and things were starting to change. I had wanted this fame, this legacy, this proof that my life had not been spared—twice—in vain. I wanted that feeling more than anything else. And here it was. I'd accomplished the impossible, and now, basking in the glory of it all, I realized that it wasn't enough. It wasn't even close. But now, for the first time, I knew what was.

For the next week I stayed home with Mack. We slept late, worked out in the backyard, ate ribs, and drank beer. We got drunk and made love. We cried and we laughed and we slept.

Eventually, I decided to check voice messages and emails.

One was from Marie Robinson at the Tennessean. She wanted to write an above-the-fold feature about me and about the case. Another was from Fuad Suleyman, thanking me in broken English and offering me free liquor for life. Then there was the message from Mattie Thompson. I made an exception and called her back.

The call started with a hearty congratulations which was immediately followed by being told to expect to be asked to resign within the week. She said that prosecuting and convicting a Democratic governor hadn't sat well with the Democratic President. She suggested I go ahead and clean out my desk so I'd be spared any public humiliation when the axes started falling. I thanked her for her belief in me and her steadfast support, but I didn't go in. There was nothing there I wanted or needed. Not anymore. I wanted to put Lonnie Black and the entire situation in my past for good. But not before taking care of a few loose ends.

Nashville National Cemetery was cold the day I visited Agent Lawrence Beard's grave. It was Christmas Eve, and the grounds were decorated with beautiful wreaths, lights, and a massive Christmas tree that stood in front of the even bigger limestone archway at the main entrance. I had missed his funeral during Mack's recovery, but after stopping by the administration building to get his burial location, I walked through the arch, then followed a tunnel that ran below a railroad track that divided the cemetery into two halves and found Larry without much trouble.

Even though I didn't believe the soul remained under six feet of dirt when someone was buried, something about the festive time of year, the bitter cold, and the bare trees made me want to talk to my friend. So, for the next hour, that's what I did. I told him about the investigation, the Suleymans, Zeke Gibson, the trial, and the win. I bragged about how I might end up talking about the case with Lesley Stahl on *60 Minutes* and Gayle King on the CBS morning show. But, in the end, there was just one thing I really wanted to say. So, I knelt on the cold ground, wiped the ice and leaves off his flat gravestone, and told him.

"Thank you."

My next stop was all the way out in Cocke County. I had called Sheryl Lee Everett to ask if I could pay her a visit, and she reluctantly agreed. Her trailer was much smaller than Dobb and Cazzie's, and as I pulled up, I wondered how she could ever fit all the kids inside. She opened the door before I knocked and nodded me in. It was much cleaner than I expected and had a surprisingly warm, homey feel. Her oldest daughter was gone, and her two youngest kids were playing an old Xbox.

After accepting the coffee she offered, we sat in the kitchen and found our footing. I asked her how she was doing, and she said about the same. Then I thought of the young Cole girl, and how she had hugged my leg so tight I couldn't feel my toes.

"Where are Dobb and Cazzie's kids?" I asked, dreading the answer before it came.

"Had to put 'em in the system," she said. "It cut my heart in two, but there wasn't no other choice. They both started acting crazy, havin' nightmares, waking up screamin' bloody murder, not eatin' or drinkin'… I'm pretty tough, I guess, but I damn sure ain't no superwoman."

I felt a pain in my chest and a gnawing in my gut. Those poor kids had lost the game before it even started.

I couldn't think about that failure any longer, so I asked her if she had heard about Black's conviction.

"You think I live on the moon or somethin'?" she said. "Better late than never, I guess."

"It never would've happened at all if it hadn't been for you," I said. "I wanted to come and tell you that."

She stayed quiet, even after I pulled out a checkbook.

"If you'll let me, I'd love to pay you for all your time and effort… You earned it."

She turned and looked at her two kids. "All right," she said. "If you wanna hand out money, I'm not dumb enough to turn it down."

I wrote her one check for fifteen thousand dollars. Then I wrote another for the same amount. "The first is for the kids' money that was lost. The second check is yours."

She looked at them, then up to me. Then Sheryl Lee stood and walked to the front door. I understood it as my invitation to leave, so I stood and walked outside. Surprisingly, she followed and pulled the door closed behind us. She hugged herself against the cold and shifted her weight from one foot to the other. "I went and saw John yesterday," she said. "He told me an interestin' story."

I waited for her to continue.

"I'd decided not to tell you, but…" She waved the checks in the air.

"What is it?" I said.

"Well, he told me he got close to the last round of one of them inmate chess tournaments they have inside," she said. "John said the fella that beat him offered to give him some lessons, but they had to be quick 'cause he was gettin' out soon."

"That's good," I said, not knowing what else to say.

"John said the guy told him he still had another twenty-two years to go, but he had a powerful stepsister that got some strings pulled."

Now I was really listening.

"Guess who his sister turned out to be?"

CHAPTER SEVENTY-NINE

Brittany stood behind Ruthie Mae's reception desk, staring at me with an annoyed look on her symmetrical face. "Get out," she said, "or I'll call the cops."

"For what?" I asked. "Visiting without an appointment?"

That confused her for a bit, and while she was thinking of a reply, I walked past her and into Ruthie Mae's office. "Shit-fire," she shouted, "not again!" She ran after me yelling, "I'm sorry, Ms. Potter, please don't fire me!"

I was face to face with Ruthie Mae when the secretary arrived.

"Nobody is getting fired, honey," she said. "Just go take your lunch. I'll be fine."

"But—"

"Go on, now, sugar, and get you something to eat," Ruthie said. The blonde gave me a dirty look and turned on her heels. "She wants to practice law," Ruthie continued, nodding toward the doorway the woman had passed through. "I'm not one to stomp on dreams, but Lord have mercy, it's hard to see it."

Ruthie lit a cigarette and poured a scotch on the rocks. "You want one?" she said. "Or both?"

I shook my head no.

"Congratulations," she said. "It was a helluva performance. One for the ages."

"I learned from the best," I said, nodding to her.

An awkward silence fell as Ruthie took another sip and drag. "Presley, darlin', things just ain't always black and white. I know you hate me now, and I don't blame you, but I hope you know it wasn't personal. I consider you family. You're like a daughter to me. Always have been and always will be."

"Family, huh?" I said. "Does that mean your stepbrother would be my step-uncle?"

Her face went rigid.

"It's funny, you know. After all these years of being 'family,' I had no idea you even had a stepbrother. Especially one in prison for murder. That's something I thought you might've told me. Seeing as how I'm like your daughter, and all."

"I don't know what you heard, but—"

"Leon talked to a friend of mine's husband inside," I said. "Told him how his high-powered sister was gonna pull some strings to get him released early. Said it was a miracle. But we know better than to believe in miracles, don't we?"

Ruthie Mae finished her drink, then poured another.

"It's actually a relief for me," I said. "At least there's a good reason you stabbed me in the back. I just thought you'd gone crazy."

"How much do you want to stay quiet?"

I poured myself two fingers of whiskey and took a sip.

"Fifty thousand?" she asked me. "A hundred?"

"You say we're family, but real family would know better than to ask me that question."

"If it's not money, then what?" she said. "You want me to quit my practice? What?"

"On the contrary," I said. "I want you to stay right here and keep working." She looked at me warily. I reached into my back pocket and pulled out a rolled-up piece of paper and handed it to Ruthie.

"If I wanted you gone," I said. "You would be gone."

She unrolled the sheet. It was the commutation document for her stepbrother, signed by Governor Black. "Looks like ol' Lonnie hadn't put it through yet," I said. "Oops."

Her entire body slumped. After a few seconds, she looked up. "Why not take it to the Ethics Committee? I'd be ruined."

"Come on, Ruthie," I said. "Remember what you told me after I asked you why you didn't kick me off the Black case for conflict of interest?"

She stared at me with clear, hurt eyes.

"You remember?" I repeated.

She dropped her head.

"I like a little competition," I said, repeating her words as I walked out of her office.

"And I do mean a little!"

On my drive home, my mind raced. I thought about the tragedy and triumph of the last year. The pain, the hurt, the death. I thought of Agent Beard and Sheryl Lee; Dobb and Cazzie; Dustin and Emma. I even thought of Biney Beals and Chuck Haynes. They had families, too.

People who loved them. I thought of Fuad Suleyman and his beautiful family. Then I thought of Zeke Gibson. He was a vile man, a murderer. But I had cut him a deal and set him free. The decision didn't sit well with me, but Governor Black had always been the target. I had let one bee go in order to take down the queen and the entire hive. I took some small bit of comfort in the fact I had made it clear to Gibson that if he broke another law, any law, from this day forward, I would find out about it and make it my personal mission to see to it he was put away for a very long time. By any means necessary.

Lastly, I thought of the promises I had made. The promise to keep my father's name alive. To build on his legacy. To never let his memory die. I risked my life and cost others theirs to ensure that would happen. It was tragic, but it was done.

And even if it was true I couldn't have it all, I had enough. I was a lawyer, a daughter, a wife, a sister, and a friend.

I was Presley Carter.

And that was enough.

EPILOGUE

Christmas morning was sunny and warmer than normal. Mack and I had spent Christmas Eve finally getting our decorations up and our tree trimmed. We picked the best tree of what was left on the lot by the house. It was small and spindly, but it had character. Before we went looking, Mack suggested that we skip it this year, but our tradition was to host a Christmas dinner with family, so I insisted on putting up a tree and decorations.

Since Mack didn't have any siblings, and only his estranged father was alive, the usual attendees were my mother and brother. Sometimes Mack invited one or two of his deputies who were single, divorced, or just lonely, and sometimes I did the same for my friends. But this year, it was going to be small. My brother hadn't been home since he left for California, so it would just be Mack and me, along with my mother and her new boyfriend. At least that's what I told Mack.

After getting the turkey in the oven, the sweet potatoes mashed, the green beans snapped, and the biscuits cut and set, I took off my apron.

"Where are you going?" Mack said, as I grabbed my car keys.

"Gotta go pick up a present."

"What are you talking about?" he said. "It's too late now. What's gonna be open on Christmas night?"

"I already called," I said. "But I've gotta go now."

"What is it?"

"I'm not gonna tell you. It'd ruin the surprise."

"I'm not five," he said. "Tell me."

I shook my head and started out.

"Your mom's on her way with her new beau," he said. "You're gonna leave me to deal with that on my own?"

"Just take a shot of something before they get here and be your usual charming self. I won't be gone long."

An hour later, I walked back in the house. I could smell the food as soon as I stepped inside. My husband was sitting in the living room across from my mother and her new boyfriend. She had been seeing him for a few months, but we'd never met. Before I could speak, she saw me out of the corner of her eye.

"Look who's back!" she said, as she grabbed her boyfriend's hand and led him toward me. "I swan to goodness, I just couldn't be prouder if my life depended on it!" She released Roger's hand and spread her arms and awkwardly hugged me before planting a kiss on each of my cheeks. "Please allow me to introduce my beau for the night. This is Roger Sparks, Presley. We've known each other longer than you've been alive."

The tall, thin man looked to be in his late sixties, and once again had on sunglasses. Inside. I almost said something, but his quiet, shy demeanor threw me off. I offered my hand, and he gently shook it.

"It's so nice to meet you again," he said.

"Again?" I asked, confused.

"Roger and his recently departed wife—bless her soul—were some of my and your father's best friends way back when," Mother said. "They'd come over and play Spades when you and Aaron were tee-tiny. He and your daddy even did a little business together, isn't that right, Rog?"

He grinned slightly and nodded. My gut tightened. It suddenly felt awkward.

"Where's the big present?" Mack said. "You've got me on pins and needles."

I took a deep breath, grabbed Mack's hand, and led him to the kitchen. As soon as we walked in the room, he froze. Then he let go of my hand.

"Who are they?"

"Mack, I'd like for you to meet Colter and D.J. Cole. They're some good kids and I thought you might like to meet 'em."

My mother and Roger were watching the tense moment play out. And it *was* tense. I'd expected Mack to be excited immediately, but he was quiet and still, staring at the two children sitting at the table.

"Mack?" I said. "Are you okay?"

D.J. and Colter became more and more uncomfortable the longer the silence went on. I felt terrible for putting them in the situation. I should've asked Mack first before getting their hopes up. "I'm sorry, y'all," I finally said, "but I think we should head on back."

They nodded and stood, but Mack's voice stopped them cold. "And miss out on all this food?" he said. "What do you say we cut up some turkey and throw it on a couple buttered biscuits?"

D.J. and Colter looked to each other, then to me. I knew the sound in Mack's voice was one of happiness. He was just as glad to have the kids there as I was. It had just taken him a little longer to realize it. "I'd take him up on it before he eats it all himself," I said.

Colter hurried toward the food with Mack, but D.J. stayed at my side. I was going to surprise her and her brother at the table, but she seemed sad, so I decided not to wait.

"I thought maybe we could use this tonight at dinner," I said, as I reached in my pocket and pulled out her mother's corn-on-the-cob saltshaker I had found at the family's burned trailer. "But only if you want to, of course."

The young girl's eyes filled with tears, and she nodded her head up and down.

"Go ahead and put it on the table, then get you a biscuit," I said, doing my best not to cry, too.

"This a one-time thing, or something a little more permanent?" Mother asked, nodding to the kids.

"I don't know," I said. "It just felt right for tonight."

"I love a good turkey biscuit," Roger Sparks said before strolling toward the dining room.

"Sunglasses inside at night?" I said. "Will he at least take 'em off for dinner?"

"Be nice," she said. "They're prescription, he's got sensitive eyes." Then she leaned in close to whisper.

"They're pretty though, Presley, you should see 'em. One's blue and the other's brown."

One blue and one brown, I thought to myself. Just like Daddy's killer. What were the odds?

"My Lord, honey, you look like you've seen a ghost," she said.

"Wh—what kind of business were they in?"

"What?"

"Daddy and Roger," I said. "What kind of business was it?"

"Your guess is as good as mine, sweetie. Your daddy'd flitter to and fro worse than a hummingbird. Why don't you go ask Roger? He was hoping you two could bond."

I stared at the man in the sunglasses eating a turkey biscuit in my living room and compared him to the man who shot my father all those years ago. We had been inches apart, and I remembered every detail. The masked killer was tall. So was Roger. The killer was thin. Roger was too. The killer had Heterochromia iridum. Roger's eyes were also blue and brown.

Three for three.

My mother's date and my father were friends and business associates at the time of the murder. Maybe a deal had gone bad? Maybe bad enough for murder. My head started spinning faster and faster. I lost my balance, and my mother grabbed my arms to prevent me from falling.

"What in the world?"

"I'm not feeling well," I said. "I'm gonna go lay down for a bit." I walked past the table on my way to the stairs. "Y'all go ahead and start without me. I'll be back down in a bit."

"What's wrong, honey?" Mack said.

"A little headache. It's been a long few months."

"You want me to come up and take care of you?"

"No, no, no," I said. "It's nothin'."

"You sure?"

"Positive. A couple Excedrin, and I'll be right as rain. Now y'all eat!"

I forced a laugh that calmed everyone down, then walked upstairs and into my bedroom. I had lied. No medicine could cure what ailed me now. There was only one cure, and it was hidden in the bed. I leaned forward and reached my hand between the mattress and box spring until I felt the gun. It had been there ever since Zeke Gibson's attempt on our lives. It was cold to the touch as I pressed the steel tab to release the six-bullet chamber. It was fully loaded. Ready to kill.

"Knock, knock," Roger said, as he stood in the hallway behind my door. His voice shocked me, but I pushed the chamber closed and slid the gun under my thigh.

"Yeah?" I said. "Come in."

He pushed the door open and stepped in the room. "I hope I'm not disturbing you," he said, "but your mother sent me up to check on you. She said you might have some questions for me."

I stared at the man while my finger wrapped around the trigger.

"Umm... she did?" I said, calculating the odds of self-defense standing up in court.

"About your dad?" he said, as he stepped closer. "I still miss him like crazy. Can't imagine what it's like for you."

I used my thumb to pull the gun's hammer back. The weapon was now ready to fire. Just a slight jerk of my finger against the trigger, and Roger Sparks would be no more. I was ready to do it too, but his next words stopped me cold.

"I'm so sorry it happened," he said, holding back emotions. "I loved him… I loved him like a brother."

Then Roger Sparks stepped closer and gently patted the top of my head. His touch sent electricity through my body. I knew without a doubt that it was the same hand that comforted me as a child. It was him. He killed my father. There was no doubt in my mind.

I stood up fast and aimed the gun at the shocked man.

"It was you," I said. "You killed him."

"Hold on now," he said, raising his hands toward the ceiling. "I don't know what you're talking about… I didn't kill anyone."

"LIAR!"

Roger stopped talking and turned toward the door, looking for help. None was there.

"Presley, you all right?" Mack yelled up from the dining room.

I stayed quiet, still pointing the gun at Roger Sparks's head.

"What are you doing here?" I said. "What do you want?"

"I'm here for Christmas dinner. Your mother invited me, and I accepted the invitation."

"I don't believe you."

"It's true," he said. "I swear."

"Presley?" Mack said again. I could tell he was on his way up the stairs.

I had a decision to make, and it needed to be made fast. I gripped the trigger a little tighter as Mack reached the landing and envisioned the murder in my mind.

The bullet, the body, the blood. Black blood pooling on my floor, the way it had pooled on my father's desk so long ago.

I thought of revenge, and it felt warm.

My husband's footsteps were close. It was time to decide.

"Press?" Mack said, as he stepped through the door. "You okay?"

A second before, I had uncocked the gun and stuffed it back under the mattress. It was all I could do to manage a smile, but I spread one out. "Yeah," I said. "Roger was just telling me some stories about daddy."

"Really?" Mack said. "That's cool. You must be feeling better then?"

I managed a nod.

"Good. Let's eat."

Mack held my hand and led me out of the room. As we went, I turned back and saw Roger Sparks right behind us, smiling. For the rest of the night, he acted as if nothing out of the ordinary had happened. Like I hadn't pointed a loaded, cocked handgun in his face. Like I hadn't accused him of killing my father. For the rest of the night Roger Sparks was a perfect gentleman.

Why?

Why would he act like nothing happened? Was it because he was innocent? Or because he was guilty?

I lay awake until dawn trying to figure it out, but I didn't know the answer.

Not yet.

But I knew one thing for sure.

I was going to find out.

Thank you for reading, and I sincerely hope you enjoyed *Blood is Black*. As an independently published author, I rely on you, the reader, to spread the word. So if you enjoyed the book, please tell your friends and family, and if it isn't too much trouble, I would appreciate a brief review on Amazon. Thanks again. My best to you and yours.

Scott

ABOUT THE AUTHOR

Scott Pratt was born in South Haven, Michigan, and moved to Tennessee when he was thirteen years old. He is a veteran of the United States Air Force and holds a Bachelor of Arts degree in English from East Tennessee State University and a Doctor of Jurisprudence from the University of Tennessee College of Law. He lives in Northeast Tennessee with his wife, their dogs, and a parrot named JoJo.

www.scottprattfiction.com

ALSO BY SCOTT PRATT

An Innocent Client (Joe Dillard #1)
In Good Faith (Joe Dillard #2)
Injustice for All (Joe Dillard #3)
Reasonable Fear (Joe Dillard #4)
Conflict of Interest (Joe Dillard #5)
Blood Money (Joe Dillard #6)
A Crime of Passion (Joe Dillard #7)
Judgment Cometh (And That Right Soon) (Joe Dillard #8)
Due Process (Joe Dillard #9)
Last Resort (Joe Dillard #10) Coming Summer 2023
Justice Redeemed (Darren Street #1)
Justice Burning (Darren Street #2)
Justice Lost (Darren Street #3)
River on Fire
The Sins of the Mother (Miller & Stevens #1)
Deep Threat (Billy Beckett #1)
Divine Strike (Billy Beckett #2)
Ripcord (Billy Beckett #3)

Made in the USA
Middletown, DE
23 September 2023